# EX LIBRIS

**Alexia Flick**

Alexia Flick

ALISON UTTLEY was born at the end of the 19th century, and was brought up on a Derbyshire farm. She studied maths and science at Manchester University and English at Cambridge, then taught science at a London school. Her enduring love of the countryside and her fascination with dreams and fantasy combine to make *A Traveller in Time* a mysterious and compelling read.

# ALISON UTTLEY

# A Traveller in Time

*Illustrated by Faith Jaques*

PUFFIN BOOKS

UK | USA | Canada | Ireland | Australia
India | New Zealand | South Africa

Puffin Books is part of the Penguin Random House group of companies
whose addresses can be found at global.penguinrandomhouse.com.

puffinbooks.com

Penguin
Random House
UK

First published in Great Britain by Faber and Faber 1939
Published by Jane Nissen Books 2007
Reissued in this edition 2015
001

Set in 12.5/16.5 pt Sabon LT Std
Typeset by Jouve (UK), Milton Keynes
Printed in Great Britain by Clays Ltd, St Ives plc

A CIP catalogue record for this book is available from the British Library

ISBN: 978-0-141-36111-6

www.greenpenguin.co.uk

MIX
Paper from
responsible sources
FSC
www.fsc.org          FSC® C018179

Penguin Random House is committed to a
sustainable future for our business, our readers
and our planet. This book is made from Forest
Stewardship Council® certified paper.

*In love and gratitude to Elizabeth Meagher*

# Contents

# Foreword

All my early years were spent at the farm across
the hillside from the small manor house I have
called 'Thackers' in my story, and often I climbed
to the crest and looked down the well-known
fields to the church tower with its emblazoned
shields which rose from among the barns and
haystacks of Anthony Babington's birthplace. My
father talked of Anthony Babington as if he had
recently lived in the old farmhouse of his
neighbour. He spoke of the secret passages
underground which he had entered in his own
childhood. The tunnels had been filled in, but the
memory remained. Country tradition is strong,
and they say that Anthony Babington tried to
help the Queen of Scots to escape from Wingfield
along these hidden galleries to the little manor
farm. This unsuccessful plot took place two years

before the great plot which shook England and brought the Queen to the block and Babington to the gallows.

I paddled in Thackers brook and picked bluebells in Thackers meadows: 'Squirrels, Westwood, and Meadow Doles', mentioned in Anthony's will. I played with the little girl who lived in the farmhouse and on special occasions I went to the old church among the haystacks.

Many of the incidents in this story are based on my dreams, for in sleep I went through secret hidden doorways in the house wall and found myself in another century. Four times I stepped through the door and wandered in rooms which had no existence, a dream within a dream, and I talked with people who lived alongside but out of time, moving through a life parallel to my own existence. In my dreams past and present were co-existent, and I lived in the past with a knowledge of the future. I travelled into that secondary dreamworld, seeing all things as if brightly illuminated, walking in fields and woods dazzling in their clarity of atmosphere. I sat on the stone walls in the sunshine of other times, conscious of the difference, knowing intermediate events. The painted room, the vision through the windows of the house, and many another incident came to me in dreams, and I have woven them into this story.

Time is
Time was
Time is not
– *sundial motto*

# 1. Thackers Farm

I, PENELOPE Taberner Cameron, tell this story of happenings when I was a young girl. To this day every detail of my strange experience is clear as light. I see the beautiful countryside with its woods and gentle hills stretching out infinitely green, and the little brook shimmering with sunlight as it flows under the hazel groves. I hear the murmur of woodpigeons, sleepy and monotonous in the beech wood, and the warm intimate call of the cuckoo in the orchard by the house. Ice-cold water springs from the mossy earth and I stoop with cupped hands, one clasping the other, to sip the draught, and the taste of that water is on my lips many years afterwards. I smell the hot scents of the herb garden drenched in sunshine, and the perfume of honeysuckle after rain, but stronger than these is the rich fragrance of the old house, made up of woodsmoke, haystacks, and old old age, mingled together indissolubly. All these scents and sounds are part of the story I have to tell, with light and darkness, shadows and tragedy interwoven.

I was called Taberner after my mother's family, yeoman farmers of Derbyshire stock, and Penelope is a name which was often given to members of that family in bygone days. I was born in Chelsea, and lived with my parents in Cheyne Row, near the river. My sister Alison was older than I and had different interests, and my brother Ian, who was near me in age, was her companion, so I was left very much to myself. I was a delicate girl, and often had to miss school. I was small, too, for my years, and this separated me from the others who were tall and strong.

When I was kept at home through illness I pored over many leather-backed books from my father's shelves, and found my own friends in the pages. I read legends and folklore, books of poetry and stories of knights in armour, antique tales which had been forgotten and lay thick with dust under piled-up newspapers and periodicals.

My favourite occupations were drawing and modelling, and I worked with my pencil, and a lump of clay, spending hours with them when I ought to have been out of doors taking exercise.

Our house in Cheyne Row was little and old, with four steps leading to the green front door, and a little flight going down to the basement. We had the furniture brought by my grandmother Penelope from Derbyshire, ancient oak chests with inlaid bands and carved initials, Bible boxes, tables riddled with wormholes, and a great armchair with scrolls along the front and a hinged seat which held a score of books inside it.

In the oak presses and the writing desk were queer musty smells, and from my earliest days I used to lean over them and breathe the strange mildewed odours which seemed to rise from them like incense.

When we were allowed a special treat, and it was my turn to choose, I always asked for the pleasure of rummaging in a great oak chest. My mother gave me a worn, heavy key, and I unlocked it, using both hands for it was stiff and the lock in the carved hollowed panel was unyielding. Then as the key turned I lifted the lid and stood for a moment smelling rapturously at a delicate odour of musk and old linen, and the smell of long ago which came out of the dark depths – for it was pitch black in that deep chest. Then I plunged in a hand and drew up first one object and then another, and I laid them on the table by my side. As I reached down in the chest I had to bend so low I nearly fell inside and I was fearful lest I should slip and be shut up there. So after the lid was opened a heavy cudgel was propped inside to keep the massive top from dropping upon me and making me lost for ever.

Sometimes Ian and Alison came to help, for they loved the chest as much as I, but I had an advantage. I could invent tales about the things we found – or perhaps I should say I told the stories, certain that they were true. As I picked up the cashmere shawls, the silk-embroidered waistcoats, the pistol with its mother-of-pearl and incised roses and leaves, I seemed to hear a voice telling me about them. Then even clever Alison listened to me.

'Come and hear Penelope,' she cried. 'Quick! Quick!' and they sat with wide eyes as I told the tales and Ian clapped his hands and made me blush with pleasure.

Then I folded the dresses and smoothed the silks and twisted the tarnished ribbons and tassels, and I replaced all as I had found them, for although I was untidy with my own belongings, I never dared misuse these ancient possessions.

There had never been much money in our house, with three children to feed and educate. Father wrote scientific articles which nobody printed, and Mother did all the housework except the scrubbing which was done by stout Mrs Jakes, our charwoman. Alison and I always made the beds, and Ian helped to wash up, but even then it was a busy household, and there was always some task waiting. I was the lazy one, but Alison usually discovered me hiding in the dark basement kitchen, reading in the corner, and up the stairs she fetched me, an unwilling helper, to dust and tidy the rooms.

I always answered the front door bell, it was my special privilege. Footsteps walked along the pavement in front of our house, people going to see Mr Carlyle's house farther up the street, people going to the Embankment to stare at the great barges on the Thames, people hurrying for buses, or sauntering on pleasure, and I listened to these steps, imagining their owners, inventing adventures for them. Somebody would walk up our four steps, which were stoned with sand as in Mother's country childhood, and the bell clanged and rattled. I opened the green door very gently, just a crack, with intense excitement, wondering if a fairy godmother would be waiting there. It was usually a flower woman with a basket of tulips on her head, or a man selling muffins, and nobody like the magician I had imagined. Once a boy came with bunches of cowslips, great golden balls smelling of honey and wine, and this excited me very much. I ran helter-skelter down the crooked narrow stairs to the basement calling: 'Cowslips! Cowslips from the country. Oh Mother!' but I slipped in my hurry and sprained my ankle. This was another expense for us, and I had to lie for days on the couch without even the pleasure of door-opening.

At night, when I was in bed, I had a private joy. I slept in the front attic, a little room with a view sideways to the river. Alison's bed was in a corner and mine by the window. In cold weather we had a fire in the high fireplace with its two hobs, and we roasted chestnuts or made toast and pretended we were at boarding school or caravanning, and I felt on an equality with Alison. But when my sister was asleep, at eleven o'clock or later, a fiddler used to play at the little inn across the way. I always awoke when he began, and as he walked out of the inn down the street to the riverside, I in my thoughts danced after him on tiptoe, swaying to the music, swinging in the air. Then strange and entrancing visions came to me, flowering trees waved their branches before my eyes, lilies sprang from the earth and blossomed as I watched them, and misted dreamlike figures seemed to float up the streets moving and speaking to one another, and I was with them, living another life from my own.

One day I met one of these people of my dreams on our own stairway. Ours was a steep, crooked stair, with a handrail on one side, very narrow, with rooms leading off it so suddenly that it was easy to fall headlong as one stepped from a doorway. We had a Morris wallpaper with leaves on it, like a green wood in spring, and I used to sit on the stairs, pretending I was in a forest far away from London with birds singing round me. I was sitting there one evening, with my feet tucked under me, in the blue dusk, waiting for the lamplighter to come whistling down the street to bring a gleam to the stairway. There was a street lamp near, and this shone brilliantly through the fanlight over the door and saved us from using our own gas lamp. We had no electric light, the landlord refused to have the old house wired, so we put pennies in a slot for our gas.

I was suddenly aware how quiet it was, never a sound, I might have been the only person in the world. Even the clock stopped ticking, and the mice ceased rustling in the wainscot. I turned my head and saw a lady coming downstairs from the upper floor. She was dressed in a black dress which swept round her like a cloud, and at her neck was a narrow white frill which shone like ivory. Her eyes were very bright, and blue as violets. I sprang to my feet and smiled up at her, into the beautiful grave face she bent towards me. She gave an answering smile, and her deep-set eyes seemed to pierce me, and I caught my breath as I stood aside to let her pass. I never heard a footstep, she was there before I was aware. She went by as I leaned against the wall, and I pressed myself against the paper to leave room for her full floating skirts which took all the stairway. I never felt them touch me, and this gave me a curious sensation. Soundlessly she swayed down the stairway, and I stood watching her, smelling the sweet, faint odour of her dress, seeing the pallor of the hands which held her ruffled skirts, yet hearing nothing at all.

I leaned over the rail to watch her, and suddenly she was gone. The clock ticked loudly, the sounds of the street came to my ears, the lamplighter's whistle, clear and round, fluted through the air, and the bright gleam of the gas danced through the fanlight upon the patterned wall. I ran downstairs and pushed open the door into the sitting room, expecting to see her there. The room was empty, and I went thoughtfully down to the basement where my mother was cooking, and asked about the lady.

'There is no one, child,' she exclaimed. 'You've imagined her. It is easy to think you see someone in the dusk with flickering street lights falling on the walls. It was the shadow of somebody in the street perhaps.'

I was positive I had seen the lady and I described her little pleated frill and the way her skirts hung over a quilted petticoat like the skirts in the oak chest.

Mother was very quiet, as if she were thinking what to say next. Then she changed the conversation, asking me if we would all like to make treacle toffee that night, for soon it would be Guy Fawkes's Day, and we should have fireworks as usual in our little paved yard, where the water tank stood and the tubs which we made into flower gardens each spring.

We made the toffee, and burnt our fingers as we picked up the little streaky coils which lay in alluring shapes at the bottom of the cup of cold water. I thought no more of the lady, nor did I see her again, but my mother looked at me sometimes with a curious glance, as if she were anxious about me. I overheard my father say very impatiently: 'Nonsense, Carlin. I don't believe such moonshine, for moonshine it is. You with your country superstitions! You say she has inherited second sight from your grandmother, but I think she needs a complete change from London. All three of them ought to go away for a month or two, and breathe fresh air, and these things wouldn't happen. Now let me hear no more of this.' He muttered 'second fiddlesticks' and banged out of the room.

Mother was very kind and gentle with me, as if she realized my solitary life for the first time. When I went to bed she came upstairs with me, pretending she had nothing else to do. She sat for a long time on the windowsill, talking of nice comfortable things, like Christmas presents, and pantomimes, singing happy songs of her own childhood, but I wasn't lonely, and I curled down in bed content.

That winter was very long and trying, but to me it was like other winters, with days of dreariness when things went wrong and the rain soaked me to the skin and my throat was sore, or the fog choked me as I fumbled my way to school, and days too of radiant beauty when snow fell and the church at the bottom of the street nearby wore a white bonnet on its tower. Then the gardens and trees of Cheyne Walk were like a fairytale and I ran along the paths with Alison and Ian throwing snowballs and shouting with excitement in the clear whiteness and the sharp frostiness of the air. To me it was meat and drink and I wanted to stay out all night, looking up at the sparkling stars above the Thames, catching their glimmer in the whitened boughs of the plane trees, stepping through the blue shadows on the trampled snow. But the street cleaners came every morning and swept away the beauty so that the dark pavements were bared. The wintry days passed, the sky dropping its burden of glittering crystals, the dustmen carrying it off as if it were something wicked.

My mother lighted my bedroom fire, and I sat by its glow with her, we two crouched on the hearthrug, the woollen curtains drawn over the window, and a kettle singing on the hob for cocoa. As she told her stories of her own girlhood, how she used to toboggan down the hills by moonlight, steering the wooden sledge past the holly bushes and by the wild brook to the last dip, how she cooked potatoes in a wood fire under the stars, and walked with the shepherd up the snowy fields to take care of the lambs, I could hear the faint sound of the fiddle in the inn across the road. It seemed to be part of her tales, and I thought of the little girl she described in scarlet tam-o'-shanter and scarlet shawl tied round her body, riding triumphantly down those lovely great hills with a fiddler tall and thin and outlandish playing fantastic icy tunes to her from his seat in the holly bushes.

But I got one cold after another, and then I was very ill. I don't remember that clearly, except the visits of the doctor and whispers behind the screen, and the crackle of the fire as I lay in bed with Mother sitting by me. When I came downstairs I was strangely weak and wretched, and I wanted nothing at all.

'Penelope must go away,' my mother said firmly. 'All three of them are ill with this terrible winter of snow and fogs.'

'We haven't any money,' my father groaned. 'Where can we send them?'

'I'm going to write to Thackers Farm and see if Aunt Tissie will have them for a while. She won't charge much, there are plenty of spare rooms, and the children will enjoy it.'

'Oh, Mother! Can we all go?' cried Alison. 'What is it like? Is it real country?'

'Shall I be able to ride and shoot?' asked Ian. But I said nothing.

'I don't even know if Aunt Tissie can take you, children, and I doubt if there will be much riding. Your Great-Aunt Tissie is not young, and she's old-fashioned in her ways.' My mother pondered, as if she were thinking of reasons to persuade her aunt to have three careless young people suddenly thrust upon her.

'Tell her that I can darn and mend,' cried Alison, 'and I will help with the cooking.' It was noble of her for she hated sewing and cooking.

'And I'll help Great-Uncle What's-his-name. Mother, what is his name, your uncle?' asked Ian.

'Uncle Barnabas. Yes, he might be glad of help, if it is real help and not hindrance,' my mother agreed.

She spent a long time writing the letter that night, and I sat waiting to take it to the pillar box. I wanted to push it safely deep down with a little prayer that Aunt Tissie would accept us. Mother was offering £2 a week for the lot of us, board and lodging, and we were a hungry three, but that was all she could possibly afford. We always knew about money in our house, just what everything cost, and that made us more careful.

At last the letter was sealed and I slipped it gently into the box with a fervent prayer. Then I stood for a moment by Chelsea Church, thinking of Sir Thomas More and his children who had perhaps walked there when Chelsea was a village and gardens and fields spread around. I thought of them so long, somebody stopped and asked me if anything was the matter, and blushing furiously, I hurried home again. It was always difficult to find a place to think without being noticed and questioned.

A few days later the expected letter came from Thackers. I lay in bed with a sore throat, listening to the noises in the street below, the cat's-meat man, the newsboys, the rumble of barrows and flower carts. Then the postman's step came tapping down the street, and I was sure there was a letter for us. I flew downstairs in my bare feet to the dining room where my parents were having breakfast alone.

'Go back to bed at once,' scolded my mother, but I begged to stay and curled myself by the fire to hear the news when the postman stopped at our door.

*Dear Niece Carlin* [my mother read],

*I was very pleased to receive your letter. I am sorry the children are badly. I have talked it over with Brother Barnabas, and we shall be glad to take them. I wish I could do it for nothing, but we have had some losses of stock. We had to buy hay, the crop was so light, and the hard winter has made everything dear. We will meet the children if you let us know the train, and we will do our best to make them happy.*

*I have no more news at present, dear Niece Carlin.*

*Your affec. aunt,*
*CICELY ANNE TABERNER*

Alison and Ian had come down, and we all shouted together: 'Hurrah! When can we go?' My sore throat miraculously disappeared, so that I was quite well the very same day.

Our clothes were washed and ironed and mended. Our suitcases were brought out of the corner of the top landing, and carried to our room where they stood gaping wide their mouths and swallowing all we put inside. Alison and I folded the garments, our best frocks, Alison's coral-coloured, mine green, and two small aprons with gay French stripes which Mother made for us from a piece of linen she had bought on her honeymoon. These were for housework she said, and I felt I could do anything wearing my little apron, but I never guessed where it would accompany me.

Ian hunted about seeking darkly for catapults and knives. Alison took her workbasket and chose her favourite authors. As for me I took my sketchbook, and Hans Andersen.

At last all was ready and we set off, carrying our bags to the bus for St Pancras. We settled down in the express which speeded north through the centre of England. We had to change at Derby and a different atmosphere enveloped us as we got into the slow train. It was market day, and people crowded into our carriage, stout folk with baskets of cabbage plants and bags filled with sausages and pork pies and fresh herrings, and as each large person peered in at the open door at the already full seats, the others called: 'Come along in, there's plenty of room for a little one.' They all knew one another, and we three, squeezed together in the space of one, listened to their talk. A stout lady offered us humbugs from a paper bag, and Alison stiffly refused, but I was glad to eat them. An old bearded man brought red pears out of his bulging pocket, nearly dislocating the whole carriage as he struggled to draw them forth, and again I took some and the others refused.

'And where do you three young people come from?' asked one. 'You're not belonging here, I can tell.'

'From London,' said Alison proudly, as if she had said 'From Buckingham Palace'.

'London! Harkee there, John. They've come from London. Eh! It's a tidy big place. Not like hereabouts. My sister lives there in Camden Town. I don't expect you've ever set eyes on her, but she's the very spit of me.'

The others agreed the two sisters were as alike as two peas in a pod, and they talked of that lady in Camden Town, how London had rubbed the corners off her and how she was smooth as silk.

Ian began to laugh but Alison nudged him to be quiet.

'And where may ye be going?' asked a farmer, and he settled his large shape by my side and lifted his full pockets out of the way so that they did not hurt me.

'To Thackers Farm, near Hollow,' I told him. All eyes were turned on us, and those who had not heard were now told.

'Thackers. To old Barnabas Taberner's. He wasn't at market today. Well I never! Be ye related?'

'Miss Cicely Taberner is my great-aunt,' replied Alison primly.

'And Mister Barnabas Taberner is my great-uncle,' I added.

'Then ye'll be the childer of Penelope's daughter, Carlin, as married a Scotchman, up Edinburgh way, and went to live at Lunnon. Well I never! Well, ye'll liven 'em up. It's a quiet spot, Thackers. Quieter than most, but ye'll do well there. It'll put some roses in your cheeks, and ye need 'em.'

He pinched my cheeks in a friendly manner, and then turned back to the others. Soon they were all talking of market prices, and the poor prices of cattle, and the frost of winter and deaths and births. We sat silent, looking out at the darkening landscape, with a village here and there, and woods and hills and the little wild river which ran foaming alongside.

At each station somebody got out and the rest cried goodnight, and sent messages to those at home. We felt they were all one family, they knew everybody and were friendly together. There was a general lifting down of packages and searching under seats for sacks of provender, and we joined in the chorus as we watched them set off with hands laden to be met by others who nodded and smiled back as if they knew us.

Then we came to our station, and our fellow travellers said goodnight, and started us towards the station yard where they said the cart would be waiting. As we walked down the platform with its tiny roof and little stone booking office we were hailed by an enormous old man wearing a great top hat and widely flapping trousers. His red smiling face was wreathed in whiskers, and he waved a large hand and beckoned to us.

'Be ye Niece Carlin's childer from Lunnon?' he asked, and we said we were.

'I'm your Uncle Barnabas,' said he and he shook hands, imprisoning our fingers in his great palms so that mine ached for half an hour afterwards.

'Welcome,' said he. 'I'm right glad to see ye. Come along, for ye'll be starved after your journey. Come along to the cart that's waiting over there.' He nodded to the darkness, and swept up all our bags as if they were straws. I sniffed the cold, scented air as if I could never get enough of it. There was not a light in the countryside, never a house, nothing at all except the river which we could hear roaring in its rocky bed. Then we saw the cart with its couple of lamps, and rugs and cushions piled upon the seat. Uncle Barnabas went to the horse's head and spoke to her, and the solitary porter carried some packages from the van and stowed them under the seat with our luggage.

'Get up, all on ye,' said Uncle Barnabas. 'We'll have to squeeze tight, for I didn't know you were so bigly growed. The little 'un must sit on the stool as I luckily brought down with me.' He drew out a scarlet stool and I perched myself upon it. He wrapped us round with rugs and tucked us up tightly. When he settled himself on the seat he nearly overwhelmed us with his vastness, and sent the shafts of the cart down so that we had to rise again as he readjusted the seat. At last we were all ready, and the horse, which had been looking round to see what all the pother was about, started off.

Through a long winding valley we drove, between wooded hillsides, with here and there a cottage or a farm with its point of light. We left the river, and turned into another more open valley, with scattered cottages. At last we came to a sharp bend by a little brook which had wandered about by our side, singing and chattering, for some time.

'It isn't far now,' said Uncle Barnabas, who had been silent for most of the drive. I found out later when I knew him better that he seldom spoke when driving, for he wished to share the peace of the country. 'It isn't far, just round the edge of the road. That's our brook, fed by our springs. Thackers brook that is.' He nodded to it as to a friend and I nodded too.

We drove slowly up a hill, where a dark, mysterious mass of buildings and roofs was reared against the side of the valley. Near it, pricked out in black on the sky was the square tower of a church, and a huddle of pointed haystacks and gable ends of barns, clear in the primrose glow which lingered in the high parts of the hills.

The horse stopped and waited as if it wanted something, and turned its head like Balaam's ass about to speak.

'Out you get, except the little lass,' said Uncle Barnabas. 'She can sit still, for she's tired. Young folk like you walk up the hills. The horses wynd here, you see. Out you get, my dears. Me and the little lass and Sally goes up here alone.'

So out sprang Alison and Ian, and joyfully stretched their cramped limbs.

'Shall I push and help the horse?' asked Ian.

'Aye. Give a good hard shove. Sally will be grateful.'

They pushed and pressed the back of the cart and I wished I could also walk, for I was slipping off my stool all the time. There were lovely smells of flowers and wet moss and trees, and adorable noises of shuffling horses in the fields through which we passed. Creatures ran to the walls, and the lights of the cart fell upon the eyes watching us over ivy-tufts, and we saw the long head of a horse or the horns of a rough-haired bullock.

But the house was near, dogs were barking and rushing out, and there was pandemonium for a few minutes as I climbed down among them, and Uncle Barnabas tried to silence them. Ian stroked them, but I shrank back for a moment.

'They won't hurt ye. Hi! Roger! Sam! Flossie! Off ye go!' called Uncle Barnabas, and the dogs ran back to the great white porch of the house.

Then Aunt Tissie came out through a gold firelit doorway, and clasped us in the darkness. We were surprised how small and odd she was. She was a little old woman, with a clear skin and rosy cheeks and eyes as bright as stars. Her back was rounded with carrying heavy weights, but her foot was neat and trim, and she walked very swiftly, with little quick steps, like a tripping fairy.

She gave us smacking kisses, and led us into the great hot kitchen, where the fire blazed in a wide, open hearth, and a kettle sung and lights came sparkling and glittering from brass and copper and grey pewter. Such a smell of cooking there was – a brown fowl baking in front of the blaze, sausages sizzling in the frying pan, and the logs hissing and spluttering on the hearth.

'Let me have a look at ye all,' said Aunt Tissie. 'So this is Ian! Ah! He's nearly a man!' She shook Ian's hand as heartily as Uncle Barnabas had shaken it, and he swelled with pride.

'And what's your name, my dear?' she asked, turning to Alison. She kissed her again and looked admiringly up at my tall sister.

'And the little wench? She's a Taberner anyone can see! Penelope? Why there's always a Penelope in our family. Us'll be friends, Penelope, won't us?' she said, and I replied fervently: 'Yes, Aunt Tissie.'

'Now come up to your bedrooms at once, for I've got a fine tea ready for you, and I'm sure you're clemmed,' she went on in her soft rolling voice.

She took us through a narrow doorway to the back stairs, for the front stairs were for visitors, and we were relations. It was a crooked twisting stairway, with steps worn and hollow, and we stumbled up them following the flickering light of the candle to the landing.

'Here you two girls will sleep,' said Aunt Tissie, throwing open a door into a large bedroom. 'And next door is Ian's room. If you want anything, my room is at the end of the passage.'

She set the candle on the flowered chintz dressing table and then lighted another candle from ours and took Ian to his room.

'Mind your head,' I cried as Alison bumped into the oak beam which spanned the sloping ceiling, and we both laughed for we had never hit a ceiling before.

It was a lovely room with the most delicious smell of lavender and strange bitter herbs, an aroma which filled the house. I sniffed round and round, opening drawers and peeping under the glossy chintz which covered the dressing table like a frilled skirt, and I sat on the rocking chair and ran my fingertips over the curious carvings of the great chests and oak boxes.

Alison had an enormous wooden bedstead with 'Sleepe Welle' carved on the head, and a diapered blue-flowered curtain hung in thick folds from the bed-tester over the snowy pillows. I whooped with excitement and sprang on the piled-up feather bed which sank under me like a snowdrift.

'Now, my poppet,' said Aunt Tissie, coming in again. 'Don't you be lepping and cavorting on the beds. You'll spoil 'em for sleeping,' and I sidled off, ashamed.

My own bed was dark oak, smelling of beeswax, with wooden balls on the four posts. It stood on a raised platform so that I had to go up a step to get into it. There was an exquisite patchwork quilt over it, but I had no time to look closely at the myriad colours, for Aunt Tissie told us to hurry downstairs and have a hot wash and come to tea. So we brushed our hair and changed our shoes and ran to peep at Ian's room.

It was as exciting as ours, with its yellow wooden bed, and a bunch of lilies and roses painted upon the head in a circle. A patchwork quilt covered it, but it was plainer than mine.

'Just lift this up,' said Ian.

'It's like padded armour,' I cried, for it was quite heavy and seemed to be stuffed with blankets.

I looked round at the corner washstand with a bowl sunk in a hole, and the sheepskin mat on the bare, white boards.

But Aunt tinkled a bell at the bottom of the stairs, and we scuttled down laughing with our bobbing candles to the great kitchen, to wash at the sink in rain-tub water, which made me think of moss and autumn leaves, to rub our faces on lavender-scented towels from an oak press in the corner, to warm our hands in front of the blazing fire, where logs crackled and hissed. Tea was on the round table in front of the hearth, and we all sat down to the spread of toasted oatcakes, roast chicken, and yellow cheesecakes, and queer little knobbly loaves as big as our fists, and golden pats of butter with pictures of corn-sheaves upon them.

There sat Uncle Barnabas with his round, red face, framed in whiskers, and little Aunt Tissie who looked as old as ninety, I thought, but her face was fresh as a girl's and she was spry as a goldfinch and nipped about the room as quickly as a mouse as she opened the oven door and drew out a plate of spiced teacakes, or ran to the dairy for a jug of cream. She told me to carry the candle for her, and I felt the cold stones under my feet as if I walked in the Tower of London. I smelled the iciness of the dairy like a dungeon under a castle, but it was all white and beautiful with cheeses and bowls of milk and dishes laden with pats of butter, and I could hardly resist leaping up and down with excitement, and a shivery thrill which came over me.

'Now, my dear, don't do that! You'll spill the candle grease. Don't be a flibberty-gibbert, my dear,' said Aunt, and I followed as sedately as I could after her, but my feet wouldn't move quietly, they felt they must dance as if they were bewitched by the strangeness of everything.

That first evening was a glow of firelight and golden reflections, a babble of voices with rich warm accents, and the all-pervading odours of herbs from the bunches round the ceiling. I talked little, nor did I listen, but I sat by the hot fire in a corner watching the sticks crackle, and the lights flutter on the copper dishes. Uncle Barnabas was near me and I found myself pressing close to him, for he had a smell of something delicious. Afterwards I discovered it was cow-cake, but I leaned against his rough coat and shut my eyes. Candles were lighted, we stumbled upstairs. With us went Aunt Tissie, bearing the copper warming pan filled with red ashes from the heart of the fire. She rubbed it up and down over our sheets and kissed us goodnight. Somehow I got undressed and tumbled into the snowy bed which lay with arms waiting to enfold me.

## 2. I Pass Through the Door

WHEN I awoke the next morning I lay wondering who was clattering in the street below, for there was a rattle of wheels and the click of a horse's hoofs on cobbles under the window. Then I remembered that here was no street but Thackers with its farmyard and fields and woods around it. I sprang from my bed and leaned down from the casement window with its sprigged curtains. Below was the yard, and beyond a little grassplat and a bed of daffodils nodding their heads at the lambs playing in the croft beyond the wicket gate.

Ian waved to me from the stable door.

'Hello Pen! I'm going down with the milk. You can go too if you're quick as lightning.'

I tossed on my clothes, dipped my face and arms in the cold spring water, and gave my hair a rapid brush. Then I rushed downstairs to the kitchen, where Aunt Tissie was frying bacon in the largest frying pan I had ever seen, over a roaring blaze which crackled and spat in the wide fireplace.

'That's just like the frying pan at Drury Lane,' I told her as she turned round, and she gave me a resounding kiss.

'This old pan here has always been at Thackers, from ancient days,' she told me. 'Drury Lane? Where's that? Whose farm's in Drury Lane?'

'It's a theatre, where they have pantomimes,' I explained, laughing at her astonished eyes.

'Theayter?' she asked. 'I don't hold with no theayters. As for pantymimes, we've plenty of those here.'

'Have you pantomimes?' I asked doubtfully. 'Where?'

She pricked and turned the bacon and then made little pancakes which she tossed in the dark chimney and caught in the wide frying pan before she piled them on a dish.

'In the yard, where the hens are fed and one gets a morsel and the others chase after for all the world like a crowd of humans. In the fields when the lambs leap and dance on their hind leggies. In the pigcote when the little pigs get teasing the old sow. Ah, you'll see many a pantymime here!'

'Buck up, Pen,' shouted Ian, running in for the whip.

'Now wipe your feet, young man,' said Aunt Tissie sternly, 'and don't call your sister away. She's going to have her breakfast along of us.'

'She's going down with the milk,' protested Ian.

'Nay she isn't,' said Aunt Tissie calmly. 'Tomorrow will be her turn. No more nor one can go with Jess. There's four milk churns and the horse isn't going to have anyone else.'

'Ready,' shouted Uncle Barnabas from the yard. 'Look slippy. Run ahead and open the gates,' and away went Ian. I stood at the door and watched the cart start on its daily journey with its load of bright churns. Jess the servant man gave me a nod and a wink, called 'Gee-up, Sally', and off he drove through the open gate.

We had breakfast at a great oak table, with eight stout legs holding it firm. Afterwards I put on my little apron and wiped the dishes and Alison carried them to the high cupboard with its fretted doors. Ian returned and sat at a side table with Jess, for he had found a good friend and he wanted no more of me or Alison.

'Bacon and soncy cakes?' asked Aunt Tissie and she piled his plate high. I left him eating and went upstairs to help with the beds. The stairs twisted and turned most crookedly, and the walls were whitewashed over wooden panels. Halfway up was a 'peeping window' as Aunt called it, and there Alison and I stopped, to look across the valley to the fields with men ploughing, and the woods newly green which hemmed the farms and lands.

'Aunt Tissie, I could live here for ever,' said Alison.

'Could you, my chuck?' Aunt Tissie smiled at her.

'For ever and ever,' I added, not to be left out, and the words seemed to reverberate from the white walls and oak panels, and I heard a whispering murmur, 'for ever and ever.'

I ran after my aunt who was disappearing in our bedroom. There we tossed and turned the feather beds and Aunt seized them and puffed and pommelled them till they were soft as down. We drew the linen sheets over them and tucked in the blankets, and Aunt Tissie talked in a low murmur like the brook outside the gate.

'There's plenty of walks round here, over the hills and in the dales, and there's lots of work, what with one thing and another, butter-making, cheese-making, calf and pig feeding, and the poultry yard. You can help me a bit as your mother suggested, and then go off on your own devices. There's maybe more here to please you than you thought on.'

She chuckled quietly and we looked at her rosy crinkled face all puckered with mirth, and wondered what she meant.

'You'll find out in tuthree days. My Betty is coming,' said she nodding and laughing as if she had made a great joke. Betty was three years old, she added, and she laughed again at our discomfiture.

From room to room we went, and some doors were padlocked and some opened on to stores of wizened apples and great round cheeses ripening on the floors. One door which my aunt threw open led to the best bedroom, where a great four-poster bed stood with richly carved posts and ancient hangings and heavy tasselled coverlet. By its side stood a small oak chest, unpolished, and a clumsy chair with a faded velvet cushion.

'This is where they had their bedroom. It's the only one left as it was in their day,' she said.

'Who? Who had this bedroom?' we asked, sniffing the air, and stepping softly into the room. I caught my breath, as I listened for her reply and once again I heard that echoing sigh 'for ever and ever'.

'The people who lived here once, those who owned the house a long time ago. Great folk they were, name of Babington. Maybe you've heard of them. The house and farm were theirs, but it has changed since then, and the farm divided.'

'When did they live here?' asked Alison, casually, and she fingered the silky stuffs of the bed curtains.

'Oh, many a year ago. Hundreds maybe. This farm and all the buildings and barns were theirs, and the church hard by the stackyard yonder was their family chapel. They were Papists and folk say –'

We were interrupted by a loud banging on the stairs and the bronze bell in the hall tinkled angrily as somebody shook it to and fro.

'Cicely Anne! Cicely Anne! Where be ye? Are ye staying up there all forenoon? Cicely Anne?'

Uncle Barnabas was roaring like a bull and Aunt Tissie shut the door and hurried downstairs.

'Corves to feed and all to do, and you enjoying yourself upstairs,' cried Uncle Barnabas reproachfully. 'Those childer had best come and help, not hinder.'

We went into the calf-place with Aunt and helped her to suckle the little red and white calves, and we held the cans of milk warm from their mothers to their slobbering mouths. We stroked their curly heads and pressed their tiny horns, and I slipped my fingers in their mouths to feel their young teeth.

'Don't be afeard! Put your fingers in. They won't hurt ye,' said Aunt Tissie, as we played with the pretty beasts.

All morning we worked, feeding the hens, running errands to the barns, stirring the pig food, and turning the handle of the turnip-chopper. Ian was out in the fields with Jess, helping to cart and spread manure, which was the healthiest job of all so Uncle Barnabas said.

In the afternoon Aunt took us to visit a neighbour at a farm near, and it wasn't till evening came that I thought of the best bedchamber. We sat round the fire and the newly risen wind cried in the wide chimney and moaned round the corners of the old house. Cows moved clumsily in the cow-places down the yard, thumping their horns against the oak stalls, and we could hear them when the door opened. There was the sturdy tramp of Jess across the cobbles and the clatter of horses led to the stables.

'You must come and see London, and stay with us,' Alison invited my uncle.

'Nay. We can never get away with the corves to suckle and cows to be milked, and London's a powerful way off,' said Uncle Barnabas, in his slow drawl.

'A powerful way off,' I murmured.

I listened to the sounds outside while Alison and Ian talked of London – the hooting of an owl in the church tower, and the shriek of some small creature in the wood. Sometimes I thought I heard muffled steps in the room itself, movements and clatters as if people walked there, but perhaps it was only the wind catching the heavy curtains over the doorways which led to the stone passages, or the mice racing up and down the wooden panels.

Above the fire on the broad, whitewashed chimneypiece hung a couple of shining guns, and Ian sat watching them, his fingers itching to hold one of them, to shoot in the fields and woods. In the chimney corner, on the left of the fireplace, was a circular cupboard, let into the thickness of the wall. Its door was of iron, blackleaded and bright, and upon its surface was a polished brass plate and brass hinges. On the right was a narrow window which looked over the churchyard. At night a curtain was drawn over it, but in the dusk we could see the church and the stackyard, with four great haystacks and the church tower, all huddled together, as if they were talking in the dim light of the stars.

'Who lived here once on a time?' I asked Aunt Tissie, when there was a chance to speak. 'Tell me more about the Babington family.' But again, before my aunt could reply, Ian interrupted.

'Can I go shooting, Uncle Barnabas?' he asked. I sighed. I knew he was going to ask that question, from the way he watched the guns, and I couldn't bear rabbits to be killed.

'Yes, my lad. There's plenty of rats hereabouts. You can get them but you must take care and not shoot your sisters. I'll give you a lesson, and you can buy your own cartridges from me, to teach you to be careful. Jess shall take you out shooting with him one day. Rabbits want keeping down, but you mustn't shoot the pheasants. That's not allowed. Leastways, don't do it for anyone to see, but if you can get one for Sunday's dinner I shall not say nay.'

He gave a broad wink, and Aunt Tissie shook her head at him.

'Now, Brother Barnabas!' she cried.

Ian leapt with excitement, but Uncle Barnabas said: 'Sit ye down, lad, and keep quiet. No need to hurry. Nobody touches my guns, nobody at all, neither your Aunt Cicely Anne, nor Jess, nor anyone, without my consent and permission, and remember that!'

Alison was looking at the books in the little hanging bookshelf. They were all old and fusty leather-bound books of sermons and poems, *Paradise Lost* and Thomson's *Seasons* and *Pilgrim's Progress*. But it was no use to try to read, the room was so full of exciting things. I could not keep my eyes from wandering round to the copper skimmers and wooden bowls and the rows of horse-brasses with their suns and moons, and the handsome grandfather clock with its brass face and eagle on the top and the lustre jugs and china horsemen. Then Jess, the servant, came in and sat behind us in a corner which was his own reserved seat, like a stall in a theatre, I thought, for he could watch all that went on from his high stool. He took out a knife and started whittling something, and Ian went over to him.

'What are you doing, Jess?' he asked.

'Just making a little nobby whistle, Master Ian,' said he, and very soon he had made a whistle out of an elder stick, and we were all asking him to make another.

From the oven came the smell of hot roast potatoes, and Aunt Tissie opened the door and peeped inside and cracked their skins. She set the table, moving softly and quickly from cupboard to dairy, but everything was done so smoothly that before we knew, supper was ready. Then we sat round the white cloth in the lamplight and ate the big roast potatoes in the way Uncle Barny ate his. We broke them in two, sprinkled salt over them, put lumps of butter in them, and then poured cream into them, and ate them with a spoon. We even ate the crisp, brown skin. We had never tasted anything like this in London, we told Aunt Tissie, and she was pleased.

'They don't have cream and butter in London like ours, I'm sure certain. That Jersey cow of ours, little Lusty, she gives rich milk, and I always keep hers for the house. Ours are all fine cows, and every one is a good milker, and I love 'em, all of 'em.'

'It will be my turn to go down with the milk tomorrow,' I reminded Uncle Barnabas.

'Then you'd better be off to bed. The grandfather says it's your bedtime.' He glanced up at the tall clock in the corner.

We hunted in the candle cupboard for our favourite candlesticks, for already I had chosen a pewter one with a beaded edge, and Alison had a china one with green leaves bordering it. There was an iron candlestick for Jess, very ancient, I was sure, and a collection of many kinds, so that each could be satisfied.

'You'll maybe like hot baths tonight,' said Aunt Tissie. 'Ian will help me carry up the water.'

She filled the pails with hot water and we helped to carry them to the flat, oval hip-baths which stood in each room.

When we had finished, we sat in bed, and Aunt Tissie emptied them and carried the water away.

'That's enough for tonight. Go to sleep my dears and don't dream.' She kissed us, and tucked us up, and blew out the candles.

I lay in bed wide awake long after she had gone, breathing in the rapturous odours of sweet mossy water and lavender and whitewash, and as I lay there I thought I saw a shadow move across the room, slipping lightly with swaying, billowing skirts to the opposite wall.

'Alison,' I whispered. 'Alison. Who lived here once, Alison?' but the quiet breathing from the curtained bed told me that Alison was fast asleep.

Then I too shut my eyes, and I never waked till the clattering of milk cans and the mooing of the cows under the window brought the lovely feeling of another day, with a ride to the station as a glorious beginning.

It was the following day that my adventure began, but first I must describe Thackers. It was a stone-built farm, with gables and doorways in unexpected places, with barns and cowhouses across the green grassplat and old ivy-covered buildings where fowls roosted and calves sheltered. Only a few yards away was Thackers church, with its twelfth-century tower which rose from the group of trees and haystacks so close to the farm buildings, the stables and barns, that it seemed to be part of the homestead. Round the high walls of the tower were sculptured shields, fifteen of them, with the arms of an old family emblazoned upon them, but so defaced by wind and weather that I could scarcely make out the devices from where I stood in the garden below. Pigeons flew about its slit windows and rested on the flat roof of the church; swallows nested in the eaves and there was a constant cawing of rooks from the encircling elms which dipped their boughs over Thackers farm. The stackyard adjoined the churchyard, the orchard was by the church, and fields went nearly to the doorway. We were warned to keep the wicket gate shut lest calves should wander in the ancient building. My uncle had the keys of the church, for he was verger and caretaker, and Aunt Tissie dusted the pews ready for the parson who came once a month from a neighbouring parish.

Inside the house, beyond the kitchen, were the parlour and dining room, stuffy rooms which Aunt Tissie kept neat and polished. She showed them to us with pride, but we had no desire to sit in the speckless splendour, among woolwork pictures of Abraham and Isaac, and silver cups commemorating Uncle Barnabas's success at the county shows. The kitchen was good enough for us, Ian told Aunt Tissie, and I could see she was pleased.

'That's well, my boy,' she nodded. ' 'Tis a good homely room as our family has lived in for generations.'

Just off the kitchen, down a stone passage was the dairy, where the cheese press and the wooden churn for butter-making were kept. It was a great, cold room, with sanded benches all round the white walls, and yellow bowls set on them. Around every flagstone of the speckless floor was a little rim of yellow sandstone. I watched Mrs Appleyard, the ploughman's wife, sand the benches and then outline them.

'Why do you do that, Mrs Apple?' I asked her, and indeed she was like an apple, with her round hard cheeks.

'To make it purty, my dear. It's an old custom. We allays does it this way in our countryside.'

Next to the dairy were other rooms, a pantry and storeroom and larder, all built out of stone, and very cold and bare. I entered these rooms later, in strange circumstances.

On the landing at the top of the stairs was the chest where Aunt Tissie kept her sheets and towels, and I held the lid that morning, while she stooped to put away the clean linen from washday. A waft of herbs came to me which reminded me of our chest at home, and I told Aunt Tissie about it.

'It's tansy and woodruff that you smell,' said she. 'We picks 'em in the pastures and puts 'em in the chests when they've been dried, to scare the moths away.' She showed me the little withered tansy flowers and the white ruffs of 'new-mown-hay'. Then I lowered the lid and stood for a moment looking out of the landing window. It was the middle of the morning, the sun was shining brilliantly, the lambs were racing across the field in front of the gate and leaping over a fallen tree trunk. I could see Ian in the croft, trying to catch Sally, holding out a sieve of corn and keeping the halter behind his back.

'There's your uncle going to the village,' said Aunt Tissie. 'Get yourself tidy. You and Alison can go with him.'

She went downstairs, and I followed to brush my shoes across in the barn.

'Are you coming?' called Uncle Barnabas. 'Make yourself nice for I want folk to see what pretty nieces I've got from London,' and his eyes twinkled with good humour.

He went to the coach house, and Jess ran out to help Ian with the horse. Alison and I went upstairs together for our hats and coats. Alison put on her navy felt hat in front of the little oval mirror and for some reason which I cannot explain I stood behind her, craning to see myself. I seldom bothered to look in a glass, but this old mirror, half-shadowed with silver, made such odd reflections, such misted, dim pictures of the room, twisting them and reforming them in its curved glass that I was attracted to it as to a magnet. There were two tiny drawers in the inlaid stand filled with old bits of jewellery, silver buttons, jet and amber brooches, and broken earrings. It stood on the rosebud chintz of the dressing table, and caught the light from the side window. So when Alison looked at her own charming face and adjusted her hat to the correct angle, I dodged behind her and tried to see myself, to find out if it was the girl I knew, the same Penelope, pale and shy. Even as I looked I knew there was a difference, and a stranger seemed to look back at me. I glanced at Alison's reflection and saw her brown eyes and her short curls with the blue hat perched askew, but behind her peered the eyes of another, who surely was not myself? Alison turned away and I followed, walking slowly, puzzled about the girl upstairs in the mirror. What did she want to tell me, or was it really myself? What did she know that was hidden from me? Who was I, anyway?

They were calling to me to hurry, and when I got to the bottom of the crooked staircase Uncle Barny was carrying the best whip from the hall, and Ian was already in the cart holding the reins.

'I shall want a rug, Cicely Anne,' said Uncle Barnabas, and my aunt asked me to fetch it from her bed, where·it lay. The everyday rug was kept in the coach house but we were to have the heavy Scotch plaid.

Upstairs I went again, but when I got to the landing I looked at the closed doors and did not know which was Aunt Tissie's, for there was something strange and unfamiliar about them. I hesitated and opened a door, and then stopped short, for in the room before me, down a couple of steps, were four ladies playing a game with ivory counters. They sat round a table and a bright fire was burning in an open hearth. They were young and pretty, except an older woman whose expression was cold and forbidding. Their dresses were made of stiff brocade, and their pointed bodices were embroidered with tiny flowers. On their heads they wore little lace caps, and I saw golden hair peeping out from one headdress. Each wore a narrow lace tucker round her neck, and rings glittered on white hands that threw the dice. All this I saw in the moment I stood transfixed at the door. Then a little spaniel rushed across the room and they turned and stared at me with startled eyes. They were as amazed as I, and sprang to their feet, yet there was never a sound. The older lady rose and I caught a glimpse of her scarlet shoe as she came towards me, frowning with hands outstretched as if to hold me.

'I beg your pardon,' I muttered, and quickly I shut the door, my heart pounding, and my hands trembling. I thought I had stumbled on some grand visitors of Aunt Tissie's, but then I saw there were other doors along the landing which I had not seen before. I felt caught in a net, and I opened one with desperation. I stopped dead, for a couple of stairs descended to a long, low-ceilinged passage. A maidservant wearing a round, white cap carried a tray and knocked on a door to the right. I saw the heavy carvings over the doorway as she entered. Then a servant man carried another tray to the left and disappeared. A bitter-sweet smell of spices and pungent herbs came to me, but there was never a sound of doors shutting or footsteps. I closed the door and went back to the landing, feeling rather sick and not daring to open another of those mysterious doors.

Then Aunt Tissie came thumping upstairs.

'I couldn't find the room,' I faltered, and I ran to her and took her warm hand in mine.

'Couldn't you find it, Penelope?' Aunt Tissie was surprised. 'Why, it's as plain as the nose on your face. Here it is, and here is the rug lying on my bed.' She threw open the door and I saw Aunt Tissie's large, bare room with lime-washed walls and a great wooden wardrobe. The window was wide open, and in front of it was an old dressing table with a pair of wig stands and pewter candlesticks, but there was no sign of the strange company I had just seen.

I couldn't believe my eyes and I stood in the doorway, not venturing to cross the threshold.

'Aunt Tissie. I opened a door and saw some ladies sitting in a room. Who were they?' I whispered, shy to speak about it as if I had done something amiss.

She started. 'You saw *them*? You've *seen* them?'

She looked at me with astonishment and then drew me to her arms. Down below in the yard I could hear Uncle Barny thumping and banging with his whip end, impatient to be off, but my aunt took no notice.

'It's the secret of Thackers,' she said very quietly. 'They lived here once, my dear, and some say they live here now. I've never seen them, nor has Uncle Barnabas, but my own mother saw them when she was a child, and her mother before her. My mother once told me about them, but nobody has mentioned them since, and that's fifty years since I heard. She said they sat round a table playing some game, and sometimes she saw other things but she didn't tell me all.'

'They weren't ghosts,' I cried eagerly. 'They were real, quite alive like you and me.'

'Yes, my dear, I know. They are the people who once lived here. Now, never say a word to anybody, for I wouldn't have it talked about, and nobody but yourself living has seen them, and maybe you'll never catch sight of 'em again.'

I promised to be silent, and followed my aunt downstairs. I climbed into the cart, but as we drove away I turned round and looked up at the house. There was my aunt's bedroom window with the blue curtains flapping, and Ian's room with a fishing rod sticking out, and my uncle's little room, and our own with the rosebud curtains. There was never a sign of the mysterious passage nor the room I had seen. In the yard stood Jess, a wide grin on his face, and he seemed so solid and real I waved my hand to him, and was reprimanded for my free manners by Alison.

We drove across the little bridge which spanned the brook and then took a lane to a small village on the hill, where my uncle called at a farm called Bramble Hall. He left us, with Ian holding the reins, and went round to the side of the house. It was Elizabethan, for on every pointed gable was a round stone ball, and the windows were diamond-paned and mullioned like Thackers, but Thackers was older still. An ivy-covered stone wall encircled the house, and in it was a tall, beautiful iron gate with a flight of circular steps.

Through it we could see the front door of the house, with mossy old steps dropping to the lawn and a cut yew hedge and flowerbeds. We sat there, listening to the dogs and calves and the sound of men's voices in the farmyard, but although Ian and Alison were talking to me and their world was all around me, my thoughts were far away. I felt dazed and queer, and I looked at the old Hall half expecting to see ladies in full, stiff dresses coming sweeping down the flight of rounded steps from that front door which was barred as if it hadn't been opened for a hundred years. Everyone used the side door, and the ghosts could come as they wished, to walk in the green garden, to pick the daffodils which bordered the uncut lawn where now a calf grazed and a hen clucked with her chickens.

Then Uncle came back to us with a pleased smile on his face, and away we drove over the hill crest, where we looked down on a small town with a row of shops, and a quarry with men blasting stone. We dismounted and walked again, for the way was steep and rough with loose stones, and now and then we had to drive a stray calf or wandering pig out of the path.

'What's the matter with Penelope?' asked Uncle Barnabas. 'Has she lost her tongue? She's never spoken all the time.'

Alison laughed. 'She's fey, Uncle Barnabas,' said she as I was silent. Uncle Barny looked curiously at me.

'Nay, we mustn't have no mooligrubs here,' said he.

'Have you never heard tell of mooligrubs, with all your book-learning?' he continued, when we laughed. 'It's the sulks.'

'Penelope isn't sulky,' explained Alison, kindly. 'It's just that she gets queer sometimes and then she imagines too much.'

I frowned at her to be quiet, for I detested Alison to call me 'fey'.

'Poor little wench,' Uncle Barny was compassionate. 'We'll soon get rid of that. Plenty of milk and good fresh hill air, and she'll be quite well again.'

As we walked down the steep road to the little town with its smell of limestone, its quarries and caverns and wooded cliffs, and the lovely green river gliding like a snake under the ivy-covered rocks, my mind cleared and I became gay and lively, forgetting everything in the excitement of petrifying wells with birds' nests of stone hanging in the grottoes, and caves with long underground passages, and hidden streams.

At night we sat round the kitchen fire, Aunt Tissie making a rug and we three helping her. She had a piece of sacking washed and hemmed for the background, and a great pile of strips of cloth, in scarlet, grey, and black. She and Alison had steel hooks with which they pulled the strips through, making a pattern on the sacking. Ian and I were provided with scissors to cut more strips for the workers. I cut up a waistcoat of my uncle's and a pair of narrow trousers which must have been a hundred years old, and Ian slit a soldier's scarlet coat.

Idly I turned over the contents of Aunt Tissie's wooden workbox, and from among the scissors and emery cushion and ivory needlecase I took up a curious spool of silks. It was a wooden figure of a little man, carved with ruff and curling hair, but the body was covered with a web of blue, green, and scarlet silks, wound in a cocoon.

'What's this, Aunt Tissie?' I asked, curious about every object I saw. 'Whatever's this?'

'Oh, that's an ancient thing, my silk bobbin-boy, I call it. It's been here I dunno how many years. I can't think what it was used for, such a queer little manikin. So I keep my silks wound round it, as you see.'

'It is an odd little person,' said I. 'Can I take the silks off and examine it, Aunt Tissie?' I asked, eager to leave the rug-making for a more exciting occupation.

'Yes. Wind them on some papers, and look at it, Penelope. It's been lying in this workbox for many a long year, and when I asked my mother about it, your great-grandmother, she said she played with it when she was little, and that was all she could say.'

I unwound the silks and exposed the small carved figure. The workmanship was exquisite; the pleated ruff with its pricked edge, the tiny buttons on the doublet, and the slashings of the trunk hose were all clear and delicate. The face was that of a young man, petulant, disdainful, with deep-set eyes, frowning. The figure was broken and stained, with part of the ruff snapped off, and notches where somebody had chipped off pieces to catch the ends of the silks.

'It was lost for years,' continued Aunt Tissie, as she peered with screwed-up eyes at the wooden man, 'and we found it again in some rubbish in one of the attics. Then once it got throwed on the fire, and I got it off just as it began to burn. Another time it lay in the yard, and the cattle trod on it, so you see it could tell us some tales if it could speak.'

I clasped the figure tightly in my hand, and I rubbed it against my cheeks, to get the essence of the ancient thing. It was smooth as ivory, as if generations of people had held it to their faces, and I suddenly felt a kinship with them, a communion through the small carved toy.

'You can have it to keep if you like, Penelope,' said Aunt Tissie, as if she read my desires in my flushed face. 'You seem set on it, so keep it. I can have my silks wound on ordinary bobbins.'

'Oh, thank you,' I cried. 'It's an Elizabethan person, Aunt Tissie, I believe.' I nodded my head importantly.

'Maybe, and maybe not. There's many an old thing in this house, and some are forgot and some are in use, just as they have always been.' My great-aunt bent her shrewd old face to her work, and her wrinkled eyelids were lowered over the piercing blue eyes, as if to screen them in reticence. Her full lips were pursed as if she knew a thing or two. The worn, brown hands reached for a scrap of scarlet stuff and she hooked it into the sacking.

As we worked, Aunt Tissie talked to us in her slow, warm voice, running on and on like the flickers of the fire. She told us of Thackers in the olden days, when her great-great-grandfather lived, and she reminded us that it was in the days of our own ancestors too, for the family of Taberner had lived at Thackers and served the great folk since those early days.

She said the house and farm were the country house of the family of Babington, and the church was their private chapel. Thackers was an old manor house, beloved by them, for although they were rich and owned great lands and a fine town house at Derby, they always made Thackers, where they had been born, their home. The house had been changed, and part of it pulled down after the 'trouble'.

'What was that?' we asked.

'The young squire, Master Anthony, was imprisoned and hanged for plotting against the queen,' said Aunt Tissie. 'Queen Elizabeth it was. I don't rightly know anything about the Babington Plot, but I know what happened here, a year or two earlier. He tried to help Mary,

Queen of Scots, escape from Wingfield, over yonder.' My aunt pointed to the east window. 'There's tunnels in the churchyard and garden here and there's a tunnel at Wingfield. She was going to escape down them and Master Anthony would have hidden her at Thackers. But it wasn't to be. God saw otherwise.'

'And did they find out then about Master Anthony?' I asked.

'Nay, I can't tell you. I don't expect they did, but he went to France after that,' sighed my aunt. 'They must have been anxious years, those last ones on earth.'

We asked for more, but that was all she knew, except that it happened long ago.

'We've been in the tunnels many a time, when we were children, haven't we Barnabas?' she continued. 'But they are closed and filled with earth and nobody can go into them now.'

Uncle Barnabas nodded 'Yes'. He had been down the rocky steps into a tunnel which led under the earth. The queen, the Scottish Queen Mary, was going to walk along it to Thackers, and hide there. His grandfather knew about it, and in his days you could go a long way underground. Stones closed the holes, and earth had fallen so that it was all blocked. There was a honeycomb of passages in which people could hide in those troublous days when Queen Bess reigned and the Papists plotted.

Uncle Barnabas then suggested we should have a tune. He liked a bit of music, something easy that he could understand. Could any of us play or sing, he asked, and he looked at us expectantly.

Yes, Alison played the piano and I sang a little and Ian had bagpipes at home, we told him. But the piano was in the cold sitting room, and the bagpipes were at Chelsea, and my throat was sore, we excused ourselves, for we were reluctant to perform.

'You give them a tune, Barnabas,' urged Aunt Tissie, knowing that he longed to be asked, but was too modest to suggest his own music.

'Yes, play to us, Uncle Barny,' we cried.

Aunt Tissie got out an accordion and he took it in his work-brown hands and I watched his fingers as they moved tenderly over the little white keys.

'What shall I play ye?' he asked. Then he conjured many an old air out of the instrument, and somehow they fitted in with the farm kitchen. As I looked round I could fancy the grandfather clock was staring at him with its engraved brass face, listening to the music, and the high dresser, and the great oak table, and the carved spice cupboard, with all its little drawers, each was hearkening. And others listened also, I could swear, dim figures I saw in the corners, shadows out of reach of the lamplight, coming from somewhere to listen to the old man.

Jess was working in his corner, never speaking, cleaning the harness, brushing and polishing the little brass ornaments and bells, fixing buckles and straps, doing something to halters and head-stalls, unconscious of the moving, flitting shades which passed before him. I kept in the lamplight, away from those pointed shadows, close to my aunt, and the music came dancing up to me, beckoning me to the darkness.

Then came bedtime, and we all went upstairs, I with some misgivings as I opened our bedroom door. I didn't want to see those ladies, but they were not there, the room was our own with its low rafters, its quiet beds with the little flowery valances under which Alison peered to see if a hen were brooding there.

All was safe, and we dived into the billowy mass of the feather beds and crept down to the warmth to lie for a few minutes to watch the moon which stared through the open casement at us, to listen to rustles and murmurs of the trees outside, to hear the owl hoot as he flew over the church tower. From down below came the sweet tones of Uncle Barnabas's accordion, and another music like a flute was mingled with it. I put my head on the cold linen and buried my face in its fragrance. I dragged the blankets tightly round my shoulders, and shut out all the world.

# 3. The Herb Garden

UNCLE Barnabas had a favourite seat where one could always find him. It was under a great oak in the croft, near enough to the farm for him to see all that went on, but leaving him free of the bustle and business if he wished to be quiet. He sat there in the evenings, watching the moon rise above the woods, listening to the call of owls and the rustles of nocturnal creatures. He went there when work was done, taking his rest away from us all. Sometimes I joined him, for he didn't mind my company; I could be part of the land and forget myself as he did. There we sat, my hand clasping his great warm fingers, as we waited to see the moon shadows and the starlight. Behind us in the house was the joyful preparation of supper, with Alison singing and Ian teasing. From where we sat we could see the glow in the kitchen, and the figures moving in the firelight, and it used to amuse us to watch them, unconscious of our gaze.

'They dunno know we sees 'em,' whispered Uncle Barny so softly I could scarcely hear, silent as if he didn't want to disturb the shadows round us, and a hedgehog passed us by and a rat slipped through the undergrowth.

As I sat there one evening listening to the swallows which were darting in and out of the barn, for it was early and light had not faded, I was conscious of much movement and excitement in the great farm kitchen. People walked in and out of the firelight, and came to the porch, strangers whom I did not know, women wearing full, gathered skirts, and wide aprons, and little ruffly collars, men in padded breeches and leather jackets and hunting boots. Some had bare legs and short, ragged leather trousers, and their hair was wild and tousled. They carried shining dishes and wooden bowls and leather jugs; they stooped over the fire and one lighted a slip of wood and carried the flame to candles fastened to the wall. Then I saw them more clearly, their rosy faces and brown hands and rough, uncut hair. They pushed and joked, or so I imagined, for I could not hear a sound. Through a bedroom window I espied another face, a boy older than I, with fair hair and keen, blue eyes. His face was eager and gay, and he looked at the oak tree where I sat invisible to him. He took a bow from the room behind him and fitted an arrow and shot at the tree's trunk, so that I winced and drew aside.

'Who are they?' I asked Uncle Barny. 'Who are those people and that boy?'

'Uncle Barny,' I cried, striving to make myself heard, but there was no sound except for my beating heart. 'Uncle Barny! Who are they? What are they doing there?' I asked again, and the words were like rain falling from the clouds or mists coming over the fields, making a pattern.

'Uncle Barny!' I made a desperate effort, and clutched his arm and a cry broke from my throat, a queer strangled noise.

'Hello! Have you been asleep, Penelope? Poor little wench. You've had a nightmare!' said he gently stroking my arm.

My voice had come back, and I asked, choking with the effort: 'Who are those people?'

Uncle Barnabas slowly turned his huge body and followed my trembling finger. Even as I pointed the lights dimmed, the serving men and women faded away, and there stood my Aunt Tissie with her copper kettle and Alison in her little apron, and Jess piling logs on the fire.

'Only your Aunt Cicely Anne and Alison! You've been dreaming,' said Uncle Barny again. I kept close to him and when he rose to return for supper, I went too. Everything was as usual, and there was a welcoming creak of chairs and crackle of the fire as we went into the kitchen and sat down to the table.

The surprise which Aunt Tissie had promised us arrived one morning soon after this. There was a clatter of hooves in the lane, and a young man rode up the drive on a chestnut pony.

'Here her is, Mester Taberner,' said he leaping down, and he led the pony to the barn door. 'Here her is. I couldn't get her afore, because they're thrutched with work at Bramble.'

'How do you like her, Penelope?' asked Uncle Barnabas.

'She's glorious,' I cried, patting the arched neck. 'Whose is she? Is she yours?'

'I've hired her from Bramble Hall for a bit, for you three to ride,' said Uncle Barny. 'It will do you good to learn to manage her. She's good-tempered, for I bred her myself.'

The pony nuzzled at his pocket and gave a whinny of recognition. 'Aye,' he continued, 'she's been inside Thackers afore this. Saw the door open and walked in, and helped yourself to a cake, didn't you, Betty?'

The pony whinnied and stamped her hoof, and the young man grinned.

We thanked Uncle Barny, bewildered by the good fortune, for we had always wanted a pony to ride. We once had lessons in London, when father was able to spare a little money, but we had never been on a horse outside the riding school.

Then Aunt Tissie came out with sugar and bread. 'Betty, you beauty,' she cried, flinging her arms round the pony and kissing its soft nose. 'Welcome home to your old stable, my pet.'

'Ian must look after her, groom her, fettle her, and you must take turns in riding,' said Uncle Barnabas, and he gave us a lesson in management, and showed us where to hang the saddle. Ian mounted at once and trotted round the yard and out to the field. I raced upstairs to change my apron and tunic. I flung open the door, and I fell headlong down a flight of stairs. I had dropped into the corridor where I had seen the servants pass with their jugs and tankards. For some time I lay half-stunned with surprise, but unhurt, for I had fallen silently like a feather floating to the floor. I looked round at the door, but it had disappeared; I stared at the low whitewashed ceiling and the carved doorways, and I listened to the beating of my heart which was the only sound. Then life seemed to come to the world, distant shouts of men, the jingle of harness, and the lowing of cattle. A cock crew as if to wake the dead, and I sat up trying to remember ... remember ...

'Grammercy! What's this ado?' cried a shrill voice, and a young woman came round the corner and stood with arms akimbo looking at me. 'What do ye here, wench? Ye've no occasion to come up here? I'll lay ye are peering into what doesn't concern ye. So get ye down to the kitchen. What are ye doing? Has my lady sent ye for 'owt? Who are ye?'

'Who are ye?' I echoed, struggling to my feet dazed and confused, and even my own voice sounded hollow and remote to my ears.

The young woman flared up angrily and shook a warning finger at me. Her clumsy body bent towards me and she muttered half under her breath: 'Don't ye be impertinent! Don't ye dare mock me!' but I had no intention of mocking. I had used her words to recover my wits, which had forsaken me completely.

'Haste down to the kitchen to Dame Cicely. The mistress is waiting for her posset,' said she more quietly, and she pointed down the passage. I went meekly past the closed doors with the carved lintels to a stone stairway up which a young and pretty servant girl was coming. Her round face was tanned and freckled and her little snub nose and ripe, red lips were beaded with moisture. She wore a full blue skirt kilted out of the way, and her small, brown feet were bare. A bonnet of lawn covered her ruddy hair, and she tossed her head to shake back a curl. In her hands she carried a besom made of birch twigs and a mop and a wooden bucket of hot water. She looked up and saw me, and she stopped dead, staring at me with her wide, brown eyes startled like a deer.

'Who art thou, mistress?' she asked, and she puckered her red lips and spoke with a broad accent which was homely and welcoming to me. 'Dost want Dame Cicely Taberner?'

'Yes please,' I faltered. 'Miss Cicely Taberner I want.'

'She's down in the kitchen making the bread.' The girl spoke slowly, and she put down her bucket in the corner and accompanied me with many a backward glance at my dress and surreptitious peep at my face, along the stone passage to the room I knew so well. There was the same big oak table in the middle of the floor and the same spice cupboard with its multitude of little drawers against the wall. The bare, scrubbed boards of the table were heaped with a medley of things – wild ducks, in their soft feathers, pigs' white pettitoes, bleached for cooking, a wide basket of apples, wooden and earthenware bowls and an enormous rolling pin like a truncheon. Strange smells came drifting through the air, pungent odours of spices and meats and smoke from the fire, and strange people were standing about on the flagged floor where green rushes were strewn. A great fire burned in the open hearth and round it were saucepans of brass and iron simmering in the edges of the flames and sending out the heavy odours which pervaded the room and made me feel giddy as I stood in the doorway surveying the scene. The stove with its ovens and hobs was no longer there, but hanging from the iron ratchet which Aunt used for her pig-food kettle was a large cauldron with meat simmering, and curls of blue vapour rising among the flames. On the floor in front of the blazing logs was a spit with a humpbacked boy turning the handle and watching the roasting fowls drop their fat into a dish below. He stared at me, unsmiling, his green eyes bright in the firelight, his rough mop of black hair glittering round his small, pointed face. Then he went on with his work, but his gaze never left me and I felt discomfort under the inimical stare.

I saw a woman who was surely my Aunt Tissie, grown taller, stouter, younger, and more comely, but with the same broad good-tempered face, and the same hooked nose and rounded cheeks. Her lips were parted, and her forehead wet with sweat. She was kneading the bread in a great wooden trough like the horses' manger and her plump arms were deep in the folds of the dough. A young girl was cracking and beating eggs in an earthenware bowl and tossing the shells to a corner of the room where a vast heap lay like foam. Another woman was stirring custard in a brass pan, chattering all the time. On a rack above their heads hung a hundred or more oaten cakes, big as dinner plates, drying in the fire's heat, and a barrel of meal stood on the floor with a wooden jug beside it.

The serving-girl pushed me gently forward as I lingered in the doorway, and my aunt looked up from her kneading-trough.

'Lord 'a mercy on us! Who's this?' she cried, and for a moment her cheeks paled, and the pupils of her blue eyes dilated, but her voice was deep and rich as ever, with the burr in it which always made me feel warm and happy.

'It's me! It's Penelope, Aunt Tissie,' I cried, running forward quickly, and my heart rejoiced to see my beloved aunt. The others stared open-mouthed, but Aunt Tissie carefully removed the clinging dough from her arms and dipped her fingers in the flour-barrel to dry them. She came slowly across the room to me, for I had hesitated halfway across the floor, bewildered by the strangeness that assailed my eyes and nostrils. I stood mute, like a little wild creature, wrinkling my nose at the smells of humanity which were unlike those I knew.

Aunt Tissie put her hands on my shoulders, and tilted my chin to the light. Her puzzled blue eyes gazed into mine, her fingers caressed my cheekbones and her thumbs poked my dimples.

'Who art thou, little wench?' she asked quietly, softly. 'Thou call'st me Aunt, niece Penelope? Art thou a niece of mine? What's thy name?'

'Penelope Taberner Cameron,' said I, and the words dropped from my lips one by one as I made the effort to remember. As I stood there, breathing the air which was different, feeling strange emotions in my heart, so that I was half trembling with fear, I stretched out a hand to hold the table, to get courage from the rough wood. Sounds I knew came from the open door. Cuckoo! Cuckoo! called a bird in the wood, which I glimpsed through the portal, and the doves cooed in the yard. My heart stopped its wild beating and I turned with a timid smile to my aunt who was staring at me.

'Penelope Taberner,' she repeated, ignoring the Cameron. 'I can scarcely believe it, yet thou art a

Taberner, in spite of thy dark hair cut like a youth's. A dimple in thy cheeks, and the same crooked way of smiling, and the same round mouth, and the little twist to thy eyebrow, as one or another of us always has, and always will have as long as there is a Taberner left.'

She paused in her inspection and frowned and took my hand in hers as if she would read the lines.

'Thou hastna worked hard, for thy hand is soft and white as my lady's. Where dost thou come from, my sweeting? I know of my kin round hereabouts, but I disremember you, although I can't keep stock of brother Andrew's twenty childer. Are ye one of 'em? Or are ye a daughter of Elizabeth, who had fourteen wenches as well as four boys? Where do ye come from, Penelope?'

'From Chelsea, Aunt Tissie,' said I, slowly, trying to remember more, but my mind was away, lost in the shadows which flickered across the doorway and raced over the fields outside.

'Chelsey? That's a village near London. I've heard Master Anthony talk about it, for he took Mistress Babington there once. Maybe thy mother was a serving maid to her when she was there? It's a powerful way off, and I've no relations living there, as I knows of, but I've lost count of some of 'em. There was niece Margery, but she married a farmer Ashover way, and you're not one of hers. And there's niece Sarah, and Rachel, and Mary and Susanna, and Jane and every one of 'em has a mithering lot of childer, some of 'em old enough to be wed, and many a Penelope among 'em. There's Robin and Ralph and John Taberner, all got daughters. Whose maiden be ye?'

I shook my head. All memory of my mother and father had disappeared, I knew nothing about them. Only Thackers and the unchanging landscape remained, familiar and dear to me, as if I had known it from time everlasting, as if I were part of it, immortal soul of it come back to the loved place.

'Aunt Tissie,' I pleaded. 'I've come to Thackers to learn the ways and to be with you, and to stay as long as you'll have me.' Then, with a flash of memory I added: 'My mother sent me, to be with you.'

'Well, whoever ye be, ye are more than welcome, for there's no shadow of doubt you're a Taberner, and a good-bred one, although not as strong-looking as ye ought to be. Here ye shall live, Penelope, as long as ye will. The last Penelope who lived here died a while back. She was my favourite niece, and when her father was killed in the war in the Netherlands, she came to me. It was same as a ghost come back to see the likeness beween ye, but she's in the churchyard yonder, under sod, and ye are alive and blooming like the rose.'

She looked down at me again with a kindly welcoming manner, and then she seemed to be aware of my clothes, for she gave a sharp cry.

'Where didst thou get those weeds, my chuck? Where's thy baggage? Have ye no belongings? How didst thou travel here?'

I shook my head dolefully. 'I can't tell, I can't answer,' I muttered.

'Ye don't know?' exclaimed Aunt Tissie, astonished, but not more surpised than myself. 'Nay, that beats it all. If ye weren't my own kin I should say ye were simple,' and she clucked her tongue in consternation.

The kitchen maids crowded round me and touched my dress with curious fingers. I looked down at my navy serge tunic and the little striped apron I had worn when I was helping Aunt Tissie. It wasn't I who had changed, but my surroundings, I reminded myself, as they whispered and nodded and pointed at my shoes.

'They're mebbe out of the oak chest on the landing,' said one of them, as I stood miserably blushing with the attention I had caused. 'There's a store of ancient clothes for the poor and needy, gear of well-nigh a hundred years in that chest.'

'Or she found 'em in the play-acting chest, where the mistress keeps her garments for mumming-plays and Christmas routs and junketings. Ye might have found something seemlier than that doublet if ye wanted to dress up and surprise us,' said another.

'Where have ye hidden your ordinary gear?' asked the one whom I had seen the first, who now entered the room. 'I found her on the landing near the mistress's chamber, and mebbe she's been inside poking about.'

'No, Aunt,' I cried, and tears sprang to my eyes. 'These are my own clothes, and I haven't any more.'

'Well amercy! Don't weep, my pretty! I mun make ye some more, for those are not seemly,' said Dame Cicely, and she wiped my eyes with her apron and put her arm about me to shield me from the others. 'Tabitha,' she called to the pretty girl who had met me on the stairs. 'Take Penelope upstairs to my bedchamber, and put more womanly weeds on her to cover up her long legs. She's like a lad in that garb. I wouldn't have the mistress see my niece so.'

'It's the dress of a London prentice she's wearing, and it becomes her. Leave her, Dame Cicely,' said Tabitha. 'She's bonny in them and the mistress won't mind anything on a day like this. She'll laugh mebbe, and it will do her good, for, poor soul, she has troubles enow with Master George's gambling debts and Master Anthony, God bless him, bringing anxieties to this quiet place where nothing's ever happened since Adam and Eve were on earth.'

'Have it thy own way,' laughed Dame Cicely. 'I'll tell Mistress Babington and Mistress Foljambe that my niece has come from Chelsey to help me, and she'll be right glad to have ye in the household, and whoever was your mother, ye are a Taberner, and the very image of her who died and is buried out yonder. Ye shall sleep in my bed, for it's had an empty place since she left us. Phoebe shall make a new smock for ye, and I'll lend ye a night-rail of mine, although thy little body will be lost in it.'

She looked me up and down, considering my position in the household.

'Niece Penelope, canst thou sew and cook and milk the kine?' she questioned. 'There's a-plenty of work to be done here, and no room for an idle maid.'

'I don't sew very well, and I can't cook,' I confessed.

'Maybe ye've been eddicated above thy station?' she said cheerfully. 'Canst read and write like the quality?'

'Oh yes,' said I.

'That's more nor us can do! I can't read a word, but I keep this household going. I carry my knowledge in my noddle and have no use for printed books. Receipts for cooking, and making of drinks and possets, I know them all. I remember the old ballads and I know the Psalms, so that I can sing without a Psalter. I keep a tally on the doorpost of the number of eggs and chickens and ducklings we have. I've done very well without reading and writing, and I keep my wits clear by not addling them with rubbish. But Mistress

Foljambe will be glad of thee. She'll maybe make thee her own maid.'

They all talked together, but I was too much astonished to utter a word, and I looked round the Thackers kitchen as if I had never seen it before. The passage to the dairy had gone, and the pantry was part of the big room. Aunt Tissie was different too, although I should have recognized her anywhere, whatever she wore. She had on a full dress, not much bulkier than the one she wore that morning when we sat down to breakfast at the same table, in a time that had slipped from my memory, so that I could not remember who sat there with us. The cherry-red woollen skirt was short enough to show her square, buckled shoes, rough and strong, but neatly made. Her black bodice was fastened up the front with little wooden buttons carved like acorns, each button slightly different from its fellow. A white cambric collar creased and crumpled with work was round her neck, tied at the front with a black, tasselled cord. On her thick hair was a fold of linen, like a cap, snowy and fresh, and her apron was gathered and pleated in many folds round her large waist. Her face had the same serenity, and she twinkled at me and laughed with loud laughter like a man's as she saw my astonished eyes which were open as wide as they could be in complete bewilderment.

'Thou art an odd moppet,' she cried heartily and she laughed so much that tears came sparkling into her eyes, and all the maids laughed too. But the green-eyed boy glowered at me, and covered his eyes with his hands when I peered his way.

'Ye are a sweet toad, and as like my great-niece Penelope was at thy age as two peas in a peascod. Come here, my sweeting, and give me a kiss.'

She enfolded me in her floury arms and printed a loud, warm kiss on my lips, in just the way Aunt Tissie always welcomed me when she saw me in the mornings.

'But dunno ye call me Aunt Tissie! That's a name for a she-cat! Call me Aunt Cicely. Cicely Taberner is my name, and Thackers is my home, and Heaven's my destination.'

She gave a rollicking laugh and went back to her bread-making.

'Now make thyself useful,' she continued, 'and ye mun feel at home.'

'I do, Aunt Cicely,' I murmured, breathlessly.

'Go and pile wood in the bread oven, for the loaves will soon be raised, and it's not near hot enow.'

She pointed with a stout forefinger to the heap of brushwood in the corner and I went across the flagged floor, treading softly on the rushes through which I could see the yellow-bordered stones.

I pushed the green wood in the deep oven which went into the wall at the side of the fire, on the left of the open fireplace. Above my head, slung across hooks in the wall, were longbows and spiked halberds, long-shafted with hatchet heads, but the blades were rusty and the wooden handles dark with age and wood smoke. Next to them was my aunt's warming pan, which she used for airing my bed. 'To take the chill off, mind you, for you'll be nesh, my dear, coming from London.' It was polished like a mirror, and one of the girls stood before its reflecting surface and tidied her cap. I stared fascinated, wondering at its strange companions which might have been used in an ancient war.

'Ye've mebbe never seen a longbow afore,' said Aunt Cicely as she caught my curious glances. 'They don't have 'em in Chelsey, but here we keep to the old ways, and these were used in long-ago battles by our family. We'm got many an aged thing kept from days long past, and if they could speak they'd have perilous tales to tell. The warming pan is new and as good as a mirror for the wenches to set their caps straight.'

She stopped over the trough and pommelled the dough into a great creamy-brown bolster, not white like the dough I had seen before. Then she lifted the whole trough down to the floor and set it by the fire for the bread to rise. The young boy moved aside from his place on the hearth. His eyes were fixed upon me, never for a moment did he look away, so that I felt as if a savage beast were watching my movements, ready to spring.

The custard was poured out into a shallow dish and the girl stirred it with slow, even motion, murmuring a rhyme to keep the eggs from curdling. The second maid gathered up the broken shells and put them in a tub, and crushed them into fragments.

'Them's ready for washing day, Penelope,' smiled Dame Cicely. 'We uses up all our egg shells for whitening Mistress Babington's linen. But get ye gone and gather some herbs for the possets.'

'Where from?' I asked faintly, and my voice sounded husky and dim. 'Where from, Aunt Cicely?'

'Hark 'ee now! Where from! And where should they be from? Herbs for beer in the fields and hedgerows, but for possets you mun go to the herb garden, beyond the yew hedge. Pick fennel for the fish, and rue and borage for Mistress Foljambe's health and a pinch of lemon balm for young Mistress Babington who likes it spread on her pillows. Get a-plenty of comfrey and strewing herbs and some bay for the venison stewing in the pot over the fire. Here, Tabitha will go with you and help. She'll like to get a breath of fresh air and a peep at Tom Snowball who's trimming the hedges this morning.'

Tabitha blushed and drew a ruddy curl from under the edge of her cap. I liked Tabitha's cheerful face. Her arms were as brown as nuts, her skin freckled where the sleeves were rolled back, and her face was good-natured, although she seemed quick-tempered. She lifted a lidded basket from the wall and took my hand in hers, and then we ran out of the white porch into the sunshine. Hens clucked and pecked in the sweepings from the stables, and cocks strolled lazily across the yard. Scents of sweetbriar came from the little hedge by the door, and the spaces of the stones of the path were filled with yellow musk. I looked up at the house, to seek for my room and others, which I had forgotten. The house was larger, another wing was there. There were many windows with small leaded panes in squares and hexagons and tiny casements through which I got a glimpse of striped woollen curtains and brightly woven stuffs. Some of the farm buildings had gone or were part of the house, but the church was the same. Then I noticed that the shields around the tower were clean and fresh with the carvings distinct. A mason was chiselling one of the shields, and Tabitha stopped and looked up at him.

'Thou wilt have to be speedy,' she cried, pitching her voice high. 'Thou wilt have to hurry with thy carving, Master Stone. Young Master Anthony's coming home, and he'll expect to see it finished.'

Master Stone shouted something which made Tabitha blush.

'Impudent hound!' she exclaimed. Then she pointed out the new emblazon on which the mason was working. 'A.B. and M.D. That's for

Anthony Babington and Mary Draycot. Her arms are put alongside his, as the custom is.'

We passed the oak-studded door of the church, and the yew trees in the churchyard, and took a path skirting a lawn smooth as green silk with a cedar tree in the centre. On the border grew an oak tree which I recognized as the giant tree under which I had rested with Uncle Barnabas. The forking boughs and the horizontal branch were the same, but the girth of the tree was smaller.

Uncle Barnabas! The memory shot through me and I struggled as in a dream. Where was he? Then he faded from my mind as Tabitha's warm fingers drew me on. Our path was separated from the green by a yew hedge with peacock and ball trimly cut. Through a wicket I saw a lady pacing under the cedar, reading a letter. A couple of hounds lay with their noses between their paws, half asleep, and a small spaniel danced round her flowing skirts.

I stopped to stare at the lady in her fine dress sprinkled with little embroidered flowers on the kirtle and the stiff white ruff upstanding round her neck. Then I whistled softly to the dogs.

'Good boy! Here!' I called and the lady lifted her head and stared at me in amazement just as if I had no business to be there.

'Hush, wench!' cried Tabitha. 'Have ye no sense? You mustn't call when Mistress Babington is here. Where are your manners? Haven't you been taught none in Chelsey? And whistling! Don't you know the adage: "A whistling woman and a crowing hen deserves to have their heads cut off"?'

Tabitha reproved me with angry voice. The dogs came bounding across the lawn, but when they came near me they gave little whimpers of fear and retreated with their tails between their legs. I cared nothing for Tabitha and held out my hand trying to coax them, but they ran back to the lady, growling and trembling.

'Tabitha,' she commanded in a clear, young voice, proud and haughty. 'Tabitha. Bring that boy to me, and don't talk of heads being cut off. There are too many heads lost in these days to joke about it.'

'She's no boy, Mistress. She's Penelope, niece to Dame Cicely, come from Chelsey to help her aunt. She's dressed up in some clothes from the play-acting chest, or from that press where the poor folks' weeds are kept for Mistress Foljambe's charities, Madam.'

'Come here, girl,' said Mistress Babington, and I opened the gate and went close to her. I looked up into her pale face, at her deep blue eyes in which there was unhappiness, and the crimson bow of lips unsmiling and stern. Her hair was brown with little curls on her forehead, half hidden under a white winged cap of delicate lace standing stiffly out like petals of a rose.

'You are the girl who looked into my chamber. I remember you,' she said slowly, staring at me as if puzzled.

'Curtsy to Mistress Babington,' whispered Tabitha fiercely, and I obeyed.

'What is your name?' asked Mistress Babington.

'If it please you, my lady, it's Penelope Taberner from Chelsey, London,' answered Tabitha speaking for me eagerly.

I opened my mouth to interrupt but Tabitha went on in her cheerful way as if wishful to change the lady's thoughts from London. 'We're going to gather herbs for your possets, Madam, and for Mistress Foljambe, and that's why we came this road.'

'Away with you then, Penelope, and see you obey your aunt, for she is the mainstay of this house of ours, and if you grow up like her it will be well. But don't go hunting in the play-acting chest, nor must you ape the men and whistle.'

She gave a sad little smile which made me like her, she flicked her long white fingers to dismiss me and turned away.

All the time we had talked the dogs were whimpering, but when I went through the narrow wicket in the yew hedge they returned and played round the lady's violet silk dress. She sat under the cedar tree looking after me, and I glanced over my shoulder and saw the sunlight fall through the flat boughs and fleck her dress and cap with bands of brightness.

'Who is that lady?' I asked Tabitha as we hurried along the unevenly paved path. 'Who is she and why did I have to curtsy?'

'She's Mistress Babington, Master Anthony's young wife, as is mistress here. Leastways she is mistress part of the time, but when Mistress Foljambe, Master Anthony's mother, comes from Darby then we have two to obey. But they get on well together, and we love them both. You curtsy because it is the custom. Don't you curtsy to your betters in London, or are you freer in your manners there? What ails you? You'd best have a cupful of rue tonight to clear your wits.'

She spoke severely but in a minute her face brightened as she looked through the bushes.

'Let us run down this alley where no one can see us. There's the herb garden at the end. You pick the herbs and I'll go about my own affairs. I must have speech with Tom Snowball the gardener.'

So I gathered the pungent grey-green herbs which grew on many small bushes in the Thackers herb patch where I had been before, and I sniffed the strong, clean smells which were those which permeated the Thackers kitchen, where bunches hung from the beams and walls. As I filled my large basket with the sprays and leaves I looked round at the flowers in surprise, for although my Aunt Tissie's garden had many a bloom as I knew very well, for I went there every day for a posy, this garden was more carefully tended, and lay in straight lines and squares like a patterned quilt. There were the same small daffodils, which my aunt called 'daffodowndillies' growing in masses by the walls, and white violets in snowdrifts filling the crannies of the path. Gillyvers striped and yellow sprung from the mossy walls, where a cat crouched eyeing me balefully. The beds were bordered with little low hedges of box, smooth as green walls, cut into trim shapes like the hedge. There were bushes of Lad's Love which sent out their rich fragrance, and lanes of lavender, and clumps of spraying rosemary, with many a rose tree growing alongside, already in full leaf.

I wandered about on the narrow path which led me in a maze in and out and round about a dozen flowerbeds which would soon be ablaze, each one bounded by the box hedge. Pale lilies-of-the-valley and blood-red primulas were out with bees hovering round them from the straw skeps perched on stone stools farther up the garden. Tall orange lilies, bronze-budded, stood like soldiers guarding them, and overhead darted the blue swallows.

I went back to the herb patch and filled the basket. Over it I slipped the brown lid, and clasped it with a wooden pin which dangled from it. I gazed up at the blue sky and the rounded hills and woods. Then I heard laughter and away down the alley among the lilies I saw Tabitha and a young man. He wore leather leggings and rough, heavy shoes clogged with soil and a short leather coat on his back. His eyes were bright as a hawk's, and his cheeks ruddy as a ripe wood-nut. His head was black and tousled, for he had taken off his round leather hat and stood with hair on end. He put his arm round Tabitha and kissed her with loud smacking kisses, which she seemed to enjoy. Then he saw me peeping over the hedge.

'Ah! The little spying wench from London! I'll buss thee too if thou tell'st on me!' he cried laughing, and Tabitha sprang from his arms and came back very red in the face.

'Penelope! Not a word to your aunt,' she warned me.

She took the basket and together we returned along the garden path towards Thackers. When we reached the wicket I saw four ladies sitting under the cedar tree, sewing and talking with their heads nodding together.

'Master Anthony's two sisters and his mother, staying with us. Since his marriage they spend their time between Thackers and the big house at Darby, but they all love this place best.'

I wanted to stop but Tabitha forbade me. 'It is not for us to speak before we're spoken to. Keep to your own side of the hedge,' said she.

'I've seen them before, playing a game in a room,' I explained, and I peered over my shoulder at their quilted skirts and their proud, young faces and the sad eyes of the older lady.

'Maybe. They've their own parlour upstairs, but you've no business spying! You munno enter except to wait on them,' said Tabitha, severely.

We went past the open door of the church, and from within came the faint sounds of music very sweet and gay, and a boy's voice sang a carol.

'Master Francis, playing his lute,' said Tabitha grown cheerful again, and we looked through the doorway. I saw the boy who had leaned from the window, but now his face was grave. He was gazing up at the beams of the church, unconscious of my peeping eyes, singing in his clear fresh voice, plucking the lute carelessly, and the music was cold as the voice of a stone angel in the choir.

Softly, without disturbing him, we went back to the kitchen. I unlidded my basket, and scattered the herbs on the table. Then I sat down to watch Tabitha empty a creel of fresh speckled trout and start to clean them.

Aunt Cicely took boiling water and made a posset of some of the herbs she chose from my collection.

'You've brought some wrong 'uns, as I didn't ask for,' she said, turning over the green-and-yellow sprigs. 'Why did you get basil and hyssop? Surely you know the names of all herbs. Your mother should have taught you. Even in Chelsey they grow in the fields, don't they? Or don't you go herb-gathering?'

'No, Aunt Cicely.' I shook my head.

All this time the humpbacked boy sat by the hearth turning the spit with the brown, crackling fowls trussed upon it, and his strange green eyes were fixed upon me. I tried to talk to him, but I couldn't understand the grunts he made.

'He's dumb, poor worm,' said Aunt Cicely with a hearty laugh, as if she thought it very amusing. 'No need to talk to he. He's as the good God made him. He was found by Master Anthony deserted by gipsy vagabonds, and he brought him here, near dying. Master Anthony's priest baptized him Jude, for he was found on Saint Jude's Day.'

The boy looked at her as she talked, and then pointed at me and made queer noises. I went up to him and took his hand in mine, for I was sorry for him with his ragged leather clothes, and hands scarred and blistered and scratched. A quiver went through him at my touch, and he shivered and gave a horrid cry. Then he bolted like a startled rabbit through the open door. Tabitha left her fish to catch him, for the spit had to be turned.

'What ails the lad? What did you to affright him, Penelope?' asked my aunt.

'I only touched his hand,' I faltered.

'He's timid as a hare. Sometimes I think he's got extra sense sent by our Lord to make up for those others he's lost. He knows things we don't know, he feels through his fingers what we can't understand with all our ears and tongues and minds. He warns of storms brewing, and bad luck and even death. Last night he came in with a little elder pipe, made by one of the stable boys, maybe, but he played queer music like fairies make, or even like Robin Goodfellow himself plays in the dairy, although the poor fish he couldn't hear a note, or so we think.'

She pointed to the little elder pipe which lay on the hearth and I knew I had seen one like it somewhere. I couldn't remember where, for the memory was like a faded dream, and it slipped away at once.

Tabitha came back with the boy and he sat down by the hearth, with quick glances of fear mingled with pleasure. He picked up the pipe, and then looked searchingly at me, and between our eyes a flash of knowledge swept. Once he rose and came across to the oaken stool where I sat watching Aunt Cicely and Tabitha and he touched my dress and shoes and smelled my hair, but he would not lay a finger on my outstretched hands. Then he turned back again, and kept his eyes on my movements as if I were a strange animal he did not know.

I was too much interested in all I saw to trouble about him. Our old dresser filled one side of the room, but instead of the china jugs and best dinner service there was ranged a variety of pewter plates and dishes, drinking horns and flagons, bowls of wood and earthenware. On a shelf by the fireplace were brass and pewter pans, a great fish kettle and some iron skillets, with little legs upon which they stood on the hearth. Wooden candlesticks were fixed to the wall, and one of the maids drew out scraps of tallow and put in fresh candles from the bundles hanging by their wicks. A pot of musk glowed golden on the deep windowsill over the broad, stone sink where I washed myself, and the scent filled the air. In the little window which looked on the church was an hourglass with the sand slowly trickling through, and Aunt Cicely glanced at it now and then as she went to the oven and looked at the flat loaves baking there. She put her hand in a canister and brought out some strong peppermints, which she gave to me, and I sucked them as I watched the slippery, speckled trout on their bed of grass.

'Where have they come from?' I asked.

'From the River Darrand. Master Francis catched them, ready for his brother. Master Anthony's a Papist, and this is a fast day for him. We're expecting him home from London, thank God.'

The River Darrand! That was what Uncle Barnabas called the little river by whose side we drove, but others called it the Derwent. So Uncle Barnabas was right, as he always was! Yes, I knew where the trout had been caught, and my thoughts flashed down to the lovely winding river with its fringe of alders and willows, to the black stones over which it rushed, and the water-hens and kingfishers which haunted its tossing singing waters.

'Master Anthony's the Old Faith?' questioned Tabitha. 'Don't he go to the chapel here?'

'Sometimes for appearance's sake, but a priest comes here with him and says Mass in his private room and teaches Master Francis Greek and

Latin. We all know Master Anthony is a Catholic but it doesn't do to talk about such things these days, with the persecutions of the Catholics and hatred of the priests. We have Mass in the chapel sometimes, and why not, when it is his own chapel, and the family an old Papist family? There are spies about, but not here. Thackers is such a lonely place, nobody would ever come here. If they did they would see nothing, because there is nothing to see. We're a God-fearing family, Mistress Foljambe and young Mistress Babington, and Master Francis and all who live here, and we go to chapel on Sunday and listen to parson's long sermon, and honour the queen and keep her laws.'

'Thackers,' I said to myself. 'Thackers,' and I tried to remember more.

Aunt Cicely went on in her comfortable, slow voice in the warm burr which took all alarm from my heart so that I leaned forward to hear: 'Master Anthony will have fine tales to tell of the queen's court. He's been there, on and off, for three years, since he was eighteen, although he went to London first to study law at the Inns of Court, like all proper young gentlemen.'

Aunt Cicely's hands fashioned the round, flat cakes, spiced and honeyed, as she talked. She pricked them in a device of leaves and put candied fruit on the top.

'He saw the queen sail in her gilded barge on the Thames and he's been at Greenwich Palace and mixed with the greatest in the land, has Master Anthony.'

'He's very clever, writing his poems, and reading his Latin and Greek books. He'd be welcome at court where there are many witty gallants,' added Aunt Cicely, proud in the exploits of her beloved nurseling.

'Why did he study law?' asked Tabitha, and she skewered the trout on long wires and tossed the guts to the cat and kitlings.

'All landowners must have a knowledge of law,' explained Aunt Cicely patiently, 'and his stepfather, Master Foljambe, and also the Earl of Shrewsbury, his guardian, arranged for him to prepare for the duties which would fall to him when he came of age. He is a handsome gentleman with a fine figure and in London he met others who were at the queen's court. But he was a courtier at another court before that of Queen Elizabeth, and there he learned to make pretty speeches, proper for a queen's ears.'

'Another court?' Tabitha was surprised, and I listened amazed.

'He learned the ways of a queen and the manners of courts from a more beautiful queen than Queen Bess. With his gracious manners and wit and comely looks he was welcomed at Greenwich, but I doubt whether he pleased Queen Elizabeth, for he didn't flatter her like others who flit around her throne. She's a glorious, masterful woman and everyone must admire her for the peace and prosperity she brought to England, but Master Anthony's heart is elsewhere.'

'He has his young wife waiting here, Dame Cicely,' interrupted Tabitha, eager for romance. She paused in her chopping of fennel and looked towards the window as if she sought her lover. 'Surely he doesn't love another beside Mistress Babington?'

'He was married before he was eighteen,' said Dame Cicely shortly, 'and he loves his wife in a right and proper way but his heart is given to one above all others. There are different kinds of love, Tabitha, and you know only one. There is love for your sweetheart and wife, which is different from mother-love for your childer; and there's love for your country which makes you go to fight the French and Spaniards; and there's love for God, which is the best of all. But there's another love, born of beauty in sorrow. Master Anthony loves the greatest and unhappiest lady in the land, the queen's cousin.'

Dame Cicely had dropped her voice and she looked round cautiously as she spoke. The other maids were in the far corner of the room, busy with clanking pails and brooms, singing and teasing as they swished the stone passages, splashing water on one another, stepping through the pools in the flagstones in their high iron-heeled pattens.

'Mary, Queen of Scotland,' she whispered, 'the queen's cousin and heir to the throne.'

Tabitha started and dropped the speckled trout she was holding so that it slithered to the floor and was pounced on and carried away by a great cat. Away ran the sly creature and the maids ran after with their brooms shouting 'Hi! Tibby!'

'The captive queen!' cried Tabitha in surprise.

'Hush,' warned Dame Cicely, nodding and glancing round to see if anyone had heard.

'She's got beauty and wit, and a tongue of silver, and eyes that kindle a fire in all men's hearts,' she continued warmly. 'She has no age they say, she is lovely and fresh as the dewy morning. Young Anthony was page to the Earl of Shrewsbury when he was nobbut fourteen, and he lived at Sheffield Castle, where the queen was imprisoned. His father died when he was only ten, and his mother was filled with pride when he was appointed there. Master Faljambe, his stepfather, had a hand in it, and was mighty pleased, for he was fond of his stepchildren. There, at the castle, Anthony worked at Latin and Greek and French with his tutor, and there he learned to sing many a song and turn rhymes deftly, and make up sweet airs for the lute. There, too, his young heart was caught by the loveliness of the poor prisoned queen, alackaday!'

'She must be a real beauty,' Tabitha agreed. 'I've heard my father talk about her, for he saw her walking in the gardens at Hardwick Hall where he was working before he fell sick. He said that Bess of Hardwick didn't like Mary Stuart, and called her cruel names, "Scarlet Woman", and "whore".'

Aunt Cicely frowned. 'Yes, everyone knows the Countess is jealous of the Scottish queen, of her charm and her lively ways and witty talk. Those who go to Sheffield Castle to buy and sell, to show their wares to the queen's servants and ladies – for there's a fine lot of them, nearly four hundred serving people – they say that the talk of her in the kitchen and servants' quarters is that her skin is white as milk, her lips red as the rowan berry, her veins blue as the sky and the blood of her body flushes her creamy skin like the wild roses in the lane yonder. Her voice is low, and full of tremors, stirring to young hearts. That's what they say, those who have heard her speak, although it is hard to get near her, she is guarded so closely. She is kind and loving to those who serve her, not like Queen Elizabeth, who is hard, but Mary Stuart never forgets a wrong.'

'Then she'll have a lot to remember,' said Tabitha.

'Aye! She was born for delight, but she has had little enow these last many years, pindling in captivity. Master Anthony once told me she would play with her pages and make a pretence of a banquet when they sat in the gardens, with wee silver cups of wine and dishes of tiny cakes and sweetmeats and they would eat and drink, forgetful she was a queen. She would laugh merrily and one would sing a ballad and she clapped her white hands and rewarded him with a box of comfits or a toy. There she romped with her little dogs, or fed her birds from her own lips.

Then she would remember and sit for hours, unspeaking, with her eyes staring far away, and her mouth working bitterly with her unhappy thoughts.'

'That's like Mistress Babington,' said Tabitha. 'Sometimes she plays with her dog Belle, and sometimes she sits all forlorn, and tears fall on her hands.'

'How long has the queen been imprisoned at Sheffield?' asked Tabitha. Dame Cicely counted on her fingers. 'Ten – twelve – yes twelve years come Michaelmas. I know because it was a wild, windy autumn, and one of the great walnut trees was blown down. We thought it was the sign of something, and the next thing we heard was that the Queen of Scotland was coming. Master Anthony's father went to see her travel the road with her suite, crowds of horsemen and soldiers. We thought it wouldn't be long before she was moved to London to be with the queen in her palace, perhaps, but it seems she'll stay there till she dies.'

'And now Master Anthony's coming home,' cried Tabitha, excitedly.

'Yes, and quite time too, for he ought to look after the lands his father left him, Lea and Codnor and Wirksworth, with farms and woods and lead mines and quarries and all his people waiting to welcome him back. Thackers is his home, not London.'

'Thackers is my home, not London,' I echoed. Then I remembered something, and I looked at the weapons above the fire.

'Aunt Cicely,' I cried, springing to my feet and clutching her woollen sleeve. 'Where is Uncle Barnabas?'

'Uncle Barnabas? My brother, Barnabas?' she asked astonished. 'What's the wench talking about? Your Uncle Barnabas was killed in the wars in the Netherlands. There's his dinted helmet, brought back by Abel Fletcher. 'Twas his little wench, Penelope, you favour so much.'

'Killed! Uncle Barnabas!' I burst into tears. Tabitha put her arm round me to comfort me and Aunt Cicely came round and kissed my wet cheeks.

'There! Don't take on, my dear,' said she. 'He's in Paradise, along of Sir Thomas More and all of 'em.'

But from outside there came a great clatter and noise, shouts rang through the air. Men came into the kitchen, buttoning their leather jerkins, fastening the buckles unloosened while they worked. They drew on their long boots, and their wooden heels clanked on the stones, and their spurs brought sparks. They smelled rankly of stable and byre, as they pushed and jostled and talked loudly to Aunt Cicely.

'They're coming! They've been sighted from the top of the Starth. Will Stoker was minding the swine in the woods by Cliff Rocks and he saw the cavalcade riding in the south. They'll be here in an hour, and we're going to the ford to meet them, for the river's high and they'll want help. Young Master Anthony's coming home for good!'

Horses were saddled, and men rode down the lanes, past the brook to the hills whose rounded shapes I already knew by heart. Away they went with a pennon waving in the air, with the arms of Master Anthony upon it. Tom Snowball ran to the church with Abel Fletcher and rang the bells in a joyful tumult of music. Young Mistress Babington came out of the house wearing her green riding habit and the white horse was brought round for her. Tabitha and I watched her ride away with the boy Francis to meet her husband. A flag was hoisted on the tower and Aunt Cicely and the maids hurried to prepare the rooms.

I went to the porch to see the flag flutter on high, to watch the rooks fly cawing from it in a fright, and the pigeons wheel as the ringing bells tossed in the high tower. As I gazed up in the blue, limpid air the flag faded away into a white cloud, the bells were the sheep bells in the pastures. Across the fields I could see a chestnut pony with a boy astride. I looked back to the kitchen window where Aunt Cicely and Tabitha were lifting the iron pot from the fire, but even as I looked they became dim as woodsmoke. I met the eyes of the boy Jude, who was staring at me as if he saw a ghost. I waved, but he shrank back, covering his face with his hands in terror. Then I ran out of doors, across the grassplat where white cloths were bleaching, to the gate.

'It's your turn, Penelope. Didn't you go upstairs? I suppose you hadn't time to change you were in such a hurry to get back.'

'Hurry to get back!' I echoed, softly. I had been away for hours, days it seemed, but the fingers of the grandfather clock had not moved while I was away. Like a dream which abolishes time and space, which can travel through years in a flash and to the ends of the world in a twinkling, I went into another century and lived there and returned before the pendulum of the grandfather clock had wagged once behind the bull's-eye glass. I had experienced the delights and anxieties of another age, moving quietly in that life, walking in the garden, talking and loitering and returning in the blink of an eyelid. It was neither dream nor sleep, this journey I had taken, but a voyage backward through the ether. Perhaps I had died in that atom of time, and my ghost had fled down the years, recognized only by Jude, and then returned in a heartbeat.

I looked down at my hands, from which a sweet and disturbing scent came. It was musk from the garden path of another age. I stood motionless, waiting for something to happen.

Ian rode up on the pony, Betty, and I mounted. I took the reins without speaking, and galloped up the fields, my head in a whirl, my heart pounding as I breathed the icy coldness of the air. I pulled up at the top of the hill and stared about through the gaps in the trees, trying to catch a glimpse of a company of horsemen riding on a distant slope. I listened for the sound of the horn which the fair-haired boy Francis had wound as he cantered away, for the echo was still in my ears. I looked up at the sky, at the floating clouds and the windswept, tossing trees which moaned under a rising wind. The fivefold hills were lavender, indigo, violet in the soft light, one behind another, concealing the small villages in their shadowed troughs. Life went on unseen in those misty shallows, and another life moved in the folded layers of time.

I turned the pony round and came slowly back to the farm, trying to puzzle it out. There before me was the church, with its broken shields on the tower and the latest one, which the unseen mason was shaping, was already weathered and worn. Hens clucked around the doorway, as they had always done, and a cock crowed with shrilly challenge. In the yard cattle were lowing, and the sheep with their tinkling bells came down the pasture with the dogs. I was living in the past and the present together, at Thackers, the home of my ancestors. I saw the web and woof of time threaded in a pattern, and I moved through the woven stuff with the silent footfall of a ghost.

Slowly I rode across the yard to the stable door, and Ian met me angrily.

'You've ridden too fast,' he cried. 'You galloped her up the hill and then you let her stay still, all sweating. She's all of a lather. Penelope, you don't deserve to share a pony.'

He rubbed the darkly streaked sides and I bit my lip, already forgetting. I didn't know what possessed me, except that I wanted to see someone before he disappeared, to catch a glimpse of a pageant of blue and silver somewhere in the distant woods, to hear the sound of a horn.

'Don't scold her,' said Uncle Barnabas, and I clung to his warm, work-hardened fingers. He was there, touching me, and I had had a bad dream about him. He would never die as long as Thackers existed. 'She's my brown lass, and she's done nowt amiss,' said Uncle Barnabas valiantly. He gave a hearty laugh as we went into the farm kitchen, and I started, for it was the deep laughter of Dame Cicely.

There was the fire burning unchanged, but the great cauldron of venison was replaced by a copper kettle which sang a quiet song. In front of the blaze, instead of the spit turned by a swarthy, green-eyed boy was a Dutch oven with a bird grilling in it for dinner. Instead of the long-shafted weapons, the pikes and halberds were my uncle's guns, polished and cleaned ready for use.

There on the left was a cupboard where the bread oven had been and I opened the door and looked inside. It was filled with flat-irons and crimping irons of many sizes and weights.

'Penelope! You mustn't open Aunt Tissie's cupboards like that,' cried Alison, but Aunt Tissie turned from the fire, her old face crimson with heat, the little white tucker in her dress all creased and crumpled.

'That was the bread oven once, Penelope, in old days. Even in my grandfather's time we made our bread in it, but now we cook in the ordinary oven. Times have changed but they say bread is never as sweet now as it was when they baked it by charcoal.'

She took some herbs from the table and dropped them in a brass pan on the fire. Then she called us to the table.

'Dinner's ready, my dears. Blow the whistle for Jess. He's out with the sheep. I hope you've got good appetites with your riding, for I've got something very nice, and you'll never guess what it is. Fresh trout from the Darrand! A gentleman staying at Bramble Hall caught them this morning, and their servant lad brought some down for me, seeing as I have visitors from London who don't get trout every day of the week, I'm sure.'

# 4. The Book of Hours

THAT night we sat round the great oak table in the kitchen at Thackers with Uncle Barnabas and Aunt Tissie in their high-backed chairs, and played dominoes. Even Jess joined us, for he scrubbed himself very clean and damped his hair and put on a Sunday coat in our honour. We each built a wall with our store and put out the dominoes from our black-and-white ramparts into the circle of lamplight. When the game was over we asked riddles, and Uncle Barnabas posed many an ancient riddle to puzzle our London wits.

A riddle, a riddle, it dances and skips,
It is read in the eyes though it cheats on the lips.

If it meets with its match it is easily caught,
But when money buys it, it's not worth a groat.

and the answer to that is 'A heart'.

Then Alison asked me to bring down my sketching book to show my aunt and uncle the drawings I had made at the zoo. With my lighted candle, which Aunt Tissie called:

Little Miss Etticoat, in a white petticoat,
The longer she lives, the shorter she grows.

I went through the door. I didn't much care to leave the warm fireside to go up the dark staircase where there was never a glimmer except the pale ghostly ray on the landing from the window which overlooked the church. I kept glancing about at the shadows which came out of the corners and moved alongside me, and I thought a voice might call or a hand stay me. I opened our bedroom door and found the sketch book lying in front of the mirror, and as I picked it up I saw again the reflection of my pale face. I had changed my dress for my green tussore with long, full sleeves, and I wore my coral necklace. I always felt proud of this dress, for Mother had made it for me. As I peered into the dim, smoky glass I wished those people, wherever they were, could see me. Then I leaned from the window and looked out at the dark church tower with its broken shields and the great door with the plaited stone rim. In the yard I saw the lamplight from the house fall in regular pattern upon the grassplat, I could hear the stamp of hooves in the stable, and from the field came the snuffling grunt of a grazing mare. Moths flew in and fluttered round the candle flame, and then the draught caught the little yellow flag and tore it away, and I was left in the darkness.

I never could get used to candles, I told myself in a panic as I fumbled my way across the room. In the faint light of the landing I thought I saw the doors drift out of obscurity. Dare I open one of them? I asked myself. Dare I? From down the narrow stair came Ian's laugh and then the deep voice of Uncle Barnabas. The safe world was there, and I had only to turn away, but I longed to enter that hidden timeless world where the hours and seconds were crystallized into one transparent drop, round and clear.

I put out a hand and lifted the shadowy latch, and stood on the threshold, not venturing to take a step, held breathless by what I saw. There in the room, brooding in the firelight which dappled the walls in pointed flames, was a young man. His gloomy handsome face was in the shade, his hands clasped round his knees. His hair was flaxen, curled and shining like fine gold in the light, his chin had a little beard, pointed and downy. His clothes were rich but stained and splashed with mud, his doublet open at the neck, where he wore a narrow lace collar. His leather thigh-boots stood wrinkled and drooping in the corner, and on his feet he had soft scarlet shoes with slashed toes. I stood still as a dream, watching him, hearing his sigh, seeing his breast rise and fall, and his fingers move convulsively. Suddenly he spun round and uttered a cry as he saw me.

' 'S blood! Who's there? Who are you? Speak!' he commanded, and his brilliant blue eyes flashed as he clutched the arms of his great chair and I saw the firelight gleam on a jewel which hung from a gold chain round his neck.

Quickly I shut the door, but I heard him mutter: 'A ghost! Or a wench, but a lovely little wench!'

Breathlessly I ran downstairs, stumbling headlong into the kitchen.

'You look as if you'd seen a boggart,' said Uncle Barnabas dryly. 'Is 'owt amiss?'

I was trembling with excitement, and elated because I had gone there again, and seen him – Anthony – but I was silent.

Aunt Tissie went to the cupboard and took out a bottle of cordial and a little fluted glass.

'Drink this, my chuck,' said she. 'You've had a tiring day, and the excitement of Betty has been too much for you. Now show your pictures quietly and then you must go to bed, for you look flushed and your eyes are over-bright. I'll run the warming pan over your sheets and bring a posset up to you.'

As Alison and I lay in our beds Aunt Tissie entered with the hot drink in a two-handled cup.

'Here's a sup that will do you good and make you sleep,' said she. 'We always have this same one, and always have done, right away back.' I tasted the honey and balm, and I thought of the herb posset I had seen Aunt Cicely make for Mistress Babington. It had the same sweet smell, and as Aunt Tissie leaned over to kiss me, there seemed little difference, so that I scarcely knew in which time I was living. Or was it that time never existed, that we all lived between two worlds which I had been privileged to enter?

Days passed in country delights, and for some time I did not see anything of those other inhabitants of Thackers. The mornings began with a ride over the hills to the station, before seven when the dew was heavy and the sun sent long fingers pointing the way to birds and beasts. The flowers raised their heads and drank that heavenly moisture, the pheasants ran across our path with quickly tripping feet, the fox walked unhurrying and secure. We passed through two villages along the riverside and all the way the milk churns jangled with loud music and I bumped about among them. I walked on the platform and watched the folk, the farmers with their fine sticks going to market, the cattle drovers with cudgels, the boys and girls going to a grammar school. Some nodded to me and others asked after my uncle, for I was accepted as belonging to the place. The train came puffing in with as much importance as if it were a London train. The guard and I exchanged buttonholes, for I always took a Thackers posy in my coat and the guard had a nice little greenhouse at home he told me. Then we waited till the green flag waved, the engine driver leaned from his cab, and away went the slow old train.

I had my own farm work at Thackers. I was the hen-wife, and I helped to feed the family of pigs. It was my delight to hang over the pig-cote door and watch the fourteen piglings nuzzle their mother, pushing each other out of the way, so that there were always one or two vainly trying to edge their snouts to the milk. Alison refused to join me, she couldn't get used to the smell of pigs, and when I came back carrying my cans she insisted on sprinkling eau-de-Cologne on my apron, to Uncle Barny's amusement.

'Penelope'll be the farmer's boy, not Alison,' said he. 'Penelope's my little wench,' and I felt proud of that.

Sometimes we all drove out with Uncle and Aunt in the old-fashioned pony cart. We trundled along the lanes, and walked up the hills, pushing behind to help the horse, and walked down the hills, pulling to act as extra brakes, while motor cars roared past us, 'all in a tarnation hurry to get somewhere and save a minute', Uncle Barnabas said.

Whether we went up to little villages of stone cottages, or down to the valleys where ivy-covered farmhouses nestled in the trees, where my uncle talked of the prospects of harvest, and the poorness of grassland, or my aunt compared her hens and ducklings, I thought of those bygone days, when other people rode along those same narrow lanes and perhaps tasted the butter and begged for a receipt for syllabub or pigeon-pie, and children in long, stiff clothes played whip and top like the boys and girls I saw.

I asked many questions about Thackers, trying to piece together the life there, but my aunt could not tell me much. Her own grandmother had been born there and many a one before that. Her family had lived on the farm in the time of the great people, the Babington family, who loved this little manor house more than any of their possessions. Their beloved home was Thackers, the nest in the hidden valley, with its church and farmstead, and lands compact and secure from marauding bands of soldiers and heresy hunters. There all the children were born, and there our own ancestors had lived, fitting into those other lives, serving them, faithful to them, linked to them by strong ties of duty and love. She herself felt it was only the other day they had died, and the land been sold, although it was many a year agone.

'But ask me no more,' she sighed. 'I've had no larning. Me and Uncle Barnabas, we've kept things going and had no time for books. I dunno when it happened, the great tragedy, but 'twas a long time ago. Over a hunnerd years, or more maybe. Aye, it must have been more, for Grandmother Penelope Taberner lived here nigh on a hunnerd years ago.'

'Are you talking about Queen Elizabeth and Mary Queen of Scots, Aunt Tissie?' asked Alison, in her cool, clear voice, and I felt annoyed with her for the superiority of her tone.

'That's her. The Queen of Scotland. Her that was so bonny and wrecked our Master Anthony's life, and had her own head cut off,' said my aunt in her simple way.

'Only three hundred and twenty years ago,' said Alison with faint sarcasm.

'Three hunnerd! Over three hunnerd! Well, how time flies! I never thought it would be as long ago as that. Well, well.' Aunt Tissie sighed and I felt downright cross with my sister.

> *They die forgotten as a dream*
> *Dies at the opening day'*

murmured Aunt Tissie. 'That's what we sing at church, and it's true. They're all forgot.'

'I don't forget,' I cried indignantly. 'I remember them always.'

'Oh, you! You! Penelope's fey,' laughed Alison to Aunt Tissie. 'You go and help Jess feed the pigs my dear, or they'll think they are forgotten too.'

But I didn't go to the pigs. I found Uncle Barny and slipped my arm in his and walked across the fields to see the lambs at play and view the growing corn. I longed to visit that great kitchen again, to listen to Dame Cicely, to be scolded by Tabitha, and perhaps to share that warm, intimate comradeship of the family who lived there.

One day I stood on the landing, and I saw the iron latchet and the dark outline of the lost door. A sudden stillness came over the little sounds of the house, I felt strangely light as if I were treading on air. Walls disappeared or stretched out before me in the gable of Thackers. I lifted the latch and stepped down the little stairway into the corridor of time. It was quiet in the passage and I tiptoed along it, but my feet made no sound. Gradually I became accustomed to other scents and the atmosphere of the other time. I was elated and filled with curiosity about the house. I softly lifted the latch of the first room and saw it was only a wardrobe, filled with clothes hanging from wooden pegs, faded farthingales and kirtles of taffeta and rusty silk, petticoats and velvet cloaks, and much-boned corsets which must have belonged to Mistress Foljambe and her daughters. Nothing was ever wasted in a country family, as I knew from my Aunt Tissie's store of clothing.

The next door was open and I peered inside. Tabitha was standing at the window looking out across the garden, engrossed by the view of Tom Snowball. I went into the room, conscious that I was now making a noise, that I was attuned to the atmosphere around me, but Tabitha was too much absorbed to notice me. There was a carved bed with grapevines down the posts and dark curtains drawn back. It stood against a wall, and the sheets and embroidered bedcover lay heaped on the floor. A boy's plum-coloured jacket with slashed sleeves was thrown on a low chest together with a pair of trunk hose, and a leather jacket, pinked all over with tiny cut flowers and buttoned with many leather buttons down the front. On a chair was a collection of arrows, a knife, and some goose feathers. There were pegs in the wall and upon them hung a cloak and feathered hat, and a pair of muddy thigh-boots stood by the door. I moved across the room to see a book which lay open on a table, but Tabitha turned back to toss the feather bed and tidy the room.

'God ha' mercy!' she cried, startled. 'What art thou doing here, Penelope? Thou'lt catch it if Dame Cicely sees thee peering about in Master Francis's room! Think shame on thee! Where hast thou been these days, running away from us? Didst go to Darby? Whatever wert thou doing?'

'Exploring, dear Tabitha,' I said, smiling happily.

'Exploring forsooth! Like Raleigh and Drake, maybe?' scoffed Tabitha, indignantly. 'I'll tell on thee.'

'Don't tell, Tabitha. I wanted to see what the house is like where Mistress Babington lives.'

I picked up the book. It was Ovid's *Metamorphoses,* illustrated with woodcuts, and I turned the pages with interest, for I had worked at it at school.

'Now put that down. It's not yourn. You can't read it either, for its pagan stuff, as I know, for

I once axed,' said Tabitha crossly. 'Come and toss this bed, Penelope, and then off you go.'

'I can read it! I can!' I protested.

'Well you oughtna to, for it's not for a young maid like thee. Just look at the pictures!'

I laughed and together we fluffed out the bed and straightened the pillows and coverlet.

'Is this the boy's room?' I asked, although I knew quite well.

'It's Master Francis's room, if that's who you mean, and he's very particular about it,' said Tabitha severely. 'Now don't you be a meddlesome wench, and poke your nose into business that's none of yourn. Here, get you gone, and leave that book alone, and help Dame Cicely. Away you go!'

I dropped the book reluctantly, and walked slowly along the passage. I could hear Tabitha thumping and banging about with her besom, and the sound gave me courage, so that I stepped up boldly to a handsome door which had a large key in the lock. With both hands I turned it, and pushed the door. Nobody was there, and I stood for a moment on the threshold, gazing entranced at the beautiful room with its odours of dried roses and violets, its mullioned windows and herb-strewn floor.

Then I entered, and saw the massive carved furniture of the chamber, a great four-poster bed which I recognized, with curtains and bedcover and velvet pillows. There were stools with tasselled cushions, and a cupboard, and long padlocked chest, but it was the wall which attracted me more than anything in the room. Oak and ash and walnut tree were painted upon it, with dropping fruits, and antlered deer and flying birds, as well as many animals of the wild wood. I walked across the floor forgetful of everything in my curiosity and interest in the lively drawings, which I felt sure had been done from the woods around Thackers, the dark, mysterious woods which stretched up the hillside.

I only glanced once through the many-sided little windowpanes which framed those woods, for I was afraid somebody in the yard below, a groom or leather-coated serving man would see me, and I hastened back to explore the pictures on the wall. Every beast and bird was different, and I wandered happily around, peering at wild duck and woodcock, at badger and otter and polecat, tracing their spirited actions, seeking creatures I knew.

Suddenly I heard a step behind me and I sprang nervously round.

'Wench! What are you doing here?'

I saw Mistress Foljambe, Master Anthony's mother, standing inside the doorway, with her starched, white ruff stiffly framing her proud head and her long skirts sweeping the floor. Without more ado, remembering my lesson, I curtsied to her.

'I was admiring the animals and birds on this wall,' I told her, and she seemed mollified for she smiled faintly as I spoke. 'I wish I could paint like this,' I added. 'It is the most beautiful room I have ever seen.'

'Come here, Penelope,' she said in a more kindly voice, and I went close to her, so that I could smell white violets and some other flower scents which clung to her dress.

'Do you know this is my private chamber, and none come here without my permission, not even my dear daughter-in-law, Mistress Mary Babington?' she asked, and she put her strong bony fingers on my shoulder and tilted my chin to the light.

'I've never been here before,' I explained.

'You are that niece of Dame Cicely's, are you not,' she asked, looking at me in a puzzled way, 'lately come from London?'

'Yes, Mistress Foljambe,' I replied.

'Dame Cicely says you have had lessons in reading, and can acquit yourself well. She told me, too, that you have deft fingers and can make little drawings, and sew evenly with small stitches.'

I hesitated, for my sewing was not at all neat or even, but she went to the great carved tallboy chest and unlocked it with a silver key which hung with many another at her girdle. Then she brought out a little leather-backed book fastened with silver latchets. She drew me to the window, for the room was dusky with the dark furniture and the painted wall.

'This Book of Hours is a treasure I don't show to everyone, and never to those who care nought for beautiful things,' she said. She turned the pages slowly and I looked breathless with delight at the painted pictures, with their rich blues and scarlets and heavy inlays of gold. There were tiny paintings of the babe Jesus in the manger with the ox and the ass near Him and a thatched room overhead, and cocks and hens feeding at the doorway.

'It's like Thackers,' I told her, excitedly, 'and that's our great hay barn where the babe lies.'

She laughed with pleasure and gave me a quick appraising glance before she turned another page.

There I saw the flight into Egypt, with the holy babe in His mother's arms, riding an ass down a lane where dog roses grew. But it was a lane I had ridden along, and the gate which Joseph opened led to a meadow called Westwood.

Again she turned a page and I saw the delicate miniature of Mary Magdalene washing the feet of Jesus, but the room was one I knew, the kitchen at Thackers, with the spit before the fire, and bows and arrows on the wall and Jesus Himself sat in Uncle Barnabas's chair with His feet in the brass washing bowl.

Mistress Foljambe was pleased I knew the Bible stories so well, but when I stammered through the Latin she was astonished, for she seemed to expect me to read Latin as easily as English. When I confessed I could not say the Paternoster except in English she shook her head in dismay.

'My children learned the psalms and the Paternoster when they were babes,' she told me.

She showed me other books and I read aloud to her part of 'The Romaunt of the Rose', and a fairytale called 'The Tale of Goody Two-shoes', to her satisfaction. I remarked on the change of spelling in the same words, and she reasoned with me.

'Spelling is a matter of individuality,' she told me. 'I have my favourite ways of spelling words, and I choose my letters. My sons and daughters each spell as they wish, and surely you do the same?'

'If I make a mistake I am scolded,' said I.

She insisted one couldn't make a mistake, for each spelt according to his whim. That was one of the delights of writing, one was free to invent a pretty word, and she was sure I should not be such a dullard as to spell in the same way always. 'Life would lose one of its pleasures if we were deprived of the power to write as we wish. I myself spell my name Alys or Alice or Alyce, and Babington is full of amusement for us in a weary world. It is pictured in our town house at Darby in a carving over the fire as a babe astride a tun, although some fools have made a different spelling and put a coarse ape, or baboon from the Indies, perched upon a tun, Baboon-tun.'

This was a new idea for me and I was delighted that I could spell as I pleased and decorate my words as I wished.

Then she showed me a round, gold clock, the size of a tennis ball, with a pierced and chased cover through which I could see the hours. She lifted the golden case and I saw an iron finger which moved over the hours and days, leaving the minutes to run as they wished. Roses were engraved on the rim, and flying birds about the keyhole, as if the hours measured only sweet flowers and birds' flight.

It was a treasured possession, she said, and the only timekeeper in the district except the great iron clock in the church which had been left by Thomas Babington, her husband's father, in 1558.

'Then how do you know the time, Mistress Foljambe?' I asked her.

'There is the sun in the sky, and a sundial in the garden, and Dame Cicely has an hourglass for her cooking. What more do you want?' she replied.

Then she tired of me and sent me away, but I was loath to leave a room so stored with many an object of beauty, and I had not finished looking at the birds and beasts painted on the walls.

'Get you down to the kitchen where I am sure some work awaits you,' she said as I hesitated. 'Tell your aunt I find you well instructed in the scriptures and in your mother tongue but not in Latin. Your wits are bright for you recognized the scenes in the Book of Hours. Those illuminations were made by Master Thomas Babington, a learned clerk who lived here in the reign of King Henry V, and they were taken from our woods and lanes. He was our famous ancestor who fought at Agincourt and his sword hangs in the hall, as Dame Cicely will show you. Some day I will teach you further the use of simples and the preservation of flowers and herbs and all kinds of needlecraft, for you have a knowledge of colours, and love for beautiful things. I shall keep you in my household, and train you to be a help to Mistress Babington.'

She waved me away and I left her replacing the Book of Hours and the gold watch in the chest and locking them safely.

I was not to arrive at the kitchen without another encounter, for I took the wrong turning, confused with the passages in the extra wing. Before I could recover myself, I had run full tilt into a tall young man who strode out of a room as I passed. He grabbed me angrily and shook my arm as I apologized. Then he tilted my face upward to the dim light of the leaded panes and stared at me, and I recognized the flaxen hair and the blue eyes of the man I had seen sitting by a fire disconsolate.

'The very same wench who peeked in at me,' said he. 'Who are you and where do you come from dressed in this garb? The green smock you wore that night when I had just come home was more becoming to you, for you are a likelier girl than a boy. Who are you?'

'Penelope, niece of Aunt Cicely, that is, Dame Cicely Taberner is my aunt,' I stammered.

'Penelope,' he said the word slowly, and again he repeated 'Penelope', and his voice was soft and full of dreams, as if he liked my name. Then he shrugged his shoulders. 'Where do you come from? Not from the village surely? I don't remember you there, and I know most of my people.'

'From Chelsea, Master Anthony,' said I boldly, for I was sure he was the famous heir of the Babingtons who had come home from London.

'From Chelsey?' he echoed. 'When I was newly married I took sweet Mistress Mary to Chelsey and we dwelt in a thatched cottage down by the church with the fields and flowers about us. Do you know it?' He didn't wait for my reply but continued. 'Later I went to Chelsey to visit the house of poor Sir Thomas More along with others of the court. We went by river, in painted barges, with musicians playing and flags flying, a gallant show, but it gave me no pleasure.'

'I live by the church, sir,' I interrupted eagerly, but he took no notice.

'I have had enough of court life,' he continued, low, as if I were not there. 'I was kept dallying on the outskirts of Greenwich, wasting my money, for I never got near enough to the queen to make the show I wished. So there I stayed, dissembling my love for another, concealing my religion, talking to fools, gambling away my substance, turning witty speeches, sick at heart, till I met those who showed me how I could help the one I worshipped.'

He spoke softly as if to himself, standing there at the window staring out at the lovely hillside where I had walked that day. Something stirred in my mind, and I interrupted him. 'There's a badger's holt in that wood and Jess is going to show it to me. I ought to go,' said I, but my words died away in forgetfulness, and I turned back to the young man at my side. His fingers were playing with a thin gold chain, fine as twisted hair which hung round his neck. On it I could see a gilded locket, with the letters M.R. engraved upon it. Instinctively he concealed it with his hand. Then he changed his mind, for he turned abruptly to me, and drew me into the room close by. The filmy lace of his ruffle swept my neck but his fingers were hard as iron as they pressed my shoulder and propelled me to the daylight. I forgot Jess and the badger and Thackers wood as I felt the pressure of his arm and heard his deep, low voice.

'Do you know who this is, Penelope Taberner? Have you ever seen a face like hers? Do you believe the evil they say or do you know the courage and splendour of her?'

He spoke passionately and he pushed me round to face the window of the little chamber, and then he slipped the gold chain from his neck. He pressed a catch and held the open locket in the palm of his hand.

I bent my head and gazed long at the miniature of a woman, wearing a black dress, bordered with fur, and a pointed lawn headdress winged and stiffly outspread like a lily's petals, edged with narrow lace. The oval face was palely beautiful, the hazel eyes were laughing stars under the lovely arch of the brows, the scarlet lips seemed as if they were about to utter a mocking word. In her long fingers she held a carnation, red as her lips. Round her white neck, over the open ruff, was a gold crucifix. I stared enchanted by the delicate features of the lady, by the lacy detail of her headdress, the bunch of pearls which fastened the boyish ruff, and the little enamelled Christ on the gold crucifix. I saw the transparent beauty of those fingers which seemed to twist the stem of the flower before tossing it to one the lady loved.

'She's very beautiful,' I murmured.

'She is the star of heaven and earth,' said Anthony under his breath.

'That's a lovely carnation,' I added, for I love flowers always.

' "Sops-in-wine" we country people call it,' smiled Anthony. 'Our garden is full of them in her memory. You know who she is?'

I shook my head, not venturing to guess.

'Her blessed Majesty, Mary Queen of Scotland,' said he. 'My beloved and sacred queen. One day she will be Queen of England, on her rightful throne, and the true religion will come back, and all will be well on earth as in heaven.'

I knew something. I struggled to speak. I had foreknowledge, I could remember. The very air I breathed was vibrant with sorrow and foreboding of disaster, and the words came unbidden to my lips.

'She was executed,' I whispered, but Anthony heard me.

The effect of my word was startling. He sprang back with his hands to his head as if shot. Then he raised his fist as if he would strike me, and I shrank against the wall, terrified by his twisted face.

'Unsay those words, vile wretch,' he cried. 'How dare you! Who are you to speak ill of the queen?'

I stared at him, terrified. He seized me and shook me violently and flung me back against the wall. I leaned there weeping softly, afraid of my own knowledge, scarce knowing why I had spoken.

'*Was? Was* did you say?' he continued. 'Why she is at Sheffield Castle now. I saw her only yesterday. I kissed those white hands and listened to words from those sweet lips.' The words came hissing from him in a broken whisper.

My head reeled, but he pulled me forward and held my face in his harsh hands and looked long into my eyes. Then as if satisfied that I was not mocking he was silent for a time.

What was Mary Queen of Scots to me that I should remember her and forget all else? Why did these fateful words come to my lips as I stood there in the little chamber? It must have been, I decided afterwards when I considered this happening, that her tragedy had impressed the scene, the vibrant ether had held the thoughts of the perilous ruinous adventure, so that the walls of Thackers were quickened by them, the place itself alive with the memory of things once seen and heard, for such grief was of eternity and outside time. As the scent which lay dormant in the oak chest for many years had spired upwards and detached itself, bearing a train of visions and half memories, so the spoken words, the desperate knowledge of the queen's execution three hundred years before, had lain in some pocket of the ether and had entered a mind attuned to it. The ghosts of the thoughts were hovering to take possession and to me they came. The knowledge was insignificant to me, but in the past it was of such tragic import it pervaded my mind and became the most outstanding memory. She was alive, but she was dead, and always she was immortal.

'Hast thou second sight, wench?' asked Anthony, fearfully, 'or didst thou visit Doctor Dee, Queen Elizabeth's astrologer, when thou wert in London? Did he say those words to thee? Didst thou look into his crystal show-stone and see the future as I once saw it? Queen Elizabeth consults him and he has advised her and shown to her friends and enemies.'

'Doctor Dee? I've never heard of him,' I answered, aghast at the effect of my words.

'He looked into the pink crystal ball where all things are visible, past and future, and there in a circle of darkness he saw tragic happenings for me and for her. The queen he refused to speak about, for an astrologer must beware of his foretellings, but he told me my own end and a worse one there could not be.'

Anthony's face was drawn with horror and despair, and he leaned on the windowsill, shuddering at the memory. 'But it shall not be. I will defeat my fate.' He sprang up and turned again to me.

'Forgive me for my harshness, but I was unbalanced by your sudden words. Can you swear you never saw him?' he asked.

'No, I've never seen an astrologer in my life, but once I heard my mother say she feared I had second sight.'

'My uncle, Doctor Babington of Bramble Hall, has second sight,' said Anthony slowly. 'He prophesied evil of me when I was very young. He wrote these words to Henry Foljambe, my stepfather, warning him to keep me by him, away from temptation and freedom.

' "Give him not, brother, his libertie in youth, or the Old Days he shall not see."

'My mother hated him for his ill-bodings, and she never spoke to him again, nor does he ever visit us at Thackers. My dear stepfather gave me my liberty and I went to London. Yet I know I shall never live to grow old, never know the heat of summer days and the cold of our Darbyshire snows. I shall not see my children ride up yonder woods, and hunt the deer, and marry and beget children of their own to live at Thackers. That thought haunts me, but I am driven on by unseen forces.'

I hastened to comfort him, putting my hand timidly on his sleeve, for I longed to help him in the distress I had caused.

Then he shrugged his shoulders and laughed. 'I don't know why I have told you about this except that your strange prophecy startled me. You have an air of foreknowledge which sits ill on so young a brow. Yet I know I can trust you in a world where few can be trusted. This sadness of which I have spoken is not to be mentioned at Thackers, for Thackers is an abode of peace. So keep it and hide it in your mind, Penelope.'

'We can alter the future, we have free wills, Master Anthony,' I cried, but the words came from me against my common sense, for his future was in my past. The fate of the queen was written in the archangel Michael's book.

Somehow, in the serenity of the sunny, bare chamber where we stood, with Master Anthony's blue eyes looking into mine, and that lovely jewel dangling in his fingers touching mine as he spoke, I felt all things were possible. We would put back the clock of time and save her.

He took my hands in his, and held them tightly.

'You want to save her? I can trust you with my heart? You love her too, Penelope?' he whispered.

'Oh yes, Master Anthony,' I cried passionately. 'I love her too,' and my words were true. A great love for this doomed queen swept over me, making me forget past and future in the clear present which I shared with him.

# 5. Francis Babington

I LEFT the room and went unsteadily and sadly down the twisted back staircase which led through the passage to the kitchen. I sidled past the door before Dame Cicely noticed me and went along the stone passage to the dairy, for that was a room I knew very well. I put my finger through the same thumb-hole I had always used and lifted the latch. There was the familiar ice-cold chamber with sanded benches ranged round the walls and rough oak shelves unplaned and knotted, along the whitewashed walls. A tall wooden churn with an upright dasher for butter-making stood on the floor and immense shallow bowls were set for cream. I took the copper skimmer from the shelf and dipped it into a bowl, and sipped the thick yellow cream which was sweet as nuts. Then I wandered round staring at the utensils on the shelves, the wooden prints, one carved in the shape of a Tudor rose, and another with the Babington arms upon it. There were wooden bowls, some of them worm-eaten and cracked, others fitted with covers or lined with coarse linen ready for the table. There were sieves for the milk and pewter measures shiny with use. Down on the floor was a tiny wooden bowl as big as a walnut shell filled with cream, standing on a few fresh flowers. I stared at it, wondering, not daring to touch.

The door was pushed open very quietly and an old woman entered with a bucket and mop. Her skirt was kilted, and she wore wooden shoes on her bare feet. She began to mop the floor and as she finished each flagstone she knelt down and bordered it with a rim of yellow sandstone.

'I knew you would do that,' I said to her, and she looked up from her lowly position with a toothless smile.

'Aye. It's to make it purty, my dainty lass. It's allays done that way in this countryside of Darby. Foreigners don't do it up Lunnon. Robin Goodfellow likes to see the floor clean and purty when he comes to the dairy for his sup of cream.'

'And where does he have it?' I asked, but I had already guessed.

'There's his bowl left ready. We fills it every day and sometimes he do sip it, the elvish fellow, and sometimes he don't. But we leaves it allays, for he brings good luck to the house. He sweeps out the houseplace and minds the fire from danger, and fettles the horses in stable, and does many a thing. Fairies lives in country places same as this, but not in Lunnon nowadays. Not since a long time have they lived in Lunnon. They all trooped back to the country where we looks after 'em.'

'How do they get in if the window is shut?' I asked, and I stooped over the pannikin on its posy of flowers.

'By the thumb-hole in the door, 'o course. Now don't talk about 'em any more, for they don't like folk noticing their ways. Get ye out, for I want to wash where ye stand,' said the old dame and out I went.

The door in the porch was wide open and hot sunshine poured through. I passed the kitchen and went outside towards the garden where Tabitha had taken me. Labourers and farm men were working in the fields; some came back to the yard leading horses, dragging loads of hay on clumsy rafts of wood, others were making haystacks under the church walls and the smell of new-mown hay filled the air. I had left spring behind that morning, the seasons had flown like birds on the wing. There were old men with dark, leather breeches and young men in green jerkins stained with earth and torn, chopping wood, working in the brew house, cleaning out the stables. 'Dame Cicely's niece from Lunnon,' they told one another, jerking thumbs at me, as I crossed the yard.

In the garden I wandered free, looking at the many-coloured flowers, bright blue borage, striped carnations, and tawny tiger lilies. I knelt by the beds of little yellow pansies and blue columbines which nid-nodded their heads in their encircling box hedges, and filled my pockets with camomile, and rubbed my hands in the lemon balm. An old man stepped from behind the yew hedge and came towards me, with a sickle on his shoulder and a rake in his calloused hand. He took off his leather cap and scratched his head.

'Be ye a friend of Mistress Babington's?' he asked in a deep slow voice, low like water babbling in the earth.

'No. I'm Dame Cicely's niece,' said I.

'I see ye were furrin, but if ye belongs to Dame Cicely I needner be on my bestest manners,' he said relieved and he replaced the crooked worn cap and came over to my side.

'See them oxlips?' He pointed to a group of golden-red flowers which filled a corner by the path. 'I made 'em! I got a tuthree roots of yellow oxlips from Westwood medder and planted them upsy down and they corned up like this.'

He stroked his stubbled chin and waited for my admiration.

'I did! I, Adam Dedick, did 'un!' he continued proudly, 'but it takes some skill, for ye mun get good roots, and not cover 'em wi' soil, but let the air get to 'em. I'll show ye next spring, if so be we'm above sod ourselves. It's like this, thinks I. We're buried by sexton, upsy down in earth, and up we come angels. So I puts my oxlips in upsy down and ups they come like angels.'

He laughed uproariously and I laughed too. Here was somebody who was merry and cheerful with no fears for the future.

He took me round the garden pointing out the apricot tree growing on a sunny wall with the fruit ripening under a net.

'We get many a lot of apricocks from that tree. There's never another in these parts, but here there's shelter. We grow a fine lot of strawberries on this bed,' he continued, showing me the red fruit. 'But mindye, never a one can ye pick, for they're all for Mistress Babington and the gentlefolk. Some we send to Darby to Babington House, when we pack hampers for Mistress Foljambe. But there's aplenty of wild strawberries in the lanes on the banks and you can eat 'em.'

'Here's radishes and onions all agrowing, and peas,' said he, leaning over a hedge. Then his eye grew fierce and he shook his fist.

'Them plaguey bullies eatin' buds off'en cherry trees, and eatin' off'en peas, and blackies and spinks too, all feasting like Queen Bess's courtiers. Where's that boy Jude? He oughta be here. There's no spit to turn this morning. Where is he? I'll warm him. And he's got nothing to do but to turn his clacker.'

The old man hurried off, uttering fierce curses on Jude, and a few minutes later I saw the hump-backed boy dragged by the ear, his wooden rattle in his hand. He squatted on the wall and swung the clacker so that a loud, raucous noise filled the air and away the birds flew. Then he took his elder pipe from his pocket and played an entrancing tune calling them back again as soon as Adam was out of earshot. Robins and throstles and blackbirds hopped round him, and he tossed crumbs from his pocket. He was like a bird himself I thought as I watched him through the hedge, a wild creature.

I went through the herb garden with its strong odours of medicinal possets, past a hedge of sweetbriar to the colony of beehives, where Tom Snowball was bending, so I turned hurriedly back, lest he should kiss me as he had kissed Tabitha. I saw a little fountain which sprang from the earth and filled a stone basin, and it was where my Uncle Barnabas had a water trough for his horses. I dipped my hands in it and supped the fresh spring water, and bathed my face. Then I left the garden by a wicket and started away for the woods, past the orchard wall.

In a great leafy walnut tree hung a swing and a boy was lolling there, idly reading a book. When I came near he looked up and I recognized the boy I had seen in the church.

'Who are you, tresspassing here?' he demanded, rudely enough I thought.

'Penelope Taberner,' I said. 'And I know who you are, Francis Babington.'

'Master Francis Babington,' corrected the boy. 'Yes, I've heard of you, the niece of Dame Cicely, come to help in Thackers kitchen from Chelsey,' said he in the same haughty manner which angered me.

'You entered my brother Anthony's room the night he came home and he thought you were a witchgirl.'

'I'm not,' said I indignantly. 'There aren't any witches, either.'

'Some are burnt every year,' he retorted, 'but you seem real enough. Anthony thought he had seen a ghost.' He calmly pinched my arm. I shook off his hand and turned back my sleeve to see the blackening bruise.

'And what are you doing at Thackers, Penelope Taberner?' he asked, swinging backward and forward.

'Learning manners, for one thing,' I replied crossly, for it was my home as much as it was the home of this bold youth.

'Nay, I didn't mean to be rude,' he said suddenly with a disarming smile and he sprang from his seat and sent the swing flying. 'I heard my mother speak of you, and she said you were well educated for your position, and much better read than Cousin Arabella. I'm sorry if I hurt you. You came from London to visit your aunt, I know.'

'Good day, Master Francis Babington,' I said coldly, and I turned my back and started away, angry and disappointed.

'Nay, don't go. Forgive me, sweet wench! Everybody knows me and my short temper,' he cried running after me, and taking my arm, he gently drew me back to the swing. 'I'm only Francis Babington,' said he. 'I'm the youngest brother, the nobody. Anthony is the young lord who goes to the queen's court and wears a white satin doublet and a pearl earring. George is the gambler, the spendthrift of the family, who dices with his friends and never sees Thackers. I am the stay-at-home, with no money, for all goes to Anthony and George, and no goods, for all the land is Anthony's and no clothes except cast-offs, and no fortune. All is Anthony's, but I have a small talent for music and a great love for Thackers, with its woods and fields, and a surpassing love for brother Anthony in spite of his neglect of me.'

'I love Thackers too,' said I cheerfully, for I liked the boy with his freckled face and careless clothes, too tight at the wrists, too narrow to hold his growing body. I glanced at the leather-bound book he held. It was *The Noble Art of Venerie*, and he showed me the woodcuts of dogs and horses and stags, and spoke of his own hounds, Fleet, Fury, and Blaize, and the two mares, Silver and Stella, which belonged to Anthony but which he rode.

Then he leaned forward and touched my knee, and looked into my face with intent, anxious eyes.

'What do you know of my brother Anthony?' he asked. 'Why did you go and spy upon him?'

'I didn't,' I protested. 'I don't know him at all, but I wanted to see him, because this is his home.'

'Yes. This is his home,' said Francis slowly. 'He is the heir. He possesses all the estates left by my father, lands as far as you can see, and over the hills in other valleys, farms and homesteads and faithful friends. There are no great riches, no castles, but there are woods of oak and hazel and dark holly, where hide the badger, the marten, the tawny fox. In the valleys are meadows, heavy with grass, and cornfields yellow in autumn, and cottages and good country folk. There is hunting of deer, and hawking, and the sports of the chase, and fishing in our rivers, the Darrand and Dove. That seems enough for any man, but Anthony is caught in a net.'

Francis spoke with deep feeling, his eyes flashed, and he looked like his handsome brother as he stood there under the tree's shade.

'What net is he caught in?' I asked timidly, for Francis suddenly seemed older than his years, matured by the responsibilities of his house, and not the boy who sang carols so light-heartedly in the church.

'The net of politics,' he muttered after a pause. 'A net baited to catch a young Catholic and a queen, I'll warrant. When he was in London he was persuaded to join a company of young Catholic gentry, sworn to hide Jesuit priests, and to outwit Elizabeth's Walsingham, and to help put the Scottish queen ...'

He stopped and looked at me, just as Anthony had done. Then he went on. 'You belong to Thackers, for Cicely is of our household for ever. You should know. Anthony belongs to a band of rich young gallants, a secret society, bound together by oath. Everywhere there are spies, a mesh of vagabonds and beggars, in many a disguise, and I fear my brother is being used by others stronger than he. Anthony isn't clever enough for them, he can't pretend what isn't true, he shows his feelings too easily. He is no plotter like those cursed town folk, he is a simple Darbyshire squire, and they will lead him on, and when he is safely in their toils they will destroy him. Only here is he safe, here, in the midst of his own people. One of his friends was hanged, drawn, and quartered at Tyburn. If Anthony stays here all may still be well. The land wants him, there is work to be done at Thackers. Our father died when Anthony and I were children, but our stepfather has been kind and helpful. Now Anthony is of age, and he has a young wife, but the queen has captured him.'

'The queen?' I asked, puzzled.

'Mary of Scotland. She fled to England long ago, as you must know, and there were terrible accusations against her. She threw herself on her cousin's mercy, and Elizabeth has kept her imprisoned ever since. Anthony was a page at her small court, and now he would give his life for Mary Stuart. He has sworn to deliver her, to set her free from hateful captivity.'

My eyes wandered over Thackers fields, to the cows feeding in the little field called Squirrels, to a pair of horses by the gate rubbing their necks in affection and comradeship. Afar I could see Anthony riding his grey horse, and beyond the yew hedge sat Jude with his elder pipe charming the birds, and old Adam digging and grumbling to himself. Blue smoke curled up from the chimneys, and a pigeon flew over my head. It was Thackers, a home for simple folk, and not the place to speak of queens, I thought; and other thoughts came surging up, troubling me, faces swam into my memory and disappeared as in a dream. The knowledge of a happening waxed and waned and faded to nothing.

'There is work to be done,' said Francis. 'The yeomen want him, for the fences are broken and the deer ravage the corn, harvests are bad, cattle die, and he is not here, and I am inexperienced to take his place. There is ploughing and reaping and sowing, which is better than trying to put a queen on a throne.'

But my mind was struggling with other things, for a cloud seemed to go over the sun, and his voice grew faint, and I heard other voices speaking, my aunt and Uncle Barnabas. As in a vision I saw them. My mother and father, my sister and brother were forgotten as if they had never lived, but Uncle Barnabas who seemed part of the soil itself and Aunt Tissie who was living in both centuries were ever present. They were made of Thackers earth, they were the place quickened to life and I remembered them. Then an arm shook mine and the clear voice of Francis Babington spoke insistently in my ear.

'Penelope! You are with us? You are for Mary Stuart?'

I leapt with excitement, suddenly intensely alive, and the queer half-drowned thought swam to the surface for a moment.

'Do you mean Mary Queen of Scots?' I asked slowly.

'Who else? What have we been talking about?' Francis frowned impatiently.

'She was executed.' The words framed themselves in spite of my effort to stay them. 'She died in 1587.'

'Then you are mad,' cried Francis. 'She is as alive as you, her eyes are brown as yours, her body straighter than yours will be at her age. She's at Sheffield Castle in the charge of Anthony's guardian, Lord Shrewsbury. Why do you say such things? Are you a soothsayer? Can you fortell the future? For this is the year 1582.' Francis moved away from me as if I were crazed.

'The future?' I whispered very low and my voice uttered the words without my willing it. 'I live at Thackers in the future, not in your time, Francis Babington. That's how I know about the queen.'

'That can't be,' scoffed the boy. 'It's not possible unless you are a ghost, and you are visible enough. The future hasn't happened. This is Now, and you are in Thackers croft, and Dame Cicely is in Thackers kitchen, waiting you I expect, and Anthony is out riding in the fields.'

'I belong to the future,' I said again, 'and the future is all round us, but you can't see it. I belong to the past too, because I am sharing it with you. Both are now.'

'Nay, that is nonsense. You may have some powers to know what will happen. You may have second sight. You perhaps heard from some witch or soothteller that the Queen of Scotland will be executed, but you cannot say it has already happened, for that is absurd. Prove that you are not of our time.'

'The queen was executed,' I murmured mechanically.

Francis suddenly looked at me, staring into my face, into the pupils of my eyes as if to see the little inverted image of himself.

'You are different in some way, and I half believe you.' He spoke hesitatingly and backed away for a moment. 'But I *won't* believe you,' he added quickly, jerking round. 'Such things are magic and I have nothing to do with the devil.'

I could not answer, I stood miserable and confused, and Francis went on. 'You could be hanged for what you've told me, or worse, burned in a fire, burned till your body became a black cinder.'

He spoke with vehemence, thrusting his face near mine, staring at me with horrified blue eyes so that I was frightened by his words.

'But I won't tell on you, because I think I like you, Penelope Taberner,' he added slowly. 'I believe you are a sorcerer, but you are not evil, that I will swear. You are not like the village girls, or even my sisters, your speech is different, and your voice is gentle and full of music. I think I like you. Perhaps you have bewitched me too.'

I tried to smile, for nobody was less witch-like than I. I remembered Uncle Barnabas; he would speak up for me, I thought. Then I forgot him again and there was nothing but the present.

'Whatever made you say it?' questioned Francis, but his voice was kind and sweet to me now. 'Who told you? Was it a wise woman? There's one lives at Caudle, but only the ignorant and fools go to her. Maids ask her for love potions, and servant wenches consult her. She brews them queer drinks and makes spells with adders' tongues. She is really quite harmless, but she has wisdom and reads the stars. Our uncle, Doctor Babington, has some powers, and he prophesied evil for Anthony, but my mother always said it was jealousy of his beauty. My stepfather, Henry Foljambe, gave Anthony a heavy gold chain of great value on his birthday, and Anthony with the chain about his neck climbed into one of the apple trees in the orchard yonder. He slipped, the bough broke and he was caught by the chain which nearly strangled him. There he hung, suffocating, and he would have died but my mother saw his scarlet doublet in the tree and saved him. That was an evil omen, people said, a prophecy of the manner of his own death. A cruel thing to say, and wicked. Yet the thought of this haunts my mother and Dame Cicely too.'

He sat silent, and I shivered as I too remembered something which I could not say.

'Anthony,' I whispered. 'Anthony.'

Then Francis began to talk to me of many things, asking if I could read Latin and Greek like Lady Jane Grey had done, and had I studied the science of numbers and philosophy? I said I had seen his Ovid and I too had read it, but of Greek I knew nothing, for we did French at school.

'French? Anthony's going to France on the queen's business,' interrupted Francis. 'He speaks the tongue perfectly. Mary Stuart is half French, and once she was the queen of France, but her husband died and she came back to Scotland.'

'I wish he would stay here,' sighed Francis as I was silent. 'The church roof should be mended, and new buildings made. There's a saw invented for tree-cutting I want him to buy, and two of the falcons are dead. We need another barn for wool-storing, and horses must be bought. But away he goes to Paris.'

He caught sight of my wristwatch, and examined its works eagerly. It was French workmanship, he told me, and never had he seen such a small time-keeper, although his brother's gold clock was more beautiful.

I looked down at the watch. The fingers had not moved while I had been there. Francis's fair head was bent over it, listening with a puzzled expression, and to my ears came the bleating of sheep and the ringing of church bells. The other world seemed part of the world where I found myself, and there was no division between them. Then we walked across the grass to the great thatched barn where Uncle Barnabas kept his carts and harrows. We stood under the same oak-timbered roof and Francis showed me the hunting hounds baying with bell voices, and the litter of puppies squirming in the straw. I picked up one of the pups, but the mother growled and slunk away so I let it go, saddened that always the dogs feared me, as if they alone knew I did not belong to the world and time where I found myself.

At the wide double doors was a pile of shepherds' crooks with pointed iron spikes and curled iron handles, and some pitchforks and rusty halberds. A shepherd came by carrying a crook and Francis spoke to him, and asked how he fared on the distant hills, where he had been sheep-minding, but I could scarcely understand his reply. It was full of burrs as a burdock bush, although it reminded me of Uncle Barnabas when he was talking broad to one of his friends.

The thought of Uncle Barnabas tugged at my heart, and I looked across the farm buildings seeking him. He was somewhere, alive and waiting for me. 'I must go,' I stammered, suddenly filled with desire to get away, and away I ran without another word, hastening in at the open door, but there I was met by Tabitha, and I forgot why I had gone.

# 6. Gossip in Thackers Kitchen

'HASTE thee, Penelope. Thy aunt calls thee. There's work waiting and thou in the fields roaming like a boy. Thou mun make the pastry flowers and leaves for the pies and pasties,' said Tabitha, beckoning me indoors.

I went to the kitchen and found the great baking in progress, the preparation of food for a large household. Enormous pasties were stuffed with pigeons and larks, which Margery and Tabitha had prepared, geese and capons were roasting, and Jude turned them before the fire, his eyes glancing round maliciously. I sat at the table to shape the roses and leaves out of strips of paste, to trim the pies. It was my work, Dame Cicely said, and my fingers were nimble for it. Town fingers were better than country ones when it came to making ornaments, and doubtless I had seen fine devices at the pastry cook's.

There was a ham baked in honey syrup and spiked with cloves, and brawn and pigs' pettitoes soused, and tansy puddings.

When I had finished my task the table was cleared and scrubbed and the servants' dinner was set, with pewter plates and a horn-handled knife apiece, and a polished drinking horn for the small ale and cider. I looked round for the forks but saw none, and Aunt Cicely was surprised at my inquiry. Mistress Babington had a silver fork and so had Master Anthony, but we used our fingers, and so did Master Francis. What were fingers given to us for, she asked, if not for eating? Forks were a newfangled habit from the Italians, and not for honest Englishmen.

I sat down to the table for I was very hungry, and the good smells of roasting and baking meats filled the air. I ate first some solid white pudding, heavy with lumps of fat which I carefully removed.

'You're too pernickety,' cried Dame Cicely. 'London living's spoiled you for wholesome vittles,' but secretly I dropped the scraps on the rushes for the dogs to eat. On the same plate I had a wedge of pasty stuffed with pigeon and herbs and chopped apple. I ate this with my fingers, like the others – Aunt Cicely, Tabitha, Margery, and a thin-faced girl called Moll. The men sat at a long trestle table and I was glad, for their manners were uncouth, and they spat out the food they did not like.

The drinking horns were filled with ale, made in the brew house across the yard, from our own barley. There was honey-mead for those who wanted it, but I wished for water. I knew where the spring was, for I had often filled the kettle for Aunt Tissie, and I ran out now with a leather jug.

On my way I passed a small room where a spinning wheel clacked, and a girl sat turning the wheel and spinning the wool. She nodded and smiled and I went to her. She touched my dress and wondered at its smoothness of texture, and asked if my mother had spun the wool and dyed it in Chelsey. I said we had bought it in a shop.

'Ah! On London Bridge! I've seen the water of the Thames swirling under the arches, and I've been to the shops on the bridge. My name is Phoebe Drury, and I was born at Bow, but I've been in service here for ten years. Tell me, Penelope, have you seen the queen? They say she has a dress for every day of the year and her stomachers are stiff with pearls and rubies.'

I confessed I hadn't, although I had heard of the richness of her dress. Then I went out for the water, which came bubbling from the same spring, in crystal coils jutting from the ground. As I sipped the earthy coldness of it, cupping it in my hand, I was aware once more of the continuity of life, as if I were part of events past, present, and to come, and I could choose my way among them.

They were all talking when I returned, telling tales of magic and wonders, of fire-eaters and performing animals, speaking of a bear led by a warder which danced at Darby Fair, and a horse which talked at Nottingham Goose Fair. Yes, they said, the horse could tell the hour like the nightwatchman, and it pawed the name of Queen Bess. The serving men were leaning back, drinking from their horns, joining in the discourse. They spoke of Master Anthony, how he was visiting the farms on his estates, collecting his dues, paying wages owed, hearing complaints, and being well received, because his manner was affable, with no conceit or arrogance. He was going hunting in the great woods which stretched across the hills, and the huntsmen were to meet at a little manor hidden in the woods. There was new life coming to Thackers, they said, for the news of his homecoming had spread, and pedlars came with many-coloured ribbons and laces, coifs and silks, men who had been with gewgaws to Sheffield Castle. Dame Cicely had bought a bunch of ribbons that morning, and Mistress Babington had chaffered for a silver lacing and tassels of gold for her dress. Songwriters sent ballads to please him, and presents were arriving for his birthday.

Then the old shepherd seated at the men's table spoke up in quavering high-pitched tones.

'There ain't no good coming here. There's evil abroad. I've seen a comet in the heavens when I was a-minding sheep, and it bodes no good. Something harmful's coming,' said he, mournfully. 'Young mester won't bide here, where he was born and bred. He won't bide. Stars are agin him.'

'He's going to Paris, that city of Satan,' said another, and the old shepherd shook his head. 'He won't bide here,' he repeated, 'and there's a comet in the sky.'

'All clever noblemen go to Paris and Rouen where there is much learning. There's no harm. Be silent,' cried Dame Cicely shortly. But the aged shepherd would not be silenced, and he mumbled on.

'It's for the Queen of Scotland's sake, and I dunno hold with her. She's in league with the Spaniards, and they'd utterly destroy us, like flax in the fire. I 'member things you young folk forget. I 'member tales of fire and burning in Queen Mary's reign. Those bloody days will come again if Spain gets here. Aye, we shall all be consumed like flax in the flames.'

'Master Anthony wouldn't agree to that,' said another. 'For he loves his land, but he says the Scottish queen should be set free.'

'True,' said Dame Cicely. 'So she should, for she'll be Queen of England some day, and Master Anthony will be rewarded.'

'If she doesn't die in prison first,' said Tabitha. 'I heard she was ill and like to die a time back.'

'The Scottish Queen is a murderess. She's the Scarlet Woman,' shouted a young man with a fierce, dark face. 'She plotted with Bothwell to blow up her husband, and the Scots won't have her. She shall never be Queen of England.'

Several sprang to their feet, crying out on him, and seizing him. Such a hubbub arose that Dame Cicely was in a fine to-do, shaking her hands and crying out to be silent, the mistress would hear. Blows were struck and blood flowed and dishes were overturned for loyalties divided the house and some were for one and some for another, although I could see that all were for Master Anthony and his kindred.

I slipped out of the room, filled with dismay, and I ran along the passage, past the still-room with its odours of simples, past the spinning room where Phoebe cried out to know what was the matter, but I didn't stop. I was seeking someone, looking for a dear, familiar face, a warm hand to hold, a voice to bring courage.

I crossed the panelled hall, where I had never been before. I caught a sight of the great sword and longbow hanging on the wall. They had belonged to Thomas Babington who fought at Agincourt with King Henry V, Mistress Foljambe had told me. They hung on either side of the crest.

'Foy est Tout', I read, and I stopped for a minute to look up at the words which I had seen in the church, and I whispered them to myself as I climbed the oak staircase.

Below me at the end of the room sat Anthony and his family. Francis caught the flash of my skirt as I turned the corner. Footsteps came after me, and I hurried along the passage, past the door of Mistress Foljambe's room. Through a crack I could see the walls with their painted beasts and birds but I went on. I felt that I had to get away, or I might never reach those I sought. I passed other doors each with carved fruit at the lintel, and I came to the steps at the end. I ran softly up, my feet making no noise, my step light as air. Everywhere was silent, quiet as a dreamless sleep, the footsteps had died away, no one could find me. I lifted the latch and walked through to the landing I knew so well.

The air was different, the smells were homely – odours of primroses and fresh linen, for the oak chest was open and a clothes basket full of sheets lay near. I had left the spiced and rich life behind me in summer's heat, to return to the cooler days of spring. I looked at my watch. Its fingers had not moved. The inexorable hours, the racing minutes were fused into one bright second into which I had gone undiscovered, sharing the ether with those unseen ones, breathing their rare atmosphere, living a life heightened by danger, returning with a dim memory of these things.

I looked at myself in the little mirror. My cheeks were flaming-red, my arms were sunburnt, but another sun had warmed them. The hot passions of those days flowed in my veins, I felt transfigured, old, wise, knowing a thousand things of which I had been barely conscious. Strangely moved by the knowledge that I was separated from that life by only the thinnest vapour, I went downstairs, my little watch ticking the minutes away, awakened from its sleep.

As I became accustomed to this journey in time and this transformation of scene, I found myself remembering less of the present, I became more absorbed in the past through my love for those whom I met there. Yet I knew there was a possibility I might not come back, and it was this knowledge which later on tainted my experience with fear. Sometimes I must have made the journey unknown to myself, when I slept, for they were not surprised at my reappearances, they evidently expected me. I, who had always been a dreamer, seldom awoke in the long nights at Thackers. I lay with my head nested on the downy pillow, unmoving till Aunt Tissie came into the room and the sunshine broke through the curtains. Perhaps I sped through time to the Elizabethan's home and shared the servitude of Dame Cicely, and returned while my body lay in that deep sleep. I brought no consciousness of my travelling, I lost all as one forgets a dream on awakening. When I went there in those flashes which I relate, I had an uneasy feeling that I had been there more often than I could remember. I was not a stranger, my feet moved unhesitatingly across the floors; I opened cupboards and presses aware of the contents, the taste of strange dishes was palatable to my lips. I shivered as I thought of this unknown journey, for I clung to the dear familiar things of life and I was not prepared to venture into the past unwittingly lest I should be caught and captured for ever in that time.

I only went once more, knowingly, into the secret life which moved alongside our humdrum country days before we went back to London. Whenever I stood on the landing waiting for the miracle to happen, the doors I saw were those of our own rooms, the wall was solid as reality, there was no entry into the past days.

It was after church on the last Sunday that I found my way there again. I sat in the Babington pew between Aunt Tissie and Alison, for Ian had refused to attend the monthly service and preferred to help Jess. Uncle Barnabas was left at home to look after the dinner. He said his duty was done without any psalm-singing, for already he had rung the solitary bell which went ding, ding, ding. I asked him where the other bells were, for in the old days there was a gay peal of six bells. Perhaps they had been melted down for cannon, or sold by somebody in the days of poverty which came to Thackers after Anthony Babington's death – he did not know.

I thought of this as I sat in church. Overhead were the oak rafters where a swallow flew to feed her young. Beyond I could see the carved shield with the motto: 'Foy est Tout'. Somewhere else I had seen those words, but I could not remember where. Through the windows, whose richly stained glass was now replaced by plain, the branches of the yew trees moved in the wind. Uncle Barnabas told me that villagers came to the churchyard for a hundred years for their yew bows, and the wood where we picked our bluebells was called Bow Wood because many yews once grew on its heights.

I listened to the words of the parson, a dreary man who sent us all to sleep. 'For thine is the kingdom for ever and ever,' he intoned.

'For ever and ever and ever,' I whispered again, and a mist swam over my eyes. The village people whom I knew, the blacksmith and carpenter, the postman and schoolmaster, faded away, and another congregation was there, in wimple and kirtle and leather breeches and cloth doublet. They used the same words, 'for ever and ever'.

In the pulpit was a stern man who scolded them severely for their misdeeds. Timothy Tailor had not paid his tithes, Adam Buckley had beaten his wife, Tom Snowball had slept during the sermon. I thought I saw Mistress Babington beside me, but Anthony was not in the square oak pew with the arms carved on the door. The air was hot and sultry, there was a strong smell of straw and birch branches under my feet. I staggered for I could hardly breathe.

Aunt Tissie caught me and the ghostly congregation faded away. She led me across the yard back to the farm. There was dear Uncle Barnabas in the kitchen, with a monster spoon basting the roast beef. He was much concerned over my faintness. He ought to have opened the church windows, he said.

'Lie down and bide quiet, my child,' said Aunt Tissie and she gave me a drink of hot water and ginger. Then she peeped in the oven, for I heard the clang of the iron door as I lay in my room, and she went back to church.

But through the trembling air came a whisper: 'Penelope!' – no sound at all, but the echo of some long-dead call. I rose from my bed and crept along the landing, past the oak chest to the wall. My hands glided over smooth stone, and I could find no opening. From the kitchen I could hear Uncle Barnabas whistling a hymn tune and the words came from the church over the garden.

'O God our help in ages past,' they sang. Then I touched a cold latchet, and once more found myself looking into the small, panelled room, where I had first been a visitor. Anthony Babington was there, seeking feverishly in the oak coffer, turning papers and books. His face was pale, he muttered to himself. Without noticing me he went to the fireplace and twisted a leaf carved in the foliage of the mantlepiece. A door swung back, a secret door which disclosed a priest's room with the crucifix on the wall. He knelt on the floor and prayed. Then he came out again, closing the panel so that the small slit of a room disappeared, its lines concealed in the walls.

He saw me standing in the shadows, hesitating, for I could not return by the way I had come, and I had no wish to disturb him.

'Penelope Taberner! Find my jewel,' he cried, and he seized my hands and held them as if he feared I should fade away. 'My jewel. I've lost it, I can do nothing without it. You have strange powers, so find it. Tell me where it is.'

'The locket of her? Of Mary Queen of Scots?' I asked.

He groaned. 'Yes, it's my talisman. It is lost. I meant to take it to Paris and it has gone.'

'Master Anthony, I don't know where it is,' I cried in distress, but he would not believe I had no knowledge. I promised to search in fields and woods, and do my best for him.

'If ever you find it, you will tell me. You will come and tell me,' he insisted, and his blue eyes looked as fierce as a hawk's as they stared into mine. I gave my solemn promise, and left him there among his books, for I wanted to see Francis. I went down the kitchen staircase, intending to cross the alleyway by the still room, but the door of the kitchen was wide open and a company sat round the table and sprawled on the forms listening to one who addressed them. Their talk was of the Scots queen, for a pedlar had got a glimpse of her riding with her guard on Sheffield moor, and a carpenter had seen her portrait. He was describing it as I passed, and I waited to hear the news.

'There it hung, a grand painting, done by Her Grace's embroiderer, Master Oudry. He's a Frenchman and he makes the designs for the broideries of the queen and her ladies. He showed it to me and I saw it with these very eyes.'

'How did ye manage to get in?' asked Tabitha. 'I'd give a deal to see a portrait of Her Grace.'

'I wouldna,' said another, 'I'd give naught at all,' but they silenced him.

' 'Twas this way,' said the first speaker. 'I had a small dealing with Master Oudry. I made a box to hold the skeins of silk which he has. Fifty little places to keep the skeins separate, all in a good oak box, smooth as silk itself. It was a pretty piece of work, I may tell ye, and he paid me well. He was excellently pleased with it, so I up and spoke to him. "Master Oudry," says I, although I ought to have called him Mounseer Oudry. "Master Oudry," says I. "Will ye grant me a favour? I've heard tell ye've painted the Queen of Scotland.

I've never set eyes on her, but if I could get a glimpse of your picture, I should reckon it a great honour."

'Well, he hesitated for a bit and then he took me in my working clothes into the castle apartments, past the guard, explaining I was the carpenter, and into a room where it hung. It was a good 'un, a big picture, large as life and as true maybe, although she wasn't as purty as I expected.'

'What had she got on?' asked Dame Cicely. 'I always wonder what kind of clothes queens and all uncommon mortals wear. Master Anthony has a white satin doublet for court, and a deal of trouble I had cleaning away a grease spot from the sleeve.'

'Her clothes were finer done than her face, for I expects Master Oudry was cleverer at them, being his trade, so to speak. She had black, drop earrings and black jet beadwork on her bosom, and a fine ruff edged with point lace. It had a bunch of pearls to fasten it, not ribbons like ordinary folk. There was a gold crucifix hanging by a velvet ribbon from her neck and a cross and beads at her girdle, all painted glittering and real as life. There was a cloak of lawn on her shoulders, not for warmth, just for beauty, all transparent and made very soft and light.'

'Well, you've seen something we others haven't seen,' observed Dame Cicely, and the others all began to talk of the queen and her sorrows and her captivity, arguing and quarrelling among themselves.

I went out of the house by the great porch, and round by the church. I passed into the yew walk and beyond it I saw Francis. 'Ho! Penelope! Did you hear me call you?' he asked. 'Did you know I wanted you?' and he swung his long legs over the wall and came to meet me.

'Penelope! You are dressed like a princess, like a Spanish princess at court. Where's your boy garb?'

He looked at me admiringly as I stood shyly waiting, at my best green dress with the hanging sleeves, and my dark hair tied with a green ribbon. He put his arms akimbo and began to sing a song to me, half mocking, half joyful, as if he were glad to see me again.

> *'Greensleeves was all my joy,*
> *Greensleeves was my delight,*
> *Greensleeves was my heart of gold,*
> *And who but Lady Greensleeves.*

*'Thy gown of the grassy green*
*With sleeves of satin hanging by,*
*Which made thee be our harvest queen,*
*And yet thou would'st not love me.*

*'Greensleeves was all my joy,*
*Greensleeves was my delight,*
*Greensleeves was my heart of gold,*
*And who but Lady Greensleeves.*

'That's the latest London song,' he informed me, 'which Anthony brought back with him.'

Then he called to me to follow him and he promised we would have fine sport. There were owls' nests to find, and deer to watch, and the great bull to tease. He would fetch his hawks and let me see them bring down a bird from the sky. He had a new falcon named Hover, and I should have it for my own. He would fetch his bow and shoot an arrow which would cleave the white wand set in the far fields for the Sunday games. Did I know of Robin Hood, he asked.

'Yes, I've read the ballads of Robin Hood and Little John,' I told him.

'You shall be Maid Marion to my Robin Hood,' said Francis. 'He lived in Sherwood Forest, not fifty miles away. I'll show you a great hollow oak where I keep my hunting knife, so that I can cut up the deer I slay. I'll give you a pair of antlers after my next kill.'

He promised sport indeed if I would come away to the woods, just as I was in my green dress.

I shook my head. 'I came because you called,' I said.

'It was for Anthony's locket. Did he tell you? The queen herself gave it to him, and he would rather lose his right hand than her gift.'

I explained that I didn't know where it was, I had no powers, I was no witch-girl.

'But you see into the future,' he protested. 'Can't you see it lying somewhere, can't you find it, Penelope?'

Even as he spoke he grew shadowy and dim before my eyes, his hand slipped from my arm, the warmth of his voice, the new friendliness of his glance, ebbed to nothing. I heard his voice again, vainly whispering. 'Penelope. Don't go. Penelope.' But mingled with it was the triumphant hymn which rang from the old church across the grassplat.

'O God our help in ages past,' they sang. The cedar tree had vanished, the yew hedge had gone like vapour, and only the old oak tree and the mighty yews remained as witness of the past. 'O God our help.' The words seemed to be uttered by the great tower itself, which had stood sentinel for generations, shadowing the rich and the humble ones who stood by its walls asking for aid against unseen foes. I looked up at that emblazoned tower and said a prayer for those other ones, who were near to trouble.

Then I went indoors, knowing I was going to my real home, and not the kitchen of long ago with its tumult and anxiety over the Scottish queen. By the fireside in his armchair sat my uncle. A long-handled spoon was in his hand and he basted the sirloin, just as the boy Jude had turned the spit in other days.

'What! Are you all right, my dear?' he smiled at me. 'Come and sit by an old man and I'll tell ye a tale as I've thought on, a tale that's been simmering in my mind many a year, and never come to light.'

So he talked of the woods and a curious happening there, and soon the others came home from church. The tale ended; I was quite well. It was only a faintness from standing so long, they said, and I agreed with them.

# 7. The Queen's Locket

THE LONG holiday had ended, and Mother
wrote that we must return. We had missed
enough schooling, but she hoped we had learned
some lessons not to be found in books and
made friends with those who never walked the
pavements of towns. Indeed we had! Ian's bosom
friends were Jess the ploughman, who talked like
the Elizabethans, and never went farther than
Blackpool once a year, and Jake the gamekeeper.
He spent many an hour with Jake who took him
into the preserved woods and showed him the
hens brooding young pheasants in hen coops
along a green drive. Together they kept watch for
poachers, and tracked the foxes and made a
gamekeeper's larder on an oak tree. Certainly the

gamekeeper did not walk city pavements. There was the rat-catcher too, a man with many a tale of the cleverness of rats.

'You know that rat virus we had,' said he one day when I was there. 'Well, it shines in the dark, sort of luminous like herrings' heads. What do you think those darned rats did? They never tasted it! Oh no, they was too fause, for it would have poisoned them dead. No, they carried it away and put it along their dark passages like lamps, so that they had a well-lighted road! I seed it with my own eyes.'

Alison had different friends, for all the little children in the village knew her. As for me, after Uncle Barny and Aunt Tissie there were those others, the hidden shadowy ones, who went about their own affairs in a world unseen by us; but their life was compact with sorrows and joys so intense that I marvelled the barrier was not broken down with the flood of their emotions. The air of house and barn was throbbing with the memory of things once seen and heard.

We went to the old deserted quarries to say goodbye, to see once more the broken stone huts whose floors were carpeted with the finest grass, in whose crannies ferns hung like green curtains, and over whose walls were tapestries of moss and lichen. We always crept softly up to these relics of bygone days, for we never knew what we should find. Ian expected a vixen and her cubs, or a badger remaking his holt. Alison thought we might see a tramp with billycan and savoury stew of rabbit. We saw none of these; only the queer listening silence pervaded the place as if woodland creatures and dim ghosts were watching us. We visited the meadows for the last time, and I said goodbye to my favourite fields, Westwood, Squirrels, Meadow Doles, and Hedgegrove, and as I walked there I remembered they were Anthony Babington's beloved fields which he mentioned by name caressingly.

There was Betty to go back to Bramble Hall and Uncle Barnabas said I should take her. I rode her up the long grassy lane which was a highroad in olden days. Strings of packhorses laden with 'pigs' of lead from the mines in the hills once ambled down this winding lane, and country women rode to market over the crest, with pannier basket filled with butter and eggs and fat hens hanging by their legs. Further back in history the shaggy British ponies came there with Roman lead from those ancient workings. Now all was grass-covered, rabbits scuttered along the path between the black walls, and pheasants cried *cuck-cuck* as they flew over from the woods. I rode past the little witch-wood, where the rowan trees flourished and bilberries grew, to the hamlet of farms and cottages. I trotted up to Bramble Hall and drew rein for a moment to look through the gateway at the old doorway. People were walking on the lawn, two men were playing bowls, another admired a monkey which a girl carried. The girl was handsome and petulant, and she tossed back her red-gold hair and impatiently teased the little cowering creature in her arms. She turned away to meet a lady with wide skirts of vivid blue who came slowly down the rounded steps from the open door of the house. At the same moment I saw the farmer come out from the side door and walk across the lawn to put a chicken coop out in the sunshine. Each set of figures kept distinct, neither was aware of the other, and the farmer walked through them as if they were films of smoke.

'Good morning, Penelope,' he cried, as he saw me sitting on Betty's back, staring wide-eyed through the gate. 'Come to look at the old place?

Tie Betty to the ring there by the mounting-block, and come right in.'

I obeyed him, and everyone vanished. Neither the lady nor the red-haired girl nor the men were there. The shaven lawn was rough, the front door was barred, and moss and ivy grew on the green steps.

'We never use the front door,' explained the farmer as I paused before it. 'It's rusted up, but sometimes Americans come and want to buy it. To buy my front door! They say it's genuine Elizabethan, days of Queen Bess you know, her as got shuttance of the Armada. Maybe they'd like to take the whole house, for it's an ancient place. But come along in and have a taste of gingerbread. The missis has been baking and she's a rare hand at gingerbread.'

I followed him to the side door and through an arched passage to the kitchen. His wife dusted a speckless chair for me to sit down and went to the dairy for a glass of milk.

'Thor cake we calls it,' she said cutting the fragrant, hot gingerbread. 'And so you've brought Betty back to us? Have you liked her? Has she been good? Ah, she will never forget you. Horses have long memories, better memories than people I sometimes think.'

I said goodbye to these kind friends and saw Betty turned into the field to graze. She raised her head and whinnied as I passed by, and my heart was sad to leave them all.

Our bags were packed, there was nothing more to be done and I wandered into the church. The door was wide open and I could hear the sounds of cleaning inside. Mrs Appleyard was there with her pail and brush, and Aunt Tissie was polishing the brass. I helped her for a while, but when she had finished and Mrs Appleyard had left all spotless I stayed there. It was very quiet, and I went to the crested pew, the square oak seat where the Babington family had sat so many years before. The clock ticked with a loud insistent voice, like somebody talking, and little echoes of its iron tongue came from the corners of the church. 'The belles, the clocke, and the challis of silver I bequeath to my sonne.' Anthony's grandfather had left it thus in 1558, but the chalice and the bells had gone.

'Tick, tick, tick,' went the clock, and the wheels whirred in the tower. There was a flutter of wings as a hen came to the church door, and a scurry of mice in the woodwork. I knelt down to pray for Master Anthony and for Francis, for their happiness wherever they were, and I prayed for Mary Stuart, free at last in another kingdom above that blue sky which I saw from the windows. But I could not think of her as dead, her face came before me flushed with life, her lips slightly parted, her eyes dazzling me so that I had to lower mine as if I faced a light.

I knelt there for a long time, or perhaps it was only a few minutes, but my mind recalled all that I had seen or heard, and the memories of those hidden days came vividly before me. As I crouched in the old pew, kneeling on the moth-eaten carpet, I was so still that a mouse came out of a hole in the corner and sat upright, watching me with beady eyes. Then I forgot all about Anthony Babington, as the little creature played with a crumb it had found. I made a sudden movement and away it went, like a flashing shadow out of the pew and away. I took out my penknife and pushed it down the hole, but I could not reach the bottom. Then I fetched a twig from the yew tree and scrabbled in the small cavity. The wood was rotten and I broke off pieces until I could get my finger down. Very hot and red, I fumbled in the hole, half afraid I should touch a mouse's nest. I brought out first a threepenny-bit which somebody had lost from their collection money. Then I found another object, thick and heavy, coated with dust and mould. I carried it off to the water trough, hoping for wealth, but as the dirt encrusted upon it was washed away a looped edge came to view, and I saw it wasn't a coin at all. I rubbed it with sand, and scrubbed it with a brush, and gradually the thick layer of verdigris and dirt came away and I saw it was a thin case with hinges. Even then I did not realize what I had found. I opened it with a knife and stared at the little painted picture sealed under the glass. It was the lost locket, the miniature of the queen, kept intact in its freshness, in the dry boards of the church. Mary Queen of Scots looked out at me, with her carnation held in her white fingers, and she smiled her enigmatic smile, triumphant as if she were newly risen from the dead.

I ran indoors, calling for my aunt and Alison. I rushed to the stable to find Uncle Barnabas. I shouted across the fields for Ian. Nobody else was excited. Uncle Barnabas said it had no value, it was only silver-gilt. Aunt Tissie said I could keep it to hang round my neck in memory of Thackers. Maybe a visitor had dropped it some time. It was only the picture of a lady.

'It's Mary Queen of Scots,' I exclaimed, angry at their stupidity. 'Can't you recognize her?'

They laughed. 'How do you know?' they said. 'This is an old-fashioned lady, and no great beauty. You're too romantic, Penelope.'

'It is! It is!' I cried. 'Look at the carnation in her hand. Look at the initials M.R. on the outside.'

'Dear girl. Call it what you like,' said Aunt Tissie patiently. 'Queen of Sheba, if you like. I'll give you a ribbon for it, a green one to match your dress.'

'I must give it back to Master Anthony,' I told myself. I waited on the landing, I called: 'Francis, Francis Babington.' I walked up and down the rooms, carrying the locket on its green ribbon, looking for a shadow, listening for a faint reply. All was silent, and in no manner could I get over there.

'I will leave it with you, Aunt Tissie,' I said that night, and I hung it from a nail on my bedroom wall. 'I want to leave it, for it belongs to Thackers.'

'As you like, my dear,' said Aunt Tissie amiably. 'It will be here waiting for you when you come back, pray God.'

The next morning we were up at six o'clock and started for the train at seven. Jess brought out our bulging suitcases which had expanded to twice their original sizes. Aunt Tissie filled a basket with pasties and cakes for the journey, besides packing a hamper of farm produce.

'I'm going to be a farmer when I leave school,' proclaimed Ian. 'Keep the job open for me, Uncle Barnabas,' and Uncle Barny promised he would.

I loitered upstairs at the last minute, seeking the doorway.

'Master Anthony,' I whispered. 'She's here. I have found your jewel. I promised you should have it and I can't get to you. I can't open the door to that other time where you are.'

There was no answer, and I went downstairs. They were calling me, the horse was stamping restlessly. Uncle Barny sat in the cart, and my own stool was close to his warm milky-smelling knee. I climbed in the cart, Uncle Barny flicked his whip in a curl over the horse, Aunt Tissie raised her apron and began to wave it up and down like a flag.

'Goodbye. Goodbye,' we called, and Aunt Tissie replied: 'God be with you, my dears.'

Away we jolted, along the white roads, past the woods and farms alongside the talking brook. We looked back and for a few minutes we could see the white apron tossing in the farmyard against the walls of the old house. Then the church tower with its broken emblems embowered in its clump of elms was all that remained and soon we turned the corner and we left it behind. 'With a bit of my heart,' I thought.

'It has been the best holiday we've ever had,' Ian told Mother, when she met us at St Pancras and bundled us into a cab. Our luggage had surprisingly grown, like ourselves, she told us.

'I fed the pigs every day and mixed the swill and looked after the hens,' I said proudly as the cab rumbled out of the station. 'We've brought some of our eggs for you.'

'I carted the muck, and I shot a couple of rabbits clean dead, Mother. They're in the hamper for you. I was going to shoot a pheasant too, but Uncle said I had no game licence. Can I have one for my birthday?'

'I made the butter for Aunt Tissie,' said Alison. 'She said it was the most beautiful butter she had ever tasted. There's a pat in the hamper. Do you know how to make butter? You put the cream in the churn ... Did you know butter was made from cream, and not from milk, Mother?'

'Of course I know,' laughed Mother, and she interrupted Alison's description of churning and pressing and weighing, to turn to me.

'You look much better, child. You have changed so much I hardly know you. Such rosy cheeks and such bright eyes. What have you been doing?'

'I told you, Mother,' I replied impatiently. 'I fed the pigs –'

'Penelope was fey, Mother. She spent her time thinking of the Babington family and asking Aunt Tissie questions,' laughed Alison.

'It was such an old historical house,' I excused myself, blushing, and that was all, for there was our own Chelsea street, with the great Thames flowing near us instead of the wild little brook and Chelsea Church instead of Thackers with its tower and haystacks and elms.

We settled down to the life of every day, with school on weekdays and the parks on Sundays. We fed the seagulls, and did the shopping in the King's Road. And Thackers went on with its secret life. Sometimes I thought of them all, Aunt

Tissie and Uncle Barnabas and Jess sitting in the farm kitchen, and the aristocratic family living their own troubled existence alongside, walking in the same fields, sitting under the oak tree, fishing in the river. I wondered whether Anthony found the queen's jewel before he went to Paris, and I hoped Francis had not forgotten me. Sometimes they were more real than the people round me, and then they became phantoms, swirling in dim motion, disappearing like the summer mists.

# 8. I Ride to the Fair

IT WAS a couple of years later, in June, that we returned to Thackers. I had overgrown my strength and it was arranged I should remain at the beloved farm, free to roam over the fields and breathe the life-giving air, to climb the hills and gather new health from their rocky fastnesses. I had a troublesome cough which doctor's medicine wouldn't cure and only the smell of a farmyard could take it away. Ian and Alison accompanied me for a short holiday and then I was left to my own company.

I packed my trunk this time, for I was determined that I would spend Christmas at Thackers. At the top of it lay my new green dress with hanging sleeves the colour of the grass.

I had grown out of my favourite frock and Mother had been surprised at my insistence on the same colour, but I secretly hoped to wear it in the shadowed dream-life, if I could enter its enchanted doors.

Uncle Barnabas met us at the station as before, with the glossy black mare, Sally, who turned her head to welcome us when she heard our voices. The spring cart was polished up for the occasion, the wheels glittered and the splash board was speckless. The best rug lay on the seat and the fine whip in the socket. Uncle Barnabas wore his Sunday coat, but when I kissed his red cheek I could smell the same delicious odour of cowcake and meal and hayseeds that I liked so much. He pushed his top hat back from the forehead and looked keenly at us. Ian was quite a man, old enough to leave school he was sure, and the job of farmhand was waiting for him. Alison was grown up, a bonny young lady, her school days were over. I was unchanged, but taller, and more serious, he thought.

'You won't want to suckle the calves and ride Betty, I'm sure. You've all growed up like Jack Beanstalks.' We assured him that underneath we had not changed at all; we were the three who always loved the farm.

Ian sat on the side of the cart, balanced like Jess when he had a full load of churns, and we two girls squeezed ourselves by Uncle Barnabas. There was no room for the trunk, we must manage without it for that night, said Uncle Barnabas, and Jess would bring it up in the milk cart the next morning. Maybe Cicely Anne could lend us a couple of nightgowns. Alison looked dubious as she thought of Aunt Tissie's high-necked calico garments. Then: 'Our toothbrushes,' she wailed. 'We *must* clean our teeth.'

'I've never cleaned *my* teeth,' said Uncle Barny. 'Never once in my life, and I've never been to the dentist either. Every tooth left is as sound as a bell, and do you know for why? Hard crusses and apples does it. You eat hard, knobby crusses and apples and you'll need no toothbrush.' So Alison had to be content.

We drove away from the little station down the yard where the hotel bus waited and the motor-car from the castle, but we went along the valley among the woods. I was filled with such elation I wanted to shout and sing, and as usual when

I was excited I kept very quiet. It was like being on a high swing, or riding a galloping horse, to drive behind a little fast-trotting mare which knew me, to listen to a singing river which sang a song I loved, to hear the birds in the hedges, and to see the white roses foaming over the walls.

'We're in the middle of haymaking,' Uncle Barnabas told us. 'You're just in time to help. Three more haymakers are what I want, for harvesters are scarce nowadays. Once on a time we had a crowd of Irishmen; for many a year they came, but now we have only three or four, so we are glad of all the help we can get.'

'We adore haymaking,' said Alison.

'That's more nor I do,' grunted Uncle Barnabas. '*I* don't adore it. No, I don't.'

'Can I lead the horses and go on the stack?' asked Ian.

'We'll see,' replied Uncle Barnabas. That was his favourite expression which Alison said was noncommittal and very useful at all times.

The sun was shining when we sighted Thackers, with its tower and half-made haystack, like a scented heap of dried flowers among the heavy, green trees, but the smell of Thackers was everywhere, in the lanes and woods and fields. It was a smell compounded of new-mown hay, roses, lavender, and old age, all mingled together to form a pot-pourri sweeter than that I bought in London for my mother's Christmas present. If only I could collect it and pack it in jars I should have dog roses and haystacks all the year round.

Alison and Ian were pointing out familiar objects, calling the horse which ran whinnying alongside us in the field, whistling the dogs which raced to meet us. I noticed the little things; a stone I had left for a seat under a wall was still there, a tree shaped like a witch waved her long boughs to me, the ferns were growing in the crumbled archway and under their shadow I saw a bird's nest.

Jess came out of the stable, and opened the gate at the bottom of the drive. We left Uncle riding in the cart and took a short cut through the stackyard and behind the church to meet Aunt Tissie, who stood waiting for us at the open door with sunshine gathered in her white apron, and firelight behind her making a halo of her white hair.

Even as I went across the cobbled yard to her outstretched arms, I had time to glance up at the windows. Yes, they were the four I knew, and not the row of lovely old mullions I had once seen deep in the gable which was not there, in a house that once had been. Suppose all had faded away, and I never saw that household again!

Aunt Tissie held me in her arms, looking up to me, for now I was taller than she, kissing me as if I were her own daughter. She took us into the bright kitchen where the tea things sparkled by the fire, and the grandfather clock cleared its throat and struck loudly as if to welcome us, and the canary burst into song. All the room seemed to speak as we entered, and I imagined that the dishes on the dresser, the jugs on the hooks, the guns and brass candlesticks whispered and chuckled to one another, saying: 'Here is that family from London City, and Penelope who knows our language.' So I nodded back to all the things as my eyes wandered round the room.

'You know the way to your rooms?' asked Aunt Tissie. 'I'll wet the tea and you must be quick, for I'm sure you're all clemmed.'

There was one thought as I mounted the winding stairs, and that was to see if my jewel had gone. It was still there, shining in the oblong of sunlight on the white wall. I was half disappointed it had not been taken by its rightful owner, and half glad that I could see the queen's picture.

We opened and shut the drawers, and breathed the sweet musty air of the old room. Through the windows nodded musk-scented roses and down in the garden the borders were snowy with pinks. Beyond I could see the lavender hedge and the shadow of the church tower falling over the grass, and white ducks waddling to the brook.

The rosebud skirts of the dressing table had been starched, and upon them lay a brand-new pincushion in which Aunt Tissie had stuck pins to make the word 'Welcome'. We laughed at the irregularity of the letters, for we could imagine her short fingers struggling to keep them even. A new chintz cover was on the wicker chair and a fresh patchwork quilt lay on Alison's bed. It was really a very old one brought out of the oak chest, but it looked as if it had just been made.

Ian called us to his room to see the surprise Uncle Barnabas had provided for him. It was a stuffed jay sitting on a bough in a glass case, and although I didn't like it and wouldn't have slept with it in my room, Ian was delighted.

'Jays are robbers. They suck the pheasant eggs and steal young birds,' he protested hotly.

We sat around the tea table talking nineteen to the dozen, hearing the gossip about pigs and cows and horses. A tree had been struck by lightning, and the church roof had to be mended where rain came in. The gamekeeper's wife had had a new baby and the colt won second prize at the show. We told our news too, of a play we had seen and the Lord Mayor's Show. My father had written a book but it wasn't yet published.

We washed up and put the china away before we went out to see the newly mown fields, to run down the hillside to the brook and up the opposite hill to the crest where the moorland lay golden with gorse. The moon had risen and the stars were out before we came in to supper, Ian and Alison to a meal with my aunt and uncle, I to a bowl of bread and creamy milk which I ate on a stool by the fire, just as if I were still a child.

We went to bed without candles and undressed by moonlight. Alison and I swathed ourselves in Aunt Tissie's voluminous, best nightgowns which had been airing by the kitchen fire, but they still had a delicious odour of lavender and the ancient box in which they had lain for many a year, and nothing would ever remove this smell. We danced in the patch of light on the floor holding out our full white skirts, pretending we were ghosts as we waved the long sleeves and bowed and swayed. Then we heard Aunt Tissie coming and as we didn't want to offend her by mocking at her absurd nightwear we skipped into our beds and lay there very still.

'Don't be alarmed if you hear the Irishmen singing in the yard tonight. They often sing when they come back from the Blue Bell – mournful songs I grant you, but they like them and it gives them pleasure.'

She tucked us up as if we were small children and took away our dusty shoes for Jess to clean.

'Goodnight, my children. Sleep well. I'm that glad to see you, you don't know.'

We heard nothing of the Irishmen's songs for we slept too soundly, and we didn't wake till nine o'clock, when the clatter of the horse in the yard and Jess's voice as he dragged the heavy trunk from the cart and dumped it with the milk churns roused us.

We unpacked and put on our summer frocks. Aunt gave us each a blue cotton sun bonnet, frilled and piped in an old-fashioned way, and Ian had an ancient straw hat which she insisted he should wear or he might get the sunstroke.

He looked like a Spanish brigand as he rode off bareback on the carthorse and with the wide hat flapping on his shoulders and we were like a couple of dairymaids going a-milking.

Uncle Barnabas drove the mowing machine and Jess and the Irishmen scythed round the meadows under the rose-covered hedges. Away across the fields we saw the other three men tossing the hay. Jess took us to the barn and gave us each a fork and taught us how to ted the grass. At eleven we sank down under a tree and Aunt Tissie brought out herb beer which she had cooled in the spring. Our arms were burnt, our legs were prickled and stung, our faces were freckled, but we stuck to the work, determined to show Uncle Barnabas we were worthy of our farming ancestry. All he said when we hurried off, answering the dinner bell with surprising alacrity, was: 'Well, you've not done so badly for beginners.' In the afternoon the sun was more powerful and our energy less. The tedding had brought us close to the banks where birds and beasts lived, and flowers bloomed abundantly. We found a wild bees' nest, a flock of butterflies, a writing master's nest with the scribble on the eggs. Uncle Barny said the words were: 'If ye steal me I'll harm ye,' in bird language to warn off the robber.

Then Aunt Tissie called me indoors, for I wasn't strong enough to work all day and she had promised Mother I should lie down each afternoon. I walked reluctantly back to the house, annoyed that I had to leave the fields behind, but when I got to the cool geranium-scented porch, I was glad to sit down. My legs ached, and my arms were weary with the loads I had tedded.

I walked upstairs, thinking of the book to read, but when I pushed open my door I had walked unknowingly into the past, to the manor house of the Babingtons, and there in front of me was Master Anthony writing with a quill on a pile of papers which lay before him. He swore when he saw me, springing to his feet in alarm and covering the sheets as if he feared their discovery. Then he laughed and held out his hand and smiled so kindly I thought I had never before seen him look so happy.

'Where have you been, Penelope?' he asked. 'You suddenly come upon me like a ghost walking in.'

'In London, Master Anthony, at school,' said I.

'Did your tutor teach you that Her Grace the queen escaped? Did he know that? Did he tell you she got away?'

'No,' I stammered, bewildered by his certainty. 'Did she escape?'

'Certainly she did, and in the near future too,' he laughed teasingly. 'I've been spending a profitable time in Paris, and here is my result.' He pointed to the letters and sprinkled sand from a box to dry the ink.

'Master Anthony,' I said, and I walked across the room with my back to the door. 'I found your jewel, the picture of the queen.'

'You found it? Where? Where is it?' he cried, his eyes bright with excitement. 'Where is it, Penelope?'

'In my room, hanging on the wall,' said I slowly, hesitating as I tried to bring my own room back to memory.

'Get it now, immediately,' he commanded.

'I can't go back, Master Anthony. It is safe, I wanted you to know it was found, but I can't go back.'

'Go back where?' he asked, but I shook my head. I could not explain, and besides I wanted to see Dame Cicely and Francis and the old kitchen of Thackers again.

There were footsteps running up the corridor and Francis rushed into the room shouting 'Tony! Tony! Leave your papers and come out. The horses are ready. Come along now.'

Then he saw me and started with surprise.

'Penelope! At last you've come back. I thought you had gone for ever,' he cried, and he held out both his hands and clasped mine, and then he kissed me with an eager kiss as if I were a long-lost sister.

'Penelope has found the jewel,' said Anthony.

'That's a lucky omen,' Francis said quietly. 'But it doesn't really matter, Brother Anthony. You met the queen's friends without it, and you got the letters and cipher. It doesn't matter, except that we are glad it is found by one who will love and treasure it.'

'But it is in Penelope's room. In the servants' quarters, I suppose. I have bidden her get it, but she says it is impossible.'

'It will always be impossible, Tony,' said Francis, in a grave voice, and Anthony and I stared at him as he said this. 'She cannot bring it back to the past, she can never return it to you, but you have the satisfaction of knowing it is safe.'

It was true. I could not alter the past, neither could I save the queen, nor warn Anthony of the evil which awaited him. Anthony and I looked at one another, and in that look he knew all for one long moment, and then I turned my head away, saddened by his fate. Like a flash I realized it all, and then the glimpse of foreknowledge was gone.

'The sun shines, Anthony. Forget these affairs of State and gallop over the hills. Penelope shall come with us. There's the little skewbald mare eager for a gallop,' said Francis.

'You can't ride like this,' he continued gaily, and he touched my blue cotton frock and sun bonnet with scornful finger. 'You're wearing your night-rail and bed-cap I believe. There's a dress belonging to my sister Alice in the wardrobe chamber. She is about your height, and it should fit you. Don it and come along.'

He hurried me into the little room opening off the painted chamber, and there he rummaged in a carved chest, tossing aside many a silk and satin embroidery. He threw out two or three dresses, all rich and lovely to my eyes, outworn by his sister and left behind at Thackers for country wear when they visited their old home. I could choose which fitted me and then come down to the stable yard where he would await me.

I slipped off my cotton frock, and tried on the elaborate riding dresses, which were heavy and thick. One of them was exactly my size, and I slipped my arms in the sleeves and drew on the skirt. It was made of Lincoln green cloth, somewhat worn and mended, but embroidered and laced, with gloves fringed and tasselled and hat and shoes to match. I struggled with the strings and gilded buttons and I squeezed myself into the narrow-waisted bodice. I pinned my hair with a silver pin and tilted the plumed hat over it. I drew the uncomfortable stiff gloves over my hands, and looked round but there was no mirror. Then, gathering my skirt high out of my way, I went downstairs to Francis who was waiting in the courtyard with the groom and horses. Tabitha came running from the kitchen, startled at seeing me, shouting with excitement and joy.

'Where hast thou been all this time?' she cried, and she clung to my arm. 'We thought thou wast losted in the woods, or gone off with the gipsies, or stolen. Only Master Francis said thou wert back at thy home, he knew for certain-sure. He told us not to worry, for thou wouldst come to us when it pleased thee, and not before.'

'I have been with my father and mother in Chelsey, dear Tabitha,' said I, shamefacedly, for I half remembered the truth but could not try to explain to her, even if I had been able, so I left her in simplicity.

'Thou shouldst not leave us like that with never a word when we all love ye,' chided Tabitha, and she gave me a sharp tap to emphasize her affection. 'Thy Aunt Cicely was put about, and Jude pointed to heaven and earth, and led us to the graveyard, which worried us. He showed us Penelope's grave, the little maiden who died, and poor fool, he must have took ye for the risen ghost of the girl!'

'Stop your idle chatter, Tabitha,' interrupted Francis. 'Don't be so curious about what doesn't concern you! She's here and going riding.'

'Well a day! Take care of thyself at the Fair, Penelope, and keep away from the bear-wards, for their savage beasts would as soon eat thee as not, for thou art a tasty morsel with thy red cheeks and bright eyes!'

Tabitha flounced off, half angry at Francis, half delighted that he had asked me to go to the Fair with him. It was an honour for a kitchen-girl she thought, and she made romance out of it.

'Her's come back, growed bigger and a lovely maid,' I heard her shout as she ran back to the kitchen. 'Her's been in Lunnon, among her kin, but her says nowt, and is mystery itself. Her's the same dream-filled wench, but I loves her like my own sister, and so does Master Francis, and better I warrant.'

Then out ran Dame Cicely and kissed me standing tiptoes, and cosseted me, and asked innumerable questions which I couldn't answer.

Anthony rode out of the yard on his grey mare on secret business to one of his manors, and Dame Cicely retreated and watched him go with deeply anxious eyes, forgetful of me. I mounted with the help of a groom and sat on a hard uncomfortable saddle, thankful that I could ride and should not disgrace myself unless my long skirts caught somewhere. We trotted along the lanes by the brook-side, curving round the steeply wooded hills, past hamlet and village to the ford. In front of us was a yeoman farmer and his wife riding pillion behind him. One hand clutched her husband's coat and another held the panniers of eggs from jolting. Francis nodded to them and spoke a few words, for they lived on the estate. They drew aside into the bushes to let us pass, and the stout red-faced woman who wore a little white ruff round her neck, smaller than the one I wore, gave me a warm smile as if she knew me for Dame Cicely's niece. They paid toll to the surly fellow who kept the ford, for the toll collector took from all who came to sell goods at the market.

We spurred our horses and galloped along the road to the hill which led to the old market-town. Men were quarrying on a bare hillside, and others were working at the lead mines which honeycombed the district. We rode along a side track through fields and commons glowing with foxgloves and sweet little pink roses and yellow pansies.

It was an important Fair and the streets and marketplace were thronged with jostling people who pushed one another with no apologies, elbowing rudely but good-humouredly, hailing acquaintances, using strange oaths, with many rough jokes and much laughter. We dismounted for a few minutes and went into the church to see the ancient carvings of cat and deer, and the stone angels. There was a miner, too, carved like one of the dwarfs which the countrymen said haunted the old lead mines, working day and night tap-tapping to lure men to follow. Francis seemed particularly interested in this carving I noticed. We knelt down before the altar, and said a prayer, along with many a countryman who had come to the Fair. Then we went out into the sunshine where a man waited with our horses.

Cows and horses stood in the marketplace and street, with men holding their halters. Some had come from Thackers, Francis said, and he rode among them to see that they were properly displayed by the cowmen and groom. Thin pigs snuffled in the ruts among the dirt, each tied by a string to its hind leg. They squealed as people prodded them and the more they shrieked the more mischievous boys poked them till there was a noise like Bedlam, which Francis thought very amusing.

We rode slowly among the crowd to see a juggler in the open square playing with eight balls at once, then turning rapid somersaults, and stealing like a cat after a small boy dressed in brown velvet as a bedraggled mouse with a long tail. The child was thin and wretched, and he ran this way and that, but the cat always caught him, to the crowd's delight.

Then came a couple of pedlars, and Francis beckoned to them and bought me a bunch of ribbons and a silver pin to fasten my 'partelet' which was really my neck handkerchief. I felt proud and happy and I looked across at the little old timbered houses among the trees with the sharp hills surrounding the town like a rampart. Anthony was a man of importance there, for he owned most of the land and men doffed their hats and bowed to Francis. Francis bought a ballad printed on a long strip of paper with a woodcut at the head. 'The Children of the Wood' it was called, and he read the first line aloud, so that people stopped to listen.

> *'When the Cock in the North*
> *Hath burgled his neste.'*

The pedlar then brought forth another ballad, written on the hanging of Edmund Campion, the priest who was a friend of Anthony's but Francis thrust it aside, turning pale with horror, and chose a ballad on the earthquake of 1580, which he read to me. Even as he paid the ballad-monger with pence from his fringed purse a drove of cattle with frightened eyes and tossing horns came along, splashing through the mud and rushing among the crowd, scattering them. We rode away to get from the pressing mob. The wooden shops were open booths with dropped shutters in the front, and ledges upon which goods were displayed. In one were dolls, hobby-horses with carved heads and painted nostrils, balls and ninepins. In another crockery, brown jars and bowls with a small device.

There was a play performed on a wooden platform of 'The Raising of Lazarus' which made the crowd shiver with terror as they saw the shrouded figure rise from his grave and come gliding towards them. While we were watching this there came a ragged vagabond, a most ill-favoured dirty scoundrel, with his legs wrapped in filthy bandages and horrible sores exposed. His evil face was bound in a blood-stained cloth, and Francis told me he had dipped it in a cock's blood to make it worse, and the sores were all painted on him. He begged loudly, and held out a bag for money and scraps, compelling people to give to him. He seized my foot and held it tightly as he pushed his vile-smelling bag under my nose, and uttered outlandish cries. Francis beat him off with his whip, and threw him some pence. He seemed to think nothing of it, but I was filled with alarm. Gipsies and rogues had their habitation in the Peak hills among the rocky caverns, Francis said, and they started from there to travel the roads of England, speaking their own thieves' language, stealing from country folk as they travelled to London. They missed the sheltered hamlets, and Thackers never saw them.

He pointed out an old man with a long tangled beard, and poor worn hands trembling so much I was filled with sorrow for him. He was a labourer without work, but his hands were skilled and he was getting a small living by peddling his wares. He carried a tray of toy lambs with painted faces and ribbons round their necks and gilded horns. He sang a wailing little song as he offered his goods:

> *'Young lambs to sell, young lambs to sell,*
> *If I'd as much money as I could tell,*
> *I wouldn't come here with young lambs to sell.*
> *Two for a penny, eight for a groat,*
> *As fine young lambs as ever were bought.'*

'Oh, give me two,' I cried, and Francis bought a couple. I tucked them in my bodice, with the tin horns caught in the laces, and the soft wool warm against my neck.

We sampled gilt gingerbread, in the shapes of men and women in ruffs and wide dresses and trunk hose. We bought flat cakes, spiced and honeyed, and sugar-breads for Mistress Babington who had a sweet tooth.

Francis looked at a leather shop filled with whips and saddles and he ordered a pair of long boots of undressed brown hide. Next to it was another toy booth with people crowding round, and I stood by, holding my mare, while Francis talked to the boot-maker and had his measurements taken. There were brightly coloured wooden peg-tops, green and scarlet, and wooden whips with leather lashes, which children in long stiff clothes bought. There were skittles carved out of wood, like those I had seen in the skittle-alley, for the men's games. But in the centre was a fine wooden doll, dressed like one which I had seen at Thackers in the wardrobe chamber. It wore a white ruff, small and stiffly pleated, and a kirtle of embroidery with beads stitched upon the bodice. Its hair was piled under a white, lace-edged coif, and on its shoulders was a cloak of velvet. It was a grand lady of a doll, and not for poor people. The crowd edged round, admiring it, calling to their friends to come and see, so I drew my little mare away, glad she was so docile among strangers.

More riders pressed through the market, and stopped to buy at the booths and to see the painted doll. Among them I saw the lovely red-haired girl who had walked in the garden at Bramble Hall. She rode swiftly up to us, calling to Francis, above the people's heads.

'Cousin Francis! Coz! Here you are! I have been seeking you. Who is this with you? I thought it was your sister, Alice, and I see it is the kitchen wench dressed in Alice's weeds, a sparrow aping a hawk.'

She spoke with strident harshness and those around laughed and nudged each other, staring at me and at the girl's mocking face, and they clustered close, scenting a quarrel, eager to take sides.

'This is Mistress Penelope Taberner, my friend, from London,' said Francis, doffing his hat in a low bow. 'You have made a mistake, Cousin Arabella. Good day to you.'

He swept off his hat again with an imperious gesture, and beckoned to me, and we rode away down the steep hillside, leaving Arabella with a frowning face, scowling after us.

Although I knew the great rounded hills which curved against the sky with contours unchanged for immemorial years, the villages nestling in their folds were smaller, with only a few cottages thatched with straw and rough huts where children peered. There were wild uncultivated stretches of moorland and wood where once I had seen cornfield and meadow. We stayed for a moment looking across the heavily forested slopes where hills were blue as speedwell against a violet distance, and down in the hollow basin lay the market town with its little stone houses jumbled together and wreathed in a smoky mist. Then we climbed higher, avoiding the rocks which jutted from the path, following a road as old as the hills themselves, the way taken by many a traveller journeying from the north of England to the south.

Below in the valley was the river, running through willow and alder thickets, and as I watched the winding stream I remembered riding to the station in the milk cart along a white road by its side, but only a grassy path was there, with anglers fishing in the Darrand.

We drew rein and gazed at the scene, at the peaceful beauty of the sun-drenched landscape, and the flecked and shadowed silver stream which sparkled as it broke over the rocks. Francis was intent on the fishermen who stood in the water with their rods and nets gathering a harvest of trout; I strove to bring to the surface of my mind the glimmering thoughts which swam like fish evading me.

'It is now,' I mused. 'All the past and the future are there, but we only see one part of it, the other is hidden in mists.'

Francis started and turned quickly to me.

'Tell me more, Penelope,' he implored. 'How did you come here? How can I go there and see the future?'

I shook my head. 'I wish I knew, I wish I could remember more and see more. My visits must be outside time, for when I return I find I have been away for only a fraction of a second, no measurable period, not a heartbeat, but in that span I feel life more intensely and all my senses are more acute. The grass is greener, the sky more translucent, as I step light-foot and silent across the border.

'I spend a whole day with you, and the fingers of my watch haven't moved. The time I left is the time I return. See,' I showed him my wristwatch. 'It was late in the afternoon when I came from . . . from . . . I forget what I was doing or where I was, but it was a sweet-smelling place, for I can smell it now. Then I talked with you, and we rode, and here we are, but the clock has not moved on.'

'It's like a dream, Penelope,' Francis mused. 'One makes visits like that in dreams. The philosophers say that a dream journey takes but a flash of time, that we may travel to the ends of the earth in a heartbeat, and that if we overstay in that mysterious world of dreams, we die.'

'That's what I fear,' I said very low, scarcely breathing. 'If I stay too long in this world of dreams, I shall die,' and I looked round at the brilliant green of the landscape and the dark rocks and the waving trees. For a moment they seemed unreal, like the painted scenery of a play with the footlights casting no shadows.

Francis did not hear me, and perhaps I never said my thought aloud, for he went on, heedlessly. 'Once I was awakened by Anthony knocking at my door. He knocked twice, he told me afterwards, with scarce a second between, but I went through a thousand adventures in that time, dreaming of a voyage to the Spanish Main with Captain Drake, fighting savages and eating strange tropical fruits, then taking ship again and seeking for the gold ships. The knock on my door was the banging of our guns at the galleons. Do you have wars, Penelope? Or is your future that Utopia about which Thomas More wrote?'

'We have wars, and there isn't Utopia yet,' I laughed ruefully.

'Tell me more about yourself, Penelope,' he added, and I remembered little things and spoke of them to him, unimportant incidents which must have been etched in my brain, and now appeared flashing across my subconsciousness with the incongruity of a dream sequence. As I recalled these memories they seemed to be fairy tales read in an old book, and I saw the pages turned, each with its picture which hung clear as light for a moment and then faded and was lost as I tried to catch it and bring it before the boy by my side. Like a dream within a dream my other life appeared before me, clearer now than when I first entered the Elizabethan times, but always ebbing and flowing in a manner I could not control.

I spoke of Chelsea and the river, of Westminster and Greenwich, but Francis asked questions which I couldn't answer, about the grandeurs and beauties of palaces, which had disappeared, and the retinue and liveries of famous men, who were only names to me.

Then Francis began to talk about Babington House, which he had lately visited to see his mother.

'You must go there, Penelope,' he said. 'In the great hall is the carved shield with our motto "Foy est Tout", splendid to see. There is a library with many books belonging to my father, and silver and tapestries. There is a square garden with a fountain, a high spout of water most diverting, not a tiny pretty trickle like the one at Thackers, for a conduit runs near. And we have flowers from foreign lands, and a tree of purple blossoms from Italy, and a cage of coloured birds.'

We rode together in silence as he pondered the riches of the Darby house. Then with the sudden charming gesture which pleased me he added: 'I love Thackers best, with its wild flowers and singing birds in the orchard, and the green woods around it. I want no town life, for it doesn't give me the pleasures of the country. Here I can track the deer, or train my falcons, and break in a wild young colt. I watch the herons' flight, and set my goshawks to bring them down, and when the hunt is up it is fine sport for every man alive. Yes, I am glad I live now, happy in my own time, not wishful for the unknown future. I am content with Thackers, and I would that Anthony were of the same mind. But it looks as if the peace of England will be destroyed, for I believe we shall have a war with Spain. The Spaniards are a proud race, and our avowed enemies. They are building mighty warships, galleons, for they are angry with Drake and his adventurers, and angrier still with the queen. We have only little warships to meet them, but we shall fight. I won't stay here guarding Anthony's lands. When I bought my ballads yonder I saw another in the fellow's hand, one written about Father Campion, Anthony's friend. He was caught and hanged, and every day there is talk of house-searchings. What the end will be I know not. Anthony is firm for the Old Faith, and the country folk say there is danger from the King of Spain. No, I won't stay here if there is fighting but I love Thackers so much!' He sighed deeply.

'Is it the Spanish Armada they are preparing?' I asked timidly.

'Yes. What do you know?' he questioned quickly.

'It is one of the famous tales of England,' I said slowly, unwilling to say more, nor could I remember much as I rode at Francis's side on that lovely hill.

'If we are attacked there will be a beacon lighted on the Carr, and on the Starth by Windystone, and on Masson, to carry the tidings across the valleys. Every hilltop will have its fire, as in my grandfather's time, when they made a chain of flame across England.'

We looked up the wooded valley to the Starth, a ride against the sky, and Carr on the opposite horizon, but we rode past cottages where children played, kicking bladders, or tossing knuckle-bones, unconscious of rumours of war. In a field by the roadside was a pond with a great willow dropping its branches like silver-green fingers, and in and out of the shadows floated a flock of Thackers' ducks.

I could see Thackers among the trees in the distance and my heart beat gladly, for I wanted to get back to the house and surroundings I knew, but Francis began to talk low and rapidly, with an urgent force and quick glances around.

'Penelope. Can you keep a secret? Shall I tell you something vital? Can you be trusted?'

'Why of course I can, Francis,' I replied, wonderingly.

'Swear it on your life. If you told, my brother and all of us would die, and then you would die too. I would denounce you as a witch-girl, and you would never again go to that future where you say you live.'

He spoke darkly, almost savagely, his manner changed from the boy who had ridden with me to that of a man.

'I have kept all your secrets,' I said, proudly. 'Nobody knows I come here. I won't be called a witch. You are absurdly superstitious, Francis.'

He drew his horse across my path and I had to stop.

'Why are we quarrelling, Penelope? I know you are true in a world where distrust abounds, but it is a life and death secret, and involves Thackers besides ourselves.'

He looked round at the trees as if he thought they might conceal someone. Then he rode to a meadow and stopped again. The meadowsweet was thick and creamy in the ditch, flowing like a stream of white blossoms, and the honeysuckle curled around the nut trees in our path. It was my favourite field, Squirrels, the five-acre, where I had walked once, long, long ago with Uncle Barnabas.

'Queen Mary of Scotland is going to be moved from Sheffield Castle to Wingfield Manor, and that is only four or five miles away from here. Anthony will try to save her, for he knows the house well, and its secrets. He is planning her escape, and if he succeeds she will get to France, where he has made arrangements for her. Not a word is written down, there can be no betrayal. She will raise a force in France and Catholics of England will rise to make her queen.'

I gasped, hardly realizing the full import of his words.

'But Queen Elizabeth?' I asked.

He shrugged his shoulders. 'She can live in prison walls for a change. I am talking treason I know. You talk treason too. What does it matter if we speak the truth where only the birds can hear?'

He pricked his horse and cantered away, calling to me to follow, and we rode up the short drive to

Thackers. Blue smoke curled from the chimneys and the smell of brewing came from the stone-built brew house in the yard. Francis helped me to dismount, and I walked stiffly across the cobbles to the white porch.

'I must see the time,' called Francis and he ran to the sundial on the lawn. 'If your little clock refuses to tell the truth, the sun cannot lie. We have been out five hours.'

I took off my riding dress in the wardrobe room and put on my cotton frock. I tucked the woolly lambs and the ribbons in my pocket, and opened the door to Mistress Foljambe's room. The bed lay tempting with its carved bedposts and embroidered cover. I would lie down for a moment before I tried to find my way back, I thought. I flung my weary body down and put my head on the crackling feather pillow. In an instant I was asleep and when I awoke Aunt Tissie was bending over me.

'How are you? Have you slept well?' she asked.

I raised myself bewildered, and then sank back with a groan. 'I have such an ache,' I murmured.

'It's the haymaking. It always gets you when you begin,' she reassured me.

'It was the ride over that rough country,' I thought, and quickly I looked at my wristwatch. It was ticking again, but not a minute had gone by. The ribbons, the woolly lambs, all had vanished like a dream. I had had to leave my sweet possessions behind me, with those who were stealing my heart away. There only remained with me a small exquisite drop of emotion which seemed to have distilled out of time for my comfort.

# 9. The Secret Passage

HAYMAKING took the whole of the June days, for the men began when I was asleep in the morning, and the work never stopped till the moon came out and the bats flew in and out of the barns. The haystacks were growing in the grassy yard by the church and the great wains of new hay came lurching top-heavy along the lanes and meadows past the tower. Sometimes I rode on top of the grey-gold load with Patrick, my favourite Irishman, beside me. I looked up at the tents of green leaves waving above me, with clear light dripping like water upon the ever-changing colours of the shadowed hay. Time and space seemed to slip away, I was riding on a cloud, not on the earth at all. Sometimes I thought I heard a voice calling: 'Penelope. Penelope.' But it was only the song of the cuckoo. Sometimes I heard the cries of huntsmen and saw dim, flying horses gallop over the fields to the opposite wooded hills, but when I raised myself it was only the cloud-shadows racing up the valleys to the horizon.

One day when I leaned idly against the churchyard wall waiting for the haycart to be emptied, I heard Anthony's deep voice talking to his wife, and for a moment I saw him. The garden at Thackers which adjoined the church changed before my eyes, the smooth lawn of other days spread from the little croft, the cedar tree came from the shade. Young Mistress Babington's hand was on Anthony's shoulder, her pretty face was white and drawn, she seemed to be pleading with him. I saw his plum-coloured cloak thrown back, and I caught the glint of a signet ring he wore.

'Mary, dear heart, I have pledged my life to save her. I am bound by sacred vows, and I am ready to die in her service. I must keep my word to the Catholic Church and the queen.'

'Your duty lies here, Anthony, at Thackers. These people are your people, Cicely and old John Darbishire, and the folk of the valleys and hills. Life is sweet, Anthony; we are only on the threshold of marriage. We should have many years of happiness before us, carrying on the work of your forefathers, caring for the land, living a quiet country life, serene and secure, in this valley where all is so beautiful. Stay here, dear Anthony. Don't leave me again. I can't bear the separation and the agony of fear for your safety.'

She stretched out her hand with a sweeping gesture to the warm, green woods and the sun-freckled fields. Out of the depths of the blue sky swooped a hawk, and the plover cowered in the bracken.

'Oh, take care! Take care!' I wanted to cry, but no voice came, and I beat my hands in vain.

Anthony put his arm round his wife, and pointed to the church tower with its row of shields. 'Foy est tout, Mary. I must keep faith with the three, Mary, Queen of Heaven, Mary the queen in captivity, and Mary my wife.'

'Mary of many sorrows.' The whisper came like a breath from her lips, the voices were silent, the figures faded, and I saw only the massive yews, sombre and remote, reminding me that they had witnessed scenes of parting and sadness for centuries, they had shared the life of Thackers with its births and deaths, and caught the essence of sorrow in their funereal boughs.

I went into the house and climbed the twisted stair to the landing, seeking to enter that remote world, but not succeeding, although I knew it was close to me. The door was waiting to be opened if only I could see it.

That evening the men worked late to finish and I raked the fields in the dusk with Alison, stopping to pick the dog roses which were like white stars in the hedges, then hastening after my sister. Dumbledores boomed as they struck our dresses, a hedgehog walked in the path, and we could hear the barking of a fox in the wood. Night creatures were about, and a vibrant stillness was in the air, so that every sound was magnified, and the voices of the men echoed against the tower. My mind was half with the haymakers, and half with those others of three hundred years before, for that time seemed very close to me. With my feet I walked the same warm ground that Anthony and Francis Babington had trod. I smelled the same roses, blooming on the hedges, creeping over old barns, undisturbed for generations, renewing themselves yet always the same. Poor Mary Babington may have wept under one of the yews and pressed her face against its trunk. Dame Cicley Taberner picked herbs in the garden and stooped over the bushes of rue and wormwood as I bent my face to the olive leaves. I rode on the last load of hay, under the prickling stars, and the horses drew me to the stackyard where I could see the great haystacks already built silvery-grey and rich with heavy fragrance.

They seemed half as high as the tower from where I crouched, and I was proud of Uncle Barnabas's famous stacks. I slid down and waited and the moon rose white-faced from the hills. It was a strange unearthly scene, the men like shadows, the dark horses, the church soaring under the new light. The fields lay smooth as lawns, pale in the moon rays, and the horses whinnied with pleasure as Ian opened the gate and turned them loose. Hay harvest was done and all the fun and the hard labour was finished. The land was resting after its close communion with man.

Aunt Tissie called me from the kitchen door, and waved her apron to me. Another voice seemed to come trilling like a bird in the night air. I shivered and ran indoors to the farm kitchen and washed my streaky face in the brass bowl at the sink. Then I changed my dress and took my supper to the garden where I sat under the oak tree, listening to the talk of the men.

'That's enow for tonight. We've done. We've beat the weather this year. Come rain, come snow, we've beat it,' said Uncle Barnabas.

'Glory be to God,' returned Patrick.

'Who's that ghostess a-sitting on the seat?' asked Uncle Barny, looking over the gate. 'Why it's Penelope! Come along in, my girl. You'll get your cough back again, and be abed, and we'll have to send for the doctor and I don't think he'll know the way for he's not been at Thackers for half a century.' So I finished my supper and went in, for there was no way to that hidden world.

We had great rejoicings the next day, for Uncle Barnabas kept up the old traditions of his forefathers, and there was ale and boiled beef and suet dumplings for the Irish. I helped to set the table on the grassplat, and Aunt boiled the beef in the round, black kettle which she fetched down from a granary loft. I had seen it before, I told her, but she said that was impossible unless I had been up in the dark chamber, poking about among the rats.

'I've seen it hung over the fire,' I protested.

'Nay, we only use it twice a year, for hay harvest and corn harvest, and sometimes for the Christmas hams,' said she.

Then I remembered it was the one I had seen in the Babington household hanging over the great open hearth with venison simmering in it.

'It's mortal old,' laughed Aunt Tissie, looking at the enormous iron vessel with its four little legs. 'Maybe over a hunnerd years. What do you think, Brother Barnabas?'

'Nigher two hunnerd,' said Uncle Barny.

'Nearer three hundred,' I added triumphantly.

I changed to my new green tussore and brushed my hair and fastened the picture of the Queen of Scots round my neck. Then I went to the harvest supper. The Irishmen were eating their meal at the long trestle table, such as those others had used in the Thackers kitchen, and Uncle Barnabas sat with them, his Sunday necktie looking very smart, his round, red face beaming on his friends, as he drank his ale and listened to the chatter and jokes which the men tossed from one to another. Ian sat there, too, practising the role of farmer, imitating Uncle Barnabas.

Aunt Tissie dished up the spotted dick as big as a cannonball and carried it out all steaming hot. I cut the slices and gave each man his portion dredged with sugar and curled with butter on the top. In the pudding a bright shilling was hidden, and each man hunted in his suety portion. I was glad when it settled on Patrick's plate, and he nodded and smiled over it. When all was eaten the Irishmen gave a concert, singing ballads, and dancing Irish jigs.

'What is that pretty picture Miss Penelope has round her neck?' asked Patrick.

'It's a locket we found a while back,' said Uncle Barny. 'It's not pure gowd; I wish it was, we could do with some of that.'

'She's a nice-looking colleen,' said another. 'Somebody must have loved her.'

'It's Mary, Queen of Scots,' I said proudly, and as I spoke I saw Francis standing by the door, in his fur-edged doublet and long, leather boots. On his wrist he carried a falcon, whose fierce eyes gazed beyond me as if seeing something afar. Nobody took any notice of the gallant and splendid figure, who strode across the yard and went out through the gate. He was unseen by all, but one of the Irishmen shivered as if he felt a cold wind, and he made the sign of the cross.

'Holy Mother! I thought there was somebody – somebody,' he muttered, but the others were unaware of his start and he drank a mug of ale. 'Somebody walking on my grave,' said he.

I left the harvest feast and crossed the lawn, following the dim figure, and as I went the sounds of the singing died away and the scene was blotted out.

Anthony sat under the tree, reading a book called *A Booke of Divers Prayers for Sunday Sayntes*. I stood waiting for him to look up. Perhaps I was invisible to him as Francis had been to those at the farm. He put down the book and murmured a prayer aloud, an invocation to the queen. 'Most gracious majesty,' he whispered, and I felt that he saw the queen before him as he spoke. 'Beloved majesty, most gallant and fearless of women, defiant of fortune, uncowed by years of captivity, but never captured in soul, you will ride free of them all. Your beauty will reign over us, you who already reign in our hearts.'

Then Francis came up, and both of them saw me.

'I was thinking of the queen,' said Anthony, smiling gently, with no surprise at my appearance, as if I were part of his dream.

'Tell Penelope about her,' said Francis, taking my arm. 'She is one with us, a part of Thackers. Thackers is like a rock, sheltering us. Tell her, Anthony, for she has never seen Her Grace.' Then Anthony spoke of the valiance of the Scottish queen, of the escapes she had attempted in past days. 'She gloried in brave deeds,' he cried, his eyes flashing with adoration. She escaped from Dunbar alone, disguised as a pageboy, in 1567, when Anthony himself was a child. The tale of her bravery was told to him by his father and his childish heart was fired with her deeds. His games were of escapes, and he climbed from the Thackers windows at night, to be caught and sent back to bed. He hid himself in haystacks with a parcel of bread and wine pretending to be the fugitive queen, while his parents sought for him.

'She nearly escaped a year later disguised as a laundress,' he continued. 'Then Willie Douglas, not much older than Francis here, helped her to escape from Loch Leven in a rowing boat. Only the perfidy of the rowers who saw her lovely face when her hood was blown back by the raging wind betrayed her. Then again she escaped, and slept in the open fields with sour milk to drink and a hantle of oatmeal for food. Hunger and cold were her bedfellows, darkness her cloak, yet she never felt fear, not even when all men's hands seemed against her. Not even during that terrible ride through Edinburgh streets with the crowd crying out on her did she show fear.'

He stopped, his mind on the wonder of his queen, and I waited, enthralled by his tales of her valour.

'Now she will escape again, disguised as Anthony Babington,' said he quietly, 'and this time she will be free. My plans are carefully laid. She demands courage and self-denial from her followers and we gladly risk our lives for her. A spirit lives in that frail and beautiful body such as was never on earth before.'

'Tell her all. Let her know our plans,' implored Francis. 'She may help us by her foreknowledge.'

So Anthony told me his plans to save Mary Stuart, Queen of Scotland, she who was prisoner to Queen Elizabeth, she who was liberty itself, whose other name was Freedom. He spoke with quick, staccato words, and little gestures such as a foreigner makes. His eyes blazed like stars, and Francis stood with lowered head, listening as if he heard for the first time.

Anthony went back in memory to the old days when he was a page at the court at Sheffield, the little intimate court of the captive queen.

'But it was earlier still that I loved her,' he mused. 'I think I loved her from the very beginning of my life, and I never remember the time when I did not know her name. When my mother told me fairytales, or deeds of daring, Mary Stuart was the heroine. When I heard tales of adventure, they were stories about the Queen of Scotland. She rode through my dreams at night, starry-eyed and beautiful, she lived in my daydreams. When at last I was a young page at her court, I wrote sonnets to her, and burned them, and wrote others, protesting my admiration and devotion, then tearing them up as unworthy of my queen.'

A light came to his eyes as he spoke of those days, when he served Mary Stuart, and sang in madrigals to delight her, and she joined the fair-haired boy in his songs. She played chess with him, and made him read to her from her book of Ronsard's poems, the poet of her glorious youth. He had stumbled with the language till she laughingly bade him stop. She couldn't bear his Darbyshire French any longer, she had protested.

He spoke of Wingfield Manor, a noble house, though small, only a few miles away over the wooded hills which swept up to the sky behind Thackers. The queen was shortly to be moved there, and already preparations were being made to accommodate her and her retinue of fifty.

'Fifty! Once she had four hundred of her own household and now they only allow her fifty,' sighed Anthony. 'Sir Ralph Sadleir, who is to have charge of Her Grace, begged the Earl of Shrewsbury to keep her at Sheffield, for he would rather guard her with fifty men in that strong castle than with three hundred at Wingfield! But the earl refused to keep her any longer.'

'His sympathies are with Mary Stuart,' interrupted Francis. 'His heart has been touched by her beauty and tragedy, and the Countess Bess is suspicious and jealous of the queen, and has stirred up strife and misunderstanding. I believe the earl would be glad if Mary Stuart escaped.'

'So long as she isn't in his custody,' agreed Anthony. 'He might lose his head otherwise. So it is much better for the queen that she is going to a country house, unfortified, with scarce room for the men who will guard her.'

Then he told me that at Wingfield there was a secret passage underground of which only the earl and the family of Babington knew. It led to Thackers but nobody was certain where was the exit, for it had been unused for many generations and was broken down and silted with earth and crumbled rocks. If they could reopen this ancient tunnel the queen could enter and escape. At the Wingfield end it went only a short distance and was blocked by fallen debris. It was obviously too dangerous to work there and the passage must be cleared from the Thackers end.

At Thackers there were two or three false entrances and they were digging to find the true tunnel. One passage had already been excavated, but it went to the solid rock and now another was being explored. Tom Snowball was working with other men, trusty lead miners, who were used to breaking the rocks and tunnelling in their search for lead in the hills. They were devout Catholics, who had come over from Tandy, where there were lead mines, and they would work underground.

'Why was there a tunnel, Master Anthony?' I asked.

'Nobody knows that, Penelope,' he replied. 'It must have been dug hundreds of years ago, in more troublous times even than ours, for the escape of fugitives from Wingfield, which is a very old manor. Many great houses had their secret passages, with false openings to screen the real ones, and we are seeking among the mounds of grass and piled rock in the churchyard.'

'The queen will enter at Wingfield, and she will creep along the narrow passage to Thackers, maybe in floods of water, and she will bend, and have to go down on her hands and knees in places, but she won't care!' cried Francis. 'It will be a fine adventure, and when she comes to Thackers, she will be cared for, hidden away for a night to rest, and then off to France when it is safe. She will go disguised as Anthony, for they are the same height, or maybe like a market woman riding pillion, dressed in Dame Cicely's oldest clothes, and Anthony garbed like a farmer.'

'At our darling Thackers she will hide,' I thought, 'and she will sleep in the best bedchamber, under the patchwork quilt. Aunt Cicely will warm the bed with the warming pan, for the queen will be cold and tired after her journey. I shall carry hot water upstairs and wash her feet, and fetch a clean towel from the press for her lily-white hands.'

'She will go muffled half-face, riding through the hills and woods, and nobody will recognize her when she is dressed in a man's clothes. I shall ride with her as her brother or servant,' Francis continued.

'And I too,' I implored. 'I can ride and endure hardships. Take me too, Francis.'

He laughed and shook his head, but Anthony did not hear. He was deep in thought, his eyes on the distance. He strode across the lawn and entered the house, and in a minute I could see him at his open window, quill in hand, writing rapidly.

'And if she doesn't escape? Suppose she is caught, or somebody tells?' I asked, with a queer, half-memory of disaster nagging at me like an aching tooth. What it was I could not remember, but Francis knew, for he stopped me from thinking of it, and I never said the words of my fatal pre-knowledge.

'Come with me,' said he, and he ran back across the cobbled stable-yard, where lately I had left the harvest supper. Horses stamped, grooms whistled, a servant woman laughed and talked and fluttered into the house, her white folded cap bright and clean. At the great door of the kitchen stood my Aunt Cicely, in her white apron over her dark blue bodice and padded, quilted petticoat. Her thick leather shoes were clasped with narrow thongs, and she tapped the stone sill impatiently with her wooden heel. Her hands were on her hips, she was full of laughter, and her head bobbed in its little white ruff, nodding to me as I came through the gate, as if she had lately seen me.

'There you are, my chuck! Master Francis has found you!'

A rich smell of roasted meats came steaming out, and I could hear the sounds of frizzling and hissing fats.

A voice sang a hunting melody, and the thin lovely tones of a harp came from the house. I asked Aunt Cicely who it was, for the music was strangely beautiful.

'A wandering minstrel from Galway. He's travelling the country, playing his songs, and he'll sleep here a few nights before he goes on. We are glad to get the news these bards bring, for they sit in kitchen and hall, and they hear many things which would be hidden. This man has been at Sheffield Castle, and although he did not see Her

Grace, he brought secret word that she will move in September. He is a devout man, and with his songs he can go where others cannot, for he is simple, without any guile or treachery.'

I saw the old man with tangled hair and beard, sitting in the corner of the kitchen, with the maids listening to his music. He moved thin crooked fingers over the harp strings and sang as if unconscious of his country audience. Jude stood near, watching his expression, staring at his lips as if to catch his words. Tabitha poured soup into a bowl and took it to the musician, and each one tried to honour and please him.

As the music drifted soft and clear through the room, I remembered another music there, and for a moment I saw Uncle Barnabas playing his accordion, with his work-hardened hands. I wished to enter and listen but Francis beckoned me to follow him. He took me across the grass to the church, and into the vestry where a pile of spades and mattocks rested. The church was sweet and clean, for Dame Cicely had it scrubbed each week, and fresh herbs were strewn in the pews. There was a smell of rosemary and balm, and the cool odour of green rushes from the brook-side, which were soft as velvet under my feet as I stood in a familiar pew. There was a heavy tapestry curtain across one end of Mistress Babington's pew, to screen her from the congregation, and cushions and footstools were placed ready for her. In the windows shone the lovely painted glass, and by the font was the ancient clock complaining with the wheezy voice of an old man.

Then we went to the churchyard, where Francis showed me a heap of brown earth and broken rock.

'That is where we have sunk a shaft, one gang digging, another removing the rock and soil, and timbering the room where necessary. All in the house are sworn to secrecy. The wenches in the kitchen go home at dark to the village. Only Dame Cicely and Tabitha and Phoebe stay here to look after the household, and Margery, Mistress Babington's personal maid.'

I went back to the house to help in the kitchen. Aunt Cicely was busy with her broths and roasted meats, for there was heavy work to be done, preparing for the miners, storing food for the night-work. I made the sweets for the gentlefolk, under Aunt Cicely's guidance. I ground the almonds and mixed them with honey to a paste, and then I moulded them into shapes, with colourings from a row of jars, green and brown and rosy pink. I fashioned little fruits and nuts and acorns, and laid them on a dish to dry.

Through the window I could see the miners come from the tunnel and enter the great barn. They played skittles, and slept, awaiting their turn to go back. Tabitha took them food, for they were not asked to the house.

'It's a lead vein we are seeking,' they spread the report. 'A fine vein of lead which will bring money to Thackers.' The villagers rejoiced, for they knew lead had been found on the other side of the hill at Tandy for centuries. Lead mines were worked there in Roman times and every day a train of pack mules went down the lane to the west of Thackers with panniers containing loads of lead ore to be smelted at the little 'cupellow' in the valley.

It was no lead vein they had found in the earth, as we knew quite well, but it served as a blind for the curious who might ask about the digging.

Aunt Cicely gave me the dish of sweetmeats and a silver jug of canary wine to take to Mistress Babington's parlour. I went across the hall, staying a minute to gaze up at the great sword and longbow which Master Thomas Babington had used at Agincourt, for to me they were the most romantic things in the house. Then I tapped at the parlour door and entered timidly, for I was unused to this service. But before me I saw the old parlour of Thackers, changed and made beautiful. In the window seat was young Mistress Babington in her rich blue silk dress over a kirtle of night-blue. Her ruff was stiffly starched and pleated, and round her neck hung a gold chain with a pomander which scented the room. On her fair hair was a lace coif which gave her a matronly look, although she must have been scarcely twenty-three.

She sat with a piece of embroidery before her, and I watched her needle go in and out as she deftly painted in silks a picture of Joseph's dream. There were the golden sheaves bowing down to a sheaf in the centre, and in the background were the trees of the wood's edge. Over all the sun shone with a smile on his yellow face, and long beams pointing like fingers at the sheaf. I recognized the scene as Uncle Barnabas's great cornfield on the borders of the wood, and I knew that Mistress Babington had chosen the rich old ploughland as the subject of her embroidery.

She saw me glance curiously at the work as I walked across and curtsied to her, and she smiled and showed me her stitches of yellow and gold silk. Then I held out the fluted dish with the little almond and honey sweetmeats shaped like acorns and leaves which I had helped Aunt Cicely to make, and she put one in her mouth, thanking me.

'You have made them as if you created things of beauty, instead of confections to be eaten,' she said, and I was glad, for I had taken great pains with these sweets.

Then I saw others, the girl who had scorned me at the Fair, and a priest who watched me with keenly searching eyes, so that I felt uncomfortable. Anthony laughingly called to them, and the priest walked across to me. He muttered something in Latin and pointed to the dogs, which had retreated from me with their hair on end, growling and shaking.

'Nay, Penelope is a friend,' explained Anthony. 'She's Dame Cicely Taberner's niece from Chelsey. She is of the family which has lived here as long as the Babingtons, which will live here till we go, and maybe will survive us in that future when all shall be changed. They are bound to us by generations of service; they are true as steel.

Though not of our faith they understand and are always loyal.'

The girl came forward, her dazzling white skin and her flaming hair enhanced by the rich brown velvet dress she wore. Lace-edged lawn hung from her wrists, and a ruff of lace tied with silver beads stood up round her slim, young throat.

She moved with a superb arrogance, her long body swaying in the stiff skirts like a sunflower.

'So here's the wench who rides with Cousin Francis as an equal,' she cried scornfully, and she stared at me with hard eyes and her thin scarlet lips curled in a cruel way.

'Why shouldn't I?' I retorted. 'Francis asked me to ride, and this is a free country.'

'A free country! Harkye! Not for a Babington with Queen Eliza on the throne,' snapped the girl bitterly.

'You forget yourself, Coz,' said Mistress Babington quietly. 'We are all free in this year of grace, 1584. What we shall be in a hundred years time I know not, but now we are free.'

'All except one, and she the greatest of all,' said Anthony. 'But Cousin Arabella, seat yourself, and eat a sugared comfit. These are such as we seldom have, they are so delicately made.'

He held out the sweetmeats to her, but she pushed them away.

'Cousin Anthony, Cousin Mary, will you let me be insulted?' Arabella stormed, stamping her small foot. 'Send her away, back to the kitchen where she belongs, a scullion and a dish clout.'

'Silence, Arabella! Hold your tongue, girl! This is not your house, and you must restrain yourself here. Penelope is my guest.'

'Where is your jewel? She told you she had found it. She's the one who prophesied evil, worse than my father's prophecy,' cried Arabella. 'Didn't you, wench? You can't deny it. Didn't you say Her Grace would be executed? Nay, you said stranger things than that. Have you dealings with the unholy ones? Who is a spy sent here by Walsingham's underlings?' She pushed her flaming face close to mine and suddenly boxed my ears so that I reeled. 'Answer me, slut,' she cried.

'Arabella! Silence!' shouted Anthony, white with anger. 'How dare you! Leave the room!'

Arabella swept out with her long dress trailing in a royal way, her eyes blazing, her hands twitching as if she wished to strike me again. I rubbed my smarting cheek, bewildered by the sudden onslaught. The priest hurried after Arabella and the door was shut.

'Penelope, help me to eat these sweetmeats,' said Mistress Babington in a calm voice as if nothing had happened. 'Sit down by me and forget Arabella. She is jealous of our honour, and her love for Her Grace of Scotland inflames her. You must excuse her.'

She pointed to a low velvet seat and, shaken and unhappy, I sat down. Mistress Babington went to a cupboard and brought a pierced, silver box. She removed the lid and held out golden butter drops.

'I made these myself, Penelope,' she said. 'These are made from a new substance called sugar which is too expensive a luxury for the kitchen.'

'I should think so,' said Anthony, dipping his fingers in the box. 'Twenty shillings a pound! Sugar is scarce and comes in our ships across the seas from the Spice Islands.'

'I have been talking about you to Dame Cicely,' Mistress Babington continued, 'and I want you to belong to my household. Would you like that?' Her sad eyes were fixed upon me, as she waited for my reply.

'I should like it very much,' I replied, 'thank you, Mistress Babington, but I have to go home. I couldn't stay here always, I have to go home.'

'You can read Latin with Father Hurd,' went on Mistress Babington, unheeding, 'and I will study French with you. You shall be my personal maid and companion. You will work in the kitchen with your aunt, for that is good for you. I, too, often help with baking the small breads and making the dishes for feast days. But I will train you in other ways, for you have talent. Your fingers are clever. You can draw and model, and you may become a good embroidress. I saw you admiring my tapestry of Joseph's Dream. Yes, it will be well for all of us if you are here.'

Anthony's blue eyes turned from his wife and watched me keenly as if he wished to read my thoughts.

'My wife will be very much alone, and you will be a companion for her,' said he, and his grave words had a double meaning for me which I could not miss.

Alone! How terribly alone she would be, I knew, and I realized for a moment the agony in which Mistress Babington lived, the dreams from which she awoke terrified, with thoughts of martyrdom for her husband, of hanging and all the barbarities by which traitors to Queen Elizabeth met their ends.

Then a flash of memory came to me, tearing my breast with pain. My mother and father, my sister and brother, and Uncle Barnabas and Aunt Tissie. Suppose I could never get back and those who loved me, those I loved, never saw me again. Those others – who were they? I was suddenly frightened.

'I must go,' I said breathlessly. 'They are waiting.'

'Who? Your aunt knows you are here? Who will be waiting, Penelope? You came freely from London to live here. Who waits?'

I couldn't remember, and I stood gazing round helplessly at the half-panelled walls with the candle sconces, the wide, empty fireplace, the carved stool with its fringed, velvet seat, the table with a basket of coloured wools and silks by Mistress Babington's high-backed chair, and the tapestry on her knee. I had no fear of the room, nor of the occupants, who eyed me calmly. I didn't know what it was, this sudden panic of alarm.

I stood there, looking from one to another, hesitating, when the door was flung open and Francis came in.

'Here you are, Penelope! Have they asked you to stay? You will, won't you? I'll teach you to shoot with the bow, and we will ride, and you shall learn never to fear.'

I was suddenly happy. Nothing could go wrong. I was safe.

'Yes, of course I'll stay. Why,' I laughed, 'I've nowhere else to go. This is my home! Thackers is my home.' Indeed I had forgotten all in the brightness which came in the room when the boy entered.

Mistress Babington went across the floor to a little virginal in front of the window. She lifted the painted lid, and dusted the ivory and ebony keys with a silk rag. On the lid's surface I saw a picture of blue sky and white cloud and a green flashing river flowing between dark trees, foaming over rocks.

'Do you recognize this?' she asked me, smiling.

'Isn't it the valley, where we rode to the Fair?' I asked, but doubtfully, for the artist had used his freedom of imagination to make the rocks greater, the river wilder than the one I knew.

'Yes, it is the Darrand, our beloved river. It was painted by a famous artist from Italy who once visited me. I look at this scene as I play the virginal and I feel I am walking in the valley by the river, for I love the sound of water above all things.'

'You have the brook at your door, Mary,' said Anthony, 'and I would bring the river if I could.'

He went to her and leaned over the virginal as she played a sweet tinkling air like bells in a wood, or water dropping from a spring among meadow grasses. Then Francis and Anthony sang a madrigal with her, and I listened with delight.

'And you? It's your turn, Penelope. Everybody sings in these days, music is the possession of the poorest in the land, for we are all born with an instrument of our own.'

I was shy, but I wished to please them, and I remembered that Dame Cicely and Tabitha and Margery all sang unconcernedly, with no false modesty. But I could remember nothing, except: 'It was a lover and his lass, with a hey nonny no,' which I had sung a hundred times. So I sang this falteringly, and when I finished they all applauded.

Nobody knew it, and when I said it was by Shakespeare, Anthony had not heard of him.

Mistress Babington took a manuscript book of music from a desk and showed it me with great pride. I couldn't read the notes, for they were square, and the clefs were different, curled and decorated with flourishes. Delicate pictures were drawn in the margins and the words were written in a good clear hand.

'The Caroll of Huntynge', I read, and I saw a sketch of deer under a tree. 'The carol of Christmasse', was another, and 'Lulla, Lulla, thou little tiny Child'.

Mistress Babington took the book from me and propped it on the virginal. She sang King Henry's song: 'The holly and the ivy' and we all joined in the chorus.

> *'The rising of the sun,*
> *And the running of the deer,*
> *The playing of the merry organ*
> *Sweet singing in the quire.'*

They were all songs of the countryside, she told me, and everybody in the villages could sing them, and at Christmas men would come to Thackers and all would sing together.

'Here's a new song I heard at Babington House last year when I was at Darby,' said Mistress Babington, turning the pages of the book. 'I copied it out along with others in my song book. It had come from London and it is as pretty a ballad as ever I knew.' She pointed with her slim finger and Francis began to laugh.

'That's *my* song, Sister Mary. That's a song I have taken for my own. Hearken to me sing it for you!' His eyes twinkled with mischief and he gave me a teasing sidelong look as he threw back his head and sang to Mistress Babington's accompaniment:

> 'Thy gown was of the grassy green,
> Thy sleeves of satin hanging by,
> Which made thee be our harvest queen,
> And yet thou would'st not love me.

> 'My gayest gelding I thee gave,
> To ride wherever liked thee,
> No lady ever was so brave,
> And yet thou would'st not love me.

'*Greensleeves was all my joy,*
*Greensleeves was my delight,*
*Greensleeves was my heart of gold,*
*And who but Lady Greensleeves.*'

'Aunt Cicely will want me now,' I excused myself, for my heart was aching with a strange foreboding.

I gave a low curtsy and went out, leaving Francis at his song. Then I heard other music, a dancing merry jig. It was the Irishmen singing in the yard, and I wanted to go back to them before I was caught in the web of this beloved household. I went along the passage to the kitchen, and looked in at the door. Tabitha and Margery were dipping long strips of rush-pith into fats for the rushlights, and hanging them to dry. Jude sat on the hearth whittling a little figure out of wood. He looked up as I stood there, and stayed motionless watching me. The spinning wheel clattered and all the time another music came out of the air, calling me back. The music grew louder, and the rattle of the spinning wheel and the fierce heat of the fire were lost. Those in the room grew shadowy and pale, disappearing in the light which streamed through the open door. Jude held out a hand as if bidding me stay, but I stepped through the doorway to the yard. The Irishmen were singing and Uncle Barnabas was playing his accordion just as I had left them.

I put my hand up to my neck and there hung the jewel. It was true; I could not take it to that other world. It had been found in the future and there it must remain. I carried it upstairs thoughtfully and hung it on the wall.

The Irishmen went away that night, and we all said goodbye to them, and clasped their great hard hands.

'God be with you till we meet again, Malachi and Patrick, Michael, and Andrew,' said Aunt Tissie.

'God be with you too, Mistress Taberner,' they replied, and away they went with their bundles on their backs and sticks in their hands, down the drive and away, into the moonlit night.

I sat with Uncle Barnabas on the seat under the oak tree, and we counted the shooting stars which whirled down the sky in streaks of fire. Everyone was a soul going to heaven, Uncle Barnabas told me, and we both thought of those winged beings rushing through space. Behind us were the four new haystacks, standing like great scented houses, and from them came little rustles and murmurs as the hay settled and shifted itself, breathing and sighing to the fields. The church too seemed full of tiny sounds, rumbles and whispers as if it were uneasy. Then a screech-owl swept silently from the belfry, startling me as it swooped across the lawn. Shadows and ghosts seemed to flit around us as we sat silently there. I thought of the Babington children, Anthony and his brothers and sisters. Five little children once lived at Thackers, and played around the haystacks, and hid themselves in the great barn wall, five little Elizabethan children, the two girls in long full skirts which they lifted as they ran, the boys in country smocks. In and out of the shadows they ran, calling 'Cuckoo, Cherry tree' to one another. Once I heard the click of a pickaxe and the rumble of a barrow, and I glanced up at Uncle Barnabas.

'Rats,' said he. 'Rats in churchyard. Digging holes. We mun have the rat-catcher soon, or they'll get in church and frighten folk.'

He lifted himself slowly and stiffly from his seat and together we walked indoors. There was the table spread with harvest dainties; junkets with nutmeg sprinkled on the top, raspberries and cream, and enormous curd pasties, quite three feet long, all golden brown and flecked with spice.

'They won't last long,' said Aunt Tissie, when we exclaimed at their size. 'There's some wanted for the mole-catcher, and a piece for the hedger and some for the gamekeeper.'

I didn't sleep well that night. Perhaps it was the fault of the full moon looking in at the window, or the mare cropping noisily in the field. The heavy scent of sweetbriar filled the bedroom, and I could remember Francis saying: 'This hedge is eglantine. Why do you call it sweetbriar, Penelope?'

I lay thinking of Francis's gay companionship, of Anthony's bravery, of Mistress Babington's sorrow, and as I tossed I could hear the thud of picks and shovels and the sound of feet moving softly over the grass. I got out of bed and looked through the curtains. The haystacks were silver under the moon, and the land seemed to be alert, listening. I thought I saw figures move across the yard; people walked from the dark door of the barn to the churchyard, where a lantern gleamed. Was it lantern light or only the moon rays? Were the people only shadows? I lost sight of them as they dropped to earth, and I crept back to bed, my teeth chattering; and after a while I fell asleep.

# 10. Mary Queen of Scots

I SAT AT the end of the kitchen garden one day, shelling peas for dinner. The great market basket heaped with new peas stood on the ground near me. It was very hot and the sun drew out the strong odours of rue and wormwood from the bushes at my feet. The heavy pungent smell made me think of the other household, and even as I thought of them I saw Francis standing near, sharpening a dagger on the grindstone. The whir of the stone and the hiss of the blade were familiar sounds to me, for often in the same place I had watched Uncle Barnabas grind the axe and put an edge to his tools on the same old stone. Francis did not see me at first and I sat watching him as he stooped in his green riding suit, with leather belt round his waist, and long boots.

'Francis,' I whispered, and he spun round and came to me, sticking the dagger in his belt.

'Penelope! I wanted you but I never thought you would come.' He sat down by my side, and I saw that the mossy, oak seat with ferns growing in its crevices was fresh and new. 'I wanted to warn you, Penelope,' said Francis. 'Do you know Arabella made a waxen image of you to do you harm?'

I laughed. 'How can it do me any hurt?' I asked, and I felt gay and light-hearted sitting there with Francis in the herb garden at Thackers, with the pigeons flying overhead and the little fountain playing on the lawn.

'She has it at Bramble Hall and I believe she is up to some devilry, sticking pins into it, or some tricks of sorcery. Have you any pains, Penelope? Have you had headaches or vomiting, or anguish in your belly?' he asked anxiously.

'Nothing at all. I am perfectly well,' I assured him.

'Then she will be sure you are no human girl and she will make other plans for your destruction. You must be on your guard. But there is great news. Do you know what is happening today?'

I shook my head and looked round vaguely trying to remember why I was there.

'The Queen of Scots is coming to Wingfield Manor today; we are going to see her arrive, for although her removal has been kept secret, the Galway harpist brought the news from Sheffield. She will ride with her retinue, the ladies who attend her, and her servants. We shall see her ride through the gateway. Will you come with me?'

'Oh yes! Thank you, Francis! The Queen of Scotland to come riding along our lanes!'

Then it wasn't true, that strange foreboding. I wanted to run indoors and tell them all. I sprang to my feet, and Francis arose too, and picked up his hat. There was a click of the wicket-gate and Tabitha came down the path bearing a large, lidded basket, similar to the one I had been using.

'There you are, Penelope Taberner! And we all in a ferment, with friends of Master Anthony's a-coming, and the Queen of Scots moving to Wingfield, and many a person walking the roads who may call and eat with us. Gather sweet bay and rosemary for the guests' chambers, to strew the floors, and feverfew for the grooms, for the stench of their feet in hot weather is more nor I can abide. Then cover the floors evenly.'

She then turned to Francis, who had picked up the basket. 'You are wanted, Master Francis. Master Anthony is ready, all decked in his white satin, and he wants a word with you. Ah, there is such a to-do, and here you be, as if nothing was.'

She flounced away and then turned back. 'And get some cresses from the brook and watermint for sallets, Penelope, and look sharp.'

'Be ready soon, Penelope. Have a morsel of food and change to the riding dress of my sister Alice,' Francis said, and he ran, whistling, down the garden path.

I gathered branches of rosemary and stripped the leaves from the boughs of bay. Then I found the cresses and mints growing in the shallow pool of the brook's edge, and returned through the garden for a purpose of my own. I found old Adam Dedick working near and I talked to him about the flowers that bloomed in the square box-edged borders, and as he talked I helped myself to my favourites.

'Mistress Babington likes a-plenty of flowers,' said Adam, 'and so does Mistress Foljambe. Here's a bed of sops-in-wine I've raised myself from cuttings from the Duke's place, and here's heart's-ease, although the young mistress calls 'em by a new fanciful name. "Pauncies", she says, just like that, "Pauncies". I likes heart's-ease better meself, it's more comfortable.'

'I call them pansies,' I interrupted, and he gave me a contemptuous glance. 'Pansies! Pipkins!' he said scornfully: 'Here's holy-hocks, and these is pinks, but what I likes is sweet williams and sweet johns and sweet nancies, those three, nice homely names. I shall name my grand-babbies after 'em when they're born.'

I gathered a good-sized bunch, but Adam shook his head at me when he saw it.

'Mistress Babington don't like the blossoms picked by nubbody but herself. Nay wench, you shouldna do that! You can pick the wild 'uns, the foxgloves and poppies, but you mun leave these alone!'

'Dame Cicely would let me pick them,' I protested.

'Dame Cicely isn't mistress here,' replied Adam, stoutly, 'although she rules the roost in the house. She would rather have the yarbs from the yarb garden, same as you've got in thy basket. You'd best be off, and don't be so meddlesome picking and poking. Get you gone to Dame Cicely, for I hear her calling you.'

I hid my bouquet of carnations, lilies, and damask roses under the hedge, and went indoors to my aunt. The kitchen was a turmoil of cooking and preparation, and Margery took my herbs and ran off to strew the chambers for me, for I was late.

Francis came impatiently to ask me why I was not ready. I must change my dress and ride with him to see the queen's passage. Mistress Babington would not go, it made her heart ache to think of the tragic queen so near. The country was so fair, life might be very beautiful, but underneath were cruelties, she said. She herself wished that Her Grace had remained at Sheffield, for Wingfield was too near Thackers. She would stay at home and prepare the rooms for Anthony's guests, and make her simples and ointments which would be needed for the coming winter. Wild days and much illness had been prophesied, and she must prepare, for the people turned to her in their distress.

I dressed in the little panelled room with the bare floor, next to Mistress Foljambe's painted chamber, and I hid my frock in the folds of the bed lest anyone should find it and take it away, for I felt I could not return without it. Down in the courtyard was a clatter of horses slipping on the stones, and the cries of a farrier who fastened a loose shoe. Anthony, in his beautiful white satin doublet trimmed with gold, rode off with a groom. As the squire of the estate next to Wingfield he must be there to welcome the queen when she rode up with Sir Ralph Sadleir. The earl, his guardian, had stayed at Sheffield, thankful to be rid of his important capricious captive, and Sir Ralph took his place.

It was the second time I had worn the green riding habit, and I dressed myself with pride, glancing out of the window to see Master Anthony's tossing feather as he rode down the lane. Francis was waiting with his bay horse and the little mare he had lent me, but first I ran to the hedge, stumbling over my skirts in my haste. I came back with the bunch of flowers.

'They are for Queen Mary of Scotland,' said I, and Francis was glad I had thought of it, although he doubted the wisdom of the gift.

'They will be examined by Sir Ralph, lest you have hidden a letter inside,' he warned me.

Arabella came galloping on her brown mare from Bramble Hall to join us, and rode with us, for she had no escort. She seemed quieter, more friendly, but I caught a sidelong glance at me, cruel and swift, and then she turned her head with a queer smile.

We clattered down the valley and joined a bevy of villagers on foot going to see the queen. The news had leaked out, and all were hot-foot to see the royal captive. But some stayed at home, women sat at their doors in the sunlight with their spinning wheels. What was a queen to them? They had their work to do. Children playing leap-frog, and marbles almost under the horses' hooves as we rode by. The little girls curtsied, but the boys stood bold with legs apart, or they mounted their wooden hobby horses, and pranced along the grassy ways, imitating Francis, doffing their hats, so that he frowned at them and then began to laugh and throw them coins.

At the door of the inn, under a hanging bush, was a wooden bench where old men sat drinking their barley ale. They touched their hats and Francis stopped to pass the time of day with them. I saw some young men playing skittles with wooden nine-pins down an alley, and Francis watched them, careless of the time, till Arabella angrily reminded him where we were going.

'I play with those fellows each week,' he turned to me. 'We have our score marked up on yonder sycamore, and I wanted to see how the game ran. Sometimes we play against other villages, but we always win, for we have a champion among us, Peter Dobbin, the smith. He can throw the ball at the kails and knock down every one, never missing.'

'Surely you can leave your childish games now,' scolded Arabella, but he only smiled lazily at her.

We rode up the long, winding lane and over the crest by the headland, where a stack of wood lay ready for firing, tree trunks piled in a mass against the pale sky.

'It's to send a warning of danger if a foreign foe should invade us. There are wood stacks on every peak of this country, and all the way through the length and breadth of England,' Francis said, pointing with his whip. 'Wouldn't it be glorious to see them all alight?'

'That would be war,' I said doubtfully. 'Who would invade England, Francis?'

'Nobody would dare,' cried the boy proudly. 'But the Spaniards would like to try. We've pulled their tail too often. Anthony doesn't hate them, and there I disagree with him.'

We reached a great oak wood, and threaded our way through ancient, twisted oak trees, where swineherds guarded their pigs, and woodcutters stopped their work to have a word. Francis talked to everyone, finding the men from Thackers who were there, asking after the herds. He was a friendly, happy person, careless of appearance, full of good humour. Arabella was in constant spasms of rage with him, for his unbuttoned coat, his free manners, but I thought he was right to treat the shepherds and swineherds well, instead of despising them.

At last we came to the manor house, with its high walls and great arched gateway. On the tower were the arms and quarterings of the Earl of Shrewsbury, and Arabella pointed them out with a proud gesture; but Francis's eyes were watching the serving men who ran hither and thither like ants, carrying meat for the great retinue of guards and the queen's men, taking wheat for the bread, malt for ale-brewing, oats and dried peas, and round-bellied tuns of wine which they stored in the undercroft, the vast arched room beneath the manor house.

At the oriel window in the banqueting hall stood many men with plumed hats, and slashed jackets of purple, plum, and brown, waiting to receive the queen. Then a signal was given and they trooped out to the courtyard. There was a murmur of voices and we saw a company of horsemen in the distance, two hundred of them, or more, riding rapidly towards us. We stood with a score or two of villagers, waiting, talking softly, thinking of the queen.

We three had dismounted, and given our horses in charge of a groom, so that we could be free to walk about and see the sights.

Then a few horsemen galloped up and cleared a way with angry gestures, as if they were enraged we had discovered their secret removal of the queen. Perhaps they feared there might be a plot to rescue her, for they drew their swords and kept a wide passage for the little group of women who rode disdainfully and slowly along the grassy road.

A few of us cheered, others remained silent, remembering dark deeds, and I heard murmurs of 'Bothwell. Darnley.' They were not all on her side, it was evident.

'Aye poor soul, she's suffered more nor a bit,' croaked an old woman. 'Let's give her a cheer,' but she was quickly silenced by a guard, who pushed her aside.

I clutched my bouquet of flowers and stood waiting my chance. I caught only a glimpse of the queen's chestnut hair, now faded and touched with grey, but I saw her pale, lovely face, and those bright eyes which looked round at the folk so calmly and with such assurance that several fell on their knees and asked her blessing. She smiled and moved her hand in a little gesture of charming acknowledgement, and the wind caught the snowy lace of her cuffs and swept the silk folds of her black cloak aside. Then I tried to pass through the people with my bunch held out to the queen, and she saw me and made as if to stop, and gave me a warm glance and little intimate smile which made my blood tingle. The guards marched on, and the queen was forced to move onward through the great doorway to the courtyard. One of the queen's ladies took my flowers, but at once a guard rode to her, bowed, and asked for them.

'For Mary, Queen of Scots,' I cried as loudly as I could, and he nodded, his face stern and unsmiling.

'If Sir Ralph approves,' said he coldly.

The horses and men were safe inside the walls of the great house, a house which had none of the quiet homeliness of Thackers, none of the friendliness and sweetness of the place I knew. Sheep were driven into pens in the fields nearby, and cried mournfully. Horses were stabled in the great mews beyond the walls. Grooms, stablemen, shepherds, beggars, and pedlars, all appeared from nowhere, attracted by the news that the queen had come, and there would be food and drink and leavings for many.

I thought again of Thackers. The best chamber was prepared, and some day, if God willed, she might escape from these great walls which were strong to resist attack! Once again the sense of unreality came over me, for I knew something the others did not know, and the knowledge made me feel faint. We mounted our horses and sat for a time looking at the ivied walls, thick and massive, listening, waiting, as if we expected something to happen.

'Surely a small force of soldiers could steal her away,' said Arabella. 'Even our own grooms and labourers and the village men could bear her off. I would lead them if you were too cowardly, Francis.'

She suddenly flashed with temper, as if she expected us to break down the gate and carry off the queen. 'Anthony should capture her as Bothwell did,' she went on. 'He could do it, not you.'

Francis shook his head, and turned his horse towards home. 'Our way is better,' said he. 'She will be hidden at Thackers, under their noses. We can keep her in the priest's room if there is a search, or she could hide down the tunnel. It's the best plan of all.'

We galloped most of the way home, feeling happier for the thought of the queen's rescue, for it seemed easy to help her now she was so near. Only a long hillside separated us, and at Thackers was freedom. Who would look in a little manor house, unprotected, with neither drawbridge, nor soldier, only cattle and horses and haystacks to guard her?

I changed my dress, for I was never comfortable in the long skirts and stiffly pleated ruff of the riding habit. Then I went back to the garden, looking for something I had left there. I crossed the lawn, but Mistress Babington, seated under the cedar tree, did not see me, although I passed very close to her and saw the book she was reading. Not even the birds were disturbed by my footfall and I stepped light as air back among the rose trees and box hedges.

The sun shone down, the garden was a haze of heat, much hotter than it had been on my ride. The beds of sweet william and carnation were heavy with perfume. I hurried along the path, intent on finding something I had left undone. I passed through the herb garden, and the thought flickered through my mind that I ought to help to strew the floors.

I could smell the strong odours of rue and wormwood, and I leaned forward and plunged my hands into the brown market-basket full of peas.

'Twelve peas in a pod,' I murmured inconsequently, as I split open a brimming peascod. I made my wish, as all country-bred girls have done since time began, a wish that could never come true. I worked hard and took them indoors, wondering what Aunt Tissie would say at my delay, for surely dinner was over and the men gone back to the fields.

'How quick you've been, my chuck,' said Aunt Tissie. 'Now will you gather me a bunch of parsley and a sprig of bay and some fennel for the fish which I got from the fishman. And run down to the brook for some watercress, my dear, for a salad.'

'I declare I know where you've been,' said Alison, sniffing at me. 'You've been shelling peas in the herb patch, your clothes smell of lavender and lemon balm and feverfew, as if you'd been rolling in them.'

# 11. I Revisit Wingfield

MOTHER came for a few days to Thackers, to arrange for my prolonged visit, for it was decided that I should remain after the others had returned to London. We took her round and showed the farm and the great haystacks and the corn-ricks. Autumn was the best time of the year, she said, as she tramped the woods with us and discovered the wealth of flowers which grew in the broken rocks of the quarries and the berries which ripened on many a wall and hidden bank. Sometimes we came across old lead shafts, covered with rocks to prevent cattle falling down them, their stones laced with harts' tongue ferns and London Pride. Quarries and lead mines, all were deserted, and only foxes and stoats played there.

Aunt Tissie asked Uncle Barnabas to take us for a drive before Alison and Ian went away with Mother.

'Where shall it be?' he asked. 'Shall it be Lilies Inn, or Carson, or Brasson, or Hognaston? Which would you like, Carlin?'

'Take us to Wingfield by the lanes, Uncle Barny,' said Mother, slipping her arm into his. 'It's many a year since I was there. I remember having tea at an old farmhouse there when I was a child.'

My heart thumped. I knew something important about it, something connected with the other world in which I had gone. Wingfield! It was the manor house where the queen was imprisoned long ago, a great strong house which I had seen as in a dream, where soldiers and horsemen rode with a beautiful queen.

Uncle Barnabas was pleased with Mother's choice, and he told us to get ready, for we could go that afternoon. Alison and Ian decided to walk over the hill through the oak woods, while Mother and I drove with Uncle Barny.

There was the usual excitement of getting off, for Aunt Tissie sent messages to the farmhouse attached to the Manor, and I had to take a bunch of red roses, a pot of damson cheese, and Aunt's kind regards to the farmer's wife. There was the best rug to fetch from Aunt's bed, and the best whip with the copper bands and white lash to get from the hall, and a nosebag of hay to find for the mare, and Uncle Barny's best hard hat to be brushed. Jess polished up the harness, and rubbed the trap with a chamois leather. Uncle Barnabas walked round to see that all was perfect for the drive. Ian and Alison must have been halfway before we started, but Mother only laughed.

'I'm glad Father isn't here,' she whispered to me. 'He would go crazy. He doesn't like these slow country ways, but I was born to them. A journey to another farmhouse is an important event, and we must go in our very best.'

'A journey to the house of a queen is truly an important event,' I thought, as I picked up the great bunch of roses.

When at last we got started, we went in fine style, and the children at the cottages came to the doors to see us go past, as the mare showed her paces and skipped along with her mane tossing in the wind.

I looked up at the crest where the beacon had stood ready to warn the English folk about the Armada in days long ago. There was a broken tower on it, and a quarry had cut away the grassy hill which once was so prominent. Even now it was a landmark for many miles, and we saw people standing on the top with field-glasses looking at the view.

'That's where they had the Coronation burn-fire, and the Jubilee burn-fire,' said Uncle Barny pointing it out with his whip. 'At Queen Victoria's Jubilee there was a great fire a-top, up there, and fires all across England. From the crest we could see twelve of 'em.'

'It's a splendid place for a beacon,' said Mother. 'I expect they lighted the Armada fire there.'

'Aye. I 'specks they did, but I dunno remember that,' said Uncle Barny, with a wink at me. 'But I do know they put a burn-fire on that hill when Napoleon was coming to invade England, because I heard that from my grandfather.'

I sat quietly at the back of the trap, staring at the little stone cottages and the quarrymen with their picks and closed wicker baskets. They were like people I had seen there before, corduroys for leather trousers, coats for cloaks, but the same slouching walk and eager interested stares.

We had left the river valley and were in a green land, a wide, gentle stretch of country. I was looking for the beautiful house, with thick walls and splendid gateway with strong iron-studded doors, and I was surprised when Mother said:

'There it is, Penelope. There's Wingfield Manor,' and she pointed to a ruined castle half hidden among trees. The broken walls were ivy-covered, grass grew in the courtyard, and sheep grazed there; jackdaws flew in and out of the tall, empty windows, and the stone mullions were open to the blue sky. There was an air of desolation over the ruin, stones lay in heaps where they had fallen, and little yellow gillyflowers and thick ivy spread their web of healing, trying to cover up the wounds in the lovely old house.

'Who's destroyed it like this? I thought it was a real castle!' I cried, saddened and distressed by what I saw.

'It was harmed in the Civil Wars, but nature herself has done this,' said Mother. 'I thought you knew, dear. Did you really expect you were going to see a castle, all neat and habitable?'

She laughed at my downcast face, as I replied: 'I thought there would be rooms and furniture, something left as it was in Mary Queen of Scots' time. That's why I wanted to come, not to see an old ruin. It is miserable!'

But Alison and Ian came running out to meet us, for they had arrived over the hills before us. We drove behind the ruins to the farmhouse where I delivered my presents and message to the farmer's wife. Uncle put the nosebag on Sally's head and the farmer filled it with oats. Then he drew the rug over her back and fastened her to a ring in the manor walls, and I remembered with a pang seeing that ring, when other horses were tethered there.

He went indoors to talk to the farm people, and Mother went with him, but Alison and Ian and I explored the ruins.

'That's where the Queen of Scots lived,' said Mrs Statham, the farmer's wife, running out without her hat and pointing to a wing of the house, and we stared up at the empty, gaping windows and the gaunt walls, where the ivy grew in heavy masses. Below the windows was a great walnut tree, growing in the courtyard.

' 'Tis said that tree grew from a walnut dropped from the pocket of Mister Anthony Babington, when he came to see the queen, all secret,' continued Mrs Statham. 'We make lots of walnut pickle from it, and I'll send a pot to your aunt, when you go home, seeing as the walnut tree sprang from one of your own nuts, long ago. Now you look round and don't climb up, for it isn't safe. When you've finished come back and have a sup of tea, for I'm getting it ready for your uncle and Mrs Cameron.'

I went outside the gateway and stood there thinking of the arrival of the Queen of Scots, on that September day of 1584. I went through the ivy-covered arch into a courtyard covered with short grass, and stared up at the walnut tree which hung over part of the ruin, and dropped its green-husked fruit on the grass. I walked across and hunted in the drifts of leaves for the nuts, for now the manor was destroyed there was nothing of interest. The great oriel was broken, the walls were splitting, and trees were growing out of the stones. There was nothing more to see, it was all over, the place was steeped in sorrow. I was filled with deep chagrin, as I turned the leaves aside, and broke the husks from the heavily scented nuts. I had come to see panelled rooms and a great stairway and a secret tunnel, and something else, and there was nothing but a ruin.

My head was bent to the ground, as I searched and filled my pocket. When I had finished I looked up at the windows above me, where a few minutes before I had seen the long, empty stone frames with ivy tendrils climbing through, and the sky beyond. Now they were changed, glass was in the windows, tapestry curtains hung there, and on the wall bloomed late red roses, smelling very sweet. The air was colder, the year had advanced, and I shivered in my thin clothes as the wind came sweeping down, crackling the leaves and swirling them round me.

Then I saw through a window a lady, quite near me. She was holding her needle to the light as she threaded it with fine gold thread. On her black velvet sleeve hung a bunch of coloured silks, and on her lap was a red velvet prayer-book cover. I was so close to the pane I could see the embroidery she was making, a gold fleur-de-lis and a cross. On the table by her side was an inlaid workbox, with gold clawed feet, and inside the raised lid I caught a glimpse of ivory and gold fittings, all delicate and small, scissors and thimble and needle-case.

All these things I saw in a flash, the interior of the room, with its tapestry-covered walls, and the couch and a fire glowing in the stone fireplace. But it was the lady who interested me, for I recognized her at once as the captive queen.

Mary Stuart took up her work in her long white fingers and smoothed it out. She bent over it and put in a few even stitches. She sighed and dropped it on her lap, and raised her head with a tragic gesture. She looked up at the fiery sunset, her red lips half open, and I saw her strange passionate beauty, undimmed by years, the dazzling pallor of her cheeks with a faint flush like a wild rose. Her loveliness was increased by the plain black dress she wore, so that she seemed the figure of exquisite grief. Her eyes, wide apart and calm, looked away into the depths of the ether, as if she saw the Queen of Heaven seated there in glory.

I stepped forward close to the window with hand uplifted, carried away by the sight of her. 'Take care!' I cried. 'Oh, take care! They read your letters. They find out!'

Her bright eyes looked into mine and she gave a start of surprise, and made some remark to a lady behind her who came across the room and looked out.

'There is nobody there, Your Grace,' I thought she said as her lips moved and she shook her head.

I stepped quickly back against the wall, and leaned against the stones, dazed. I knew I had no right to be there, spying through the windows, shouting warnings which could do no good.

A door opened and the queen came down to the courtyard. She stared about as if seeking me, but her glances passed without resting upon me, and I knew I was unseen. Her three little spaniels ran before her, and she picked one up and pressed her cheek against its silky head. Then she dropped it gently to the ground and they all ran yapping over the flower-borders.

'Flo, Tiny, Tray,' she called in a voice so full of music, low-pitched and clear as a bell, I held my breath, for I had never heard so sweet a voice. She passed close to me, and I looked at her lovely eyes which no longer saw me, I saw the shining braids of hair with their silver strands under the stiffened wings of the velvet cap, which in turn was covered with a black lace shawl. Her black dress was pleated over a quilted kirtle of satin, and at her neck was a lace-edged collar with pearls dropping from it. She wore a gold chain with a cross of

Jesus, and from her girdle hung a rosary of gold beads. Her shoulders were covered with a long black cloak unfastened, which she held loosely, and I could see that her fingers were swollen and hurt by constant chills.

One hand went up and touched the cross on her breast, as she looked about her.

'It is pleasant here after Sheffield, Seaton,' said she, holding her face up to the sweet-scented roses, as yet untouched by frost.

'The rooms are smaller, and more homely, Your Grace,' said the attendant lady. 'It is warmer and happier here. I pray we shall not be moved for a time.'

'Nowhere can I breathe, for there is no freedom anywhere,' said the queen with sudden passion. 'Always I am caged, and around in the villages of England are those who can walk without question, who love and marry and beget children. Children! I had a son. What lies they have told him! I sent him a toy, the gold guns, and my picture in miniature, but no reply has come. The years go by, and all that I have or may ever look to have in this world is forfeit.'

'Madam, do not distress yourself. Here you will get well and strong again. Mr Babington came a short time ago, with flowers, but Sir Ralph is keeping them back lest there should be any message.'

'Did he bring letters? I want news, news, news of the world where I belong, where I am rightful queen. They keep back all the news of Scotland and France from me, Seaton.'

'Nay, Madam, he brought no letters, or if he did he could not deliver them, for he was not allowed entrance.'

The little dogs gambolled at my feet and I softly stroked them, whispering, 'Flo, Tiny, Tray,' and I gave the little alluring call by which I always made my uncle's dogs leap joyously to me. These little creatures fled with terrified howls as my fingers touched them, and they crept close to their royal mistress's skirts, trembling and whining.

'What ails them?' she asked. 'Have they too seen a ghost? I thought I saw a dark-eyed girl in the garden, dressed in strange, foreign garb, standing under the window looking at me sorrowfully as if she read my fate, and would warn me. A phantom she must have been, for you didn't see her, and now she has faded away. The world is full of ghosts for me. There is no peace or happiness left.'

She stroked and soothed the whimpering dogs, and her face was drawn and white. Then she sat on a seat and drew her cloak around her.

'Oh, Madam,' said her lady. 'There may be freedom and happiness for Your Grace. Who knows? A new year is coming. Your cousin's heart may be softened by your sufferings. She is old, and she may change.'

'Sooner the rocks in this wild corner of Darbyshire be softened by the streams which fall from the hills than the heart of Elizabeth be touched,' said the Scots queen bitterly.

I slipped away, past the sentry who guarded the gate, into the neighbouring field. The walls dissolved, the windows were broken and vacant, and the great walnut tree spread its branches over the queen's windows and dropped its ripe fruit to the grass.

With head bent back and tears starting to my eyes I went back to the farmhouse.

'Here's Penelope,' said my mother to Mrs Statham as I entered. 'Penelope's a dreamer. I am sure she has been thinking of the Queen of Scots.'

'They don't all dream of her as comes here,' said Mrs Statham tartly. 'I wish they did. Some of them behaves as if they owns the place, talking lightly and disrespectfully, shouting and leaping from the walls, and carving their names. I have my work cut out to keep them in order. They drive the calves from the courtyard, and laugh and carry on ever so.'

I sat in the warm kitchen, and drank my tea from the old blue china, and I listened to the talk of visitors in the parlour close by, speaking in high-pitched voices, admiring the oak dresser in the hall and the carved chests and the grandfather chair in which Mr Statham sat to take his meals. They asked if they could buy the chair as a souvenir of England, for they were Americans and could pay any price within reason.

'There is no freedom. Always I am caged,' I heard another voice murmur in tones soft as a sighing wind, and two white hands holding a skein of coloured silks moved in the corner by the shadowed wall and then dropped gently as leaves fluttering to the grass.

We were very quiet on the way home, I because I was thinking of Mary Stuart, and my heart was aching for her. Mother perhaps was thinking of her also, for she sighed and whispered: 'Poor thing! Poor thing! To come to such an end, and so great and beautiful a lady.' Uncle Barny was occupied with Sally who was restive and excited. She shied at the flickering pools and darted sideways at reflections, so that Uncle had to hold her tightly as she galloped and pranced. Perhaps she too had seen something, for horses have delicate senses and see and hear more than human beings. I was glad when we got back to our own valley with its welcoming brook and the green slope where Thackers stood serene under the shadow of the protecting church, unmoved by all the troublous times it had seen.

'Did you enjoy yourself, Penelope?' asked Aunt Tissie as I climbed down from the trap and went indoors.

'Yes, very much thank you,' I replied. 'But Aunt Tissie, it was all different from what I thought, all broken, and I never knew. Nobody ever told me it was a ruin.' My lip trembled, I could not forget the lovely face I had seen, when I had stepped to the borderland of that past time.

Aunt Tissie must have guessed something was wrong, for she talked hard all the time, calling to Uncle to bring in the rug, and giving me the sugar for the mare's reward.

'It's not good for her to imagine so much,' I heard her murmur to my mother, and they had a whispered conversation.

But my day wasn't ended. I threw my hat and coat on a chair, for I didn't want to go upstairs. I couldn't bear to see Anthony's sorrow, to see his anxious face as he sat in his room, staking his life to save one who could never be saved.

I went to the table and took my place, between Alison and Uncle Barny, and I listened to my uncle tell about the Americans who tried to buy the farmer's chair.

'And did they get it?' asked my aunt.

'Nay!' and Uncle Barny said the word with a long, slow drawl, giving it as much meaning as a dozen words. 'Nay! Eli Statham wouldn't get shut of that piece of old oak where old Andrew Statham hisself sat time back an 'unnerd years, and his grandfeyther afore him, as was found dead sitting in it, many a year agone, and where Eli hisself was dandled, and cosseted when he was a babby. Nay! That chair's got lead in the back where Eli's feyther's blunderbuss went off, and there's a secret panel in the front, and the seat lifts up and holds all his farm papers. Eli was tied to the leg of that chair, to be kept out of the way when they were all in a swither over the squire's visit with a shooting party, and he up and said Boo! to the Duke hisself, as came with the squire. Now the dogs lie there, and they'd be happy nowhere else. Nay, Cicely Anne, he won't sell his old chair.'

'I should think not,' said Mother, her eyes sparkling with laughter. 'What a romantic chair, Uncle Barny! I wish I had known all those things about it when we were at Wingfield.'

I, too, wished I had seen the chair, but Mr Eli Statham had been sitting in it, with his arms along the two carved sides, and his head against a cushion which hid the back. I had seen a dog lying underneath, eyeing me in a pleasant way I found attractive after the fear of the spaniels in the courtyard.

'What happened to Mary Queen of Scots when she was imprisoned there?' I asked. 'Did she escape?'

'Now you're axing me,' said Uncle Barnabas, reproachfully. 'It's a longish time ago, and I know the underground passages were made. Mrs Statham knows about them, too, but whether the queen ever ventured along 'em I don't rightly know. She was executed, wasn't she, so she couldn't have escaped very far? Isn't that right, Cicely Anne?'

Aunt Tissie nodded. 'Yes, and poor Master Anthony was hanged, drawed, and quartered, and his young wife was left with a baby daughter, who died. But it wasn't anything to do with us or Wingfield, or our plot, but something else later, much bigger, something about Queen Elizabeth, as Master Anthony plotted against, and it was found out. No, it wasn't our little plot here. But don't think any more about it, Penelope. Don't you worry your head. It's long since, and what's done, 's done, and there's an end to it.'

'It may be happening now,' said I slowly.

'Off you go to bed if you say such nonsense,' snapped Aunt Tissie, severely. 'I've promised your mother to take care of you, and here you go talking about happening now!' She glanced across to Mother who sat silently listening.

'You do take care of me, you do,' I cried, hugging her tightly so that she squeaked, and her frown turned to a smile. Then I helped myself to another baked apple, pouring thick cream over it till it was like a snowball.

I was restless, wanting to see Francis Babington, to hear the news of work in the tunnel; but it was evening, and I didn't wish to leave the lamplight and warm cosiness of the fire, with Mother there, and Aunt Tissie reading *Pickwick* aloud, to wander with a dim rushlight in another century. But, greatly daring, I went upstairs to my bedroom. I waited on the landing. There was the same wall, with no trace of mystery, no sound of voices except those of our own family. Somewhere I knew they were talking and working, meals were served in a panelled hall, Francis was training his falcons, Anthony was perhaps away in London, and Mistress Babington was sitting anxious, wondering what would be the result of all his striving. Her fingers worked at her embroidery, the strip which I had seen, stitching the golden sheaves of corn, and the sun in the sky and the green trees bordering the field, but her thoughts were on her beloved Anthony, whose life was caught in diplomacy and intrigue, entangled in the snares of Walsingham and his spies. He was too trusting a countryman for the treacherous times. How could a plot be hatched at Thackers, with its security and sweet peace?

Not that I thought this out clearly, but I knew he was in mortal danger. I liked him for his kind words to me, for his handsome face and free bearing. He was like a prince in a fairytale in his fine embroidered coat and lace ruff, riding on his grey horse up the country lanes, or walking with head bent among the bluebells and foxgloves of Thackers fields. He liked the small manor house where he was born, and there he read his books and wrote his poems, and listened to his young wife play and sing to him in the parlour overlooking the green lawn and churchyard. The two of them went to the wood and came back with their hands full of forget-me-nots and lilies-of-the-valley, to deck the church and their own hall, and then they stopped to look at the cattle and horses, and perhaps they too admired the haystacks by the tower, for Thackers had always been a farm as well as a manor house.

I went into the bedroom, where the candlelight showed me Alison's bag half packed. I stood by the window looking out on the fields on the opposite hillside, where light came from the two farms, sparks of lamplight showing among the trees. I drew the curtains across and shut the window, for the late bats were hawking round the eaves and I did not want their company. Then I went downstairs and sat by the fire with the others. Ian was outside in the stable, sitting with

Jess, a lantern on the floor, and the horses near. The glimmer of yellow came under the stable door. Aunt Tissie's voice went on and on, and I arose and went to the porch to look out at the night. The clock whirred and began to strike nine. As I looked about me I saw the familiar hedge and thatched barn with its ploughs and harrows, and the line of light by the stable, but at the same time, as I leaned idly there, the ivied wing of Thackers came out of the mist with candlelight shining at a window. Lanterns moved to and fro, their faint light yellow through the horn shutters. The door behind me opened and Anthony passed me, unseeing. He walked across the churchyard, stopping to speak to a man who held a lantern aloft so that I could see their faces. I shivered with excitement and cold, for the trees were bare and the damp smell of earth came strong to my senses.

Then somebody touched my arm and I spun round to find Francis at my side.

'Penelope. Would you like to come down? We're digging this shaft and the work goes well. Ugh! It's cold and wet down there, for we've struck a spring.'

He fetched a cloak from the hook in the passage and put it on my shoulders, and together we went into the churchyard. He held the lantern at the head of the shaft so that I could climb down the ladder to the rocky bottom. There the tunnel began, but it was very narrow with jagged rocks piercing it like daggers, and water falling from the roof. The ground was uneven and running with darkly glittering springs. We went some distance, turning sudden corners, then descending steeply or rising according to the nature of the ground. We must have gone a quarter of a mile or more and I could see a glimmer ahead and hear the sound of pickaxes cracking the rocks.

Sometimes we had to squeeze aside as a man came along bearing a wisketful of stones, pushing past us as we waited in one of the hollows which had been made for passage and for the storage of tools. We had left the damp course where the springs cut across the way and were now in drier ground. Then I saw another dancing, glimmering light following us, and there was Aunt Cicely, brave Dame Cicely, bent nearly double, so fat she almost filled the gallery, but no other woman could be trusted to bring food to the miners. She carried jugs of hot spiced ale smelling of nutmegs and cloves, and a bottle of sack and some pasties.

'There you are, Penelope,' she cried in astonishment. 'Whatever are you doing here? I thought you were abed! Master Francis should not bring you down underground. It isn't safe for a young maid.'

'It's going to be safe for the greatest lady in England,' retorted Francis, 'so surely Penelope can come! She's treading where the queen will walk, for she may be wanted to help on the great day. Her Grace will have no woman with her, you know.'

He took a drink of sack from the leather jug, first offering it to me. Then Dame Cicely passed and went on to Anthony and the men.

'You've got on splendid, Master Anthony,' she cried, with the freedom of one who has always shared in every adventure of a big household. 'It's champion what the men have done, clearing away the rubbish and making the paths so nice. You'll be able to ride Stella along here soon! How long will it take to get there, think you?'

'A couple of months at the worst, but it all depends what obstacles we meet. We are right under the hillside now. There may be a fall farther on, but I doubt it. I think we are over the worst part. It is clear at Wingfield, but nobody dare dig there lest they should create suspicion. So all must be done at this end. What do you think of it, Tom?'

Then I recognized Tom Snowball, who was stripped to the waist, his round face covered with streaks of earth, a shield over his eyes to keep the flying splinters from hurting him.

'We shan't be long, Master Anthony. This rock is only fallen loose stuff, broken off by time. Six weeks with God's help and the power of the miners. They've split off the rocks ahead and loosened it well.'

'They use vinegar to split the rocks,' explained Francis to me. 'They are trained men, all Catholics, sworn to secrecy. If one betrayed they would all die.'

He seized a pick and worked with the men and I lifted the stones and filled the baskets to be carried away. Then I held the lantern aloft and waited in that deep pit listening to the ring of iron on stone, the murmur of voices, the drip of water, and the echoes which came from all sides. Every now and then Francis stopped and spoke a cheerful word to me, and I was proud and happy, for I had no doubt the queen would escape. Anthony, too, was elated as the work went on.

Thackers was small and insignificant, deep in the heart of England, safe and homely, and the queen was near, her cheeks cooled by the same wind, her eyes watching the same clouds. Soon she would walk along the secret way to safety.

'She will escape, won't she, pretty Pen? She will! Say yes,' he implored, snatching at my hand and tightly holding my fingers, but I could not answer Francis as surely as he wished. 'I don't know. I've never known,' I said, faintly, and with that he had to be content.

Francis saw I was tired, cramped with stooping, my feet wet, my hair streaked and plastered on my forehead.

'Come back now, Penelope,' said he kindly. 'You've been here long enough, you'll take an ague if you stay, and Dame Cicely will be filled with anger against me. Would you like to visit Mistress Babington, who would be glad to talk with you, or will you go to the kitchen to Dame Cicely and the maids?'

He laughed as he spoke, knowing my answer.

'I'd rather go to Aunt Cicely. That's where I belong, and she'll give me a warm drink, for I'm starved. I'm not fit to be seen by Mistress Babington.'

So together we struggled back, I banging my head and scratching my arms and face, but Francis avoiding the ragged ends of rock as he walked with one arm outstretched to feel the way, and the other holding the lantern to guide my feet. He helped me up the ladder into the churchyard, and there we stood, breathless, in the sweet, fresh air of evening.

'You know the way very well, don't you?' he said. 'You don't fear to go alone? Goodnight, Penelope, and don't slip away just yet.'

'Goodnight, Francis,' I answered, and he stood on the brink of the hole, holding his lantern low, shielded from any casual passer-by in the lane, but lighting my feet across the grass under the tower's shadow. I looked up at the stone shields blazed round the sides, and the last shield had the arms of Master Anthony's wife, newly carved and white as the mason had finished it but recently.

Then I walked round to the low door of the kitchen. The servants were listening to one who played a flute. A meal on the table, and I went and sat down.

'Lord bless me! Look at the wench! Where hast thou been?' asked one. 'Thou art an adventurous lass.'

'Exploring the lead mine, I guess,' said another, 'along with Master Francis.'

'Come, wash yourself, and eat and drink.'

I washed at the stone sink and wiped my face on a coarse towel Aunt Cicely took from the press. Then I brushed my hair and sat down, for I was hungry and it was late.

'Near nine o'clock and past bedtime,' said Aunt Cicely. 'Maids have to rise at four, milking done, floors mopped, and food prepared by six.'

'A song, Dame Cicely,' begged Tabitha. 'Penelope and me, Margery and you, just enough of us for a round. You can sing a catch with us, can't you, Penelope?'

I wondered what they would sing and whether I should know it, but when they took their parts and we set to sing 'Three Blind Mice' I could take my place with ease, for I had sung this round at Thackers. Aunt Cicely began, followed four bars later by Tabitha, then Margery and I joined in, and there we were all holding our places, singing the ancient nursery rhyme, laughing till our sides ached as first one and then another soared high and low like a peal of bells.

'Let's have another,' begged Margery. 'You choose, Dame Cicely.'

'Then it shall be:

> '*Hark! Hark! Hark!*
> *The dogs do bark,*
> *Beggars are coming to London Town.*
> *Some in rags, and some in bags,*
> *And some in velvet gowns.*

'We all know that, for it isn't so old. It was sung when the monasteries were closed in the troublous days of King Harry, now passed away thank God. Homeless labourers and pedlars and shepherds roamed the land with nowhere to sleep, with no bread and no work. There were thousands of labourers turned away, workless and desperate, when the great houses of the monks were taken by the king. Then black deeds were done, for the men were starving, and folk had to lock and bar their doors lest they should be murdered in their beds. But some of the lowly ones got high office, and beggars wore silk. These were the most cruel of all. That was a sad time for England and we haven't got over it yet. I wasn't born, but my grandmother told us of the savage dogs we kept at Thackers to guard us. Now the land is peaceful, or it ought to be.'

I thought of the men underground, working to save a queen. I thought of Master Anthony's troubled face and of the queen herself pacing the rooms of that stone house across the hill only a few miles away. I knew Aunt Cicely also thought of these things, but she was too wise to refer to present anxieties, and she brought only an atmosphere of goodwill and comfort and merriment to keep the heart brave in adversity.

So we sat by the embers of the fire and sang our song, each taking her own part. In the corners crouched Jude, and as he watched me I felt there was more kindliness in his glance. He sidled across and dropped a small, carved manikin in my hand, a tiny figure of wood, with ruff and doublet and hose, and he looked up into my face as if to read my thoughts.

'He's taken a liking to you, Penelope,' said Dame Cicely. 'He's been carving that little man for many a day for you.'

I thanked him and examined the lovely thing, and he nodded his shaggy head and touched my dress and retreated once more to watch me. 'The bobbin-boy,' I thought, and I held it against my cheek.

Above our heads dangling in the firelight hung bunches of horehound and goosegrass, cummin and mugwort, which I had helped to gather. The brass and pewter skillets on the shelves were all polished, for Tabitha rubbed them with sandstone from the hillside. Dame Cicely couldn't abide any dirt. There was a harsh smell of salted meat from the vats in the larder, where the store of pickled beef and fish lay ready for the winter months, and the strong smell of smoky taper and guttering candles.

On the wall I noticed a motto, beautifully printed in black letters and mounted in a heavy wooden frame.

*'Feare Candle in Hay-loft, In Barne and In Shedde,'* it ran. Dame Cicely said that Master Francis had once written it as one of his exercises with the holy clerk, and Master Anthony had framed it and hung it there for all to read and act upon. It was Master Tusser's proverb for all who lived on farms where fires were a terrible danger. Over it was our own candle cupboard with iron and pewter sticks spiked and rounded. Aunt Cicely bade Tabitha reach down one and get a light from the fire to

take us to bed. We trooped out of the door and up the narrow stair which I knew so well to our bedrooms in the garrets over the cow-places and dairies.

I went first with Tabitha and Margery and Phoebe, for I was curious to see their bedchamber. They had one enormous bed, with a padded and quilted cover, and a straw mattress.

'This holds six of us at Christmas and Michaelmas and Holy days,' said Tabitha, unbuttoning her bodice. 'The maids come from Babington House and stay here and we all sleep together. We have some fun, I can tell you, and we draw lots for who shall sleep in the middle. Those on the outside are pushed out and fall on the floor and those in the middle are warm as roast chestnuts.'

There was a plain oak stool, and that was all the furniture, beside some pegs on the wall, for the coifs and ruffs. There was no looking glass or bedroom set, but this didn't matter for the girls washed downstairs with water from the trough as I also had washed at the sink. They tossed off their clothes and piled them on the floor. Their shoes they had already left downstairs, as Aunt

Tissie, Uncle Barnabas, and Jess always removed theirs before going to bed.

I sat on the stool and talked to them, watching their bobbing shadows on the rough, stone walls, listening to the tales they told of witchcraft and spells and wonders. Margery lived at Wirksworth where we had ridden to the Fair, and she found it quiet at Thackers, but Tabitha had always lived near and she loved the place. The windows were tightly shut, but enough air crept in from the crannies and rat holes. There were no curtains and the stars seemed very bright as I sat in that whitewashed chamber. It was a room I knew, one where we kept our store of Indian corn and oats, a garret I had visited with Uncle Barnabas. I thought of him as I sat there watching the three girls in the great wooden bed. For a vivid moment I remembered him, but the girls began to hum a carol of Michaelmas, and then a mummer's song, and they chatted so that I forgot all but the present. Had I ever seen a play, they asked. They had seen a pageant where devils and angels and good men and bad performed. Flames of fire came from the devils' mouths, and there were winged beasts, a terrible sight, and angels splendid with gold crowns.

I yawned sleepily, and said goodnight, for the candle guttered out. Then I turned to find the room I shared with Dame Cicely, where I must have slept sometimes unremembering. I opened the door of an apple chamber, whose odour was rich and spicy, and I rejoiced for it was our own apple room. Next door was the cheese chamber with great round cheeses like full moons covering the stone floor, and there was a scamper of mice and a pungent smell which made me retreat quickly. Then I found myself in the passage and there was the wardrobe room and Mistress Foljambe's chamber with its painted trees and birds. By the fire sat Mistress Foljambe, and with her Mistress Babington, and the older woman stroked her daughter-in-law's hair.

My foot was light as a dream, I seemed to float along. I felt I could walk anywhere and see past or future. I pushed open Master Anthony's door and entered his room. He had come back and now he sat at the table with a quill, writing fast. Every now and then he rubbed his cheek with the soft feather, and pondered and consulted a tablet. Then, scratch, scratch, he began again. In a corner of the room, sitting with his head bent, was a priest. Those dark, gleaming eyes were fixed on

Anthony's golden hair, and now and then he said a word, dictating, advising.

I realized that Anthony was writing in cipher, which could only be read by those who had the key. My eyes were clear, I could see past and future. I knew, as those who dream know, that Walsingham had this key and that he would intercept this letter and read it to Elizabeth. I wanted to warn him, I opened my lips, but no words came. I put out my hands, but they touched nothing.

I suddenly felt very cold and tired, and there before me was the door I sought. I opened it and walked through, not into any room of the past but into our own warm, apple-scented landing. I ran downstairs and sat in the empty chair between Aunt Tissie and Alison. The grandfather clock was striking nine, and Aunt Tissie still read the tale of Mr Pickwick. But I leaned forward with my head on her knee and shut my eyes.

'Poor lamb,' I heard Aunt Tissie say as Mother shook me awake. 'She's fair done up with going to Wingfield.'

'It's not that,' I muttered. 'I've been so far since then.'

Aunt Tissie came trotting upstairs with the copper warming pan, and I followed, carrying my pewter candlestick and guttering candle.

'She'll be as right as rain tomorrow,' prophesied Aunt Tissie, but I felt right as rain the minute I climbed into bed and smelled the lavender sheets.

# 12. Arabella

ALISON and Ian went back to Chelsea with Mother, and I was left at Thackers. I spent my days helping Uncle Barnabas on the farm or wandering alone in the woods, seeking branches of golden beech leaves and mountain ash berries to deck the farmhouse window corners. Some of my woodland treasures I put in the church, on the altar, and I filled stone jars with autumn flowers and placed them against the white walls. I was seldom out of sight of the beloved church tower, which I began to look upon as a watch tower, set in that green place for the safety of all in the valley and hillside, but especially the guardian of the thatched barns and haystacks and the farmhouse buildings clustered under its shade like chickens under a hen's wings. Round my neck I wore the locket of the queen, and in my pocket I carried the worn, wooden bobbin-boy once made by Jude. These two reminded me, if ever I should forget, that Thackers was once the home of people living courageously and simply, in the way my aunt and uncle lived, giving and not asking in return, fearlessly accepting what life offered. I thought much of Francis, and wished I could see him again, for the days were slipping by and I was shut out from the intimacy of the great adventure which was moving swiftly towards its end.

One day when it was raining in torrents I wrapped a coat over my head, and ran to the hay barn where Uncle Barnabas was working. Jess had brought a load of turnips, and the chopper was going at full speed grinding them into morsels for the sheep. I helped to trim the turnips and feed them to the machine, and now and then I took up a handful of the nutty fragments and ate them.

'Thou'lt spile thy dinner,' warned Uncle Barnabas. 'Thou art that finnicky with thy food, and yet thou canst eat the sheep's fodder,' and he grinned cheerfully in the dusky barn. The rain pattered on the roof and bounced in the yard, in millions of upturned fountains. There was a continuous splash and murmur of water as the spring rushed through the troughs and cascaded away over the grass.

'Has it always been like this?' I asked. 'Was it like this in Mistress Babington's time?'

'Whose? Oh hers!' He went on feeding the chopper, ruminating on my question, and the delicious smell of oil cake filled the barn as he broke the oblong slabs. The engine thumped and the long belting quivered and whirred in the engine-room above our heads.

'I suppose so. You see how the spring comes out of the earth, Penelope,' he said at last. 'There's a power of water behind it. That's like life. It's got a power behind it, that carries folk on to struggle and not give in. This spring at Thackers has never gone dry. It goes on for ever and ever.'

'Goes on for ever and ever.' Perhaps that was why Anthony Babington sacrificed all, knowing life always goes on. I went to the half-door and stared down the hillside towards the hidden brook tossing its brown waters under the little bridge. There was no bridge in those days, I knew, for the horses walked across and the women used stepping stones.

The rain came faster than ever, pools glittered with the whirling drops, and the manure heap was a quagmire. Jess staggered out from the cowhouse with a pointed sack over his head, wheeling a barrow which he emptied on the heap. Then he lurched back and I watched him disappear like a shadow in the blackness of the doorway. Then another sound came to mingle with the hiss of rain and the rattle of the chopper, and I raised my head to listen to it.

'Music!' I said, turning to Uncle Barnabas. 'There's music coming from the church.'

'I can hear nowt,' said Uncle Barny, 'but this chopper makes such a tarnation racket.'

'There is! Listen, Uncle Barnabas,' I cried. 'Who can it be?'

'It's maybe Mrs Pluck, practising for Sunday, but why she wants to come on a bad afternoon like this, I dunno,' he replied, and he trimmed the turnips and fed the whirling chopping machine, with never a moment's respite. 'Dunno talk to me,' he continued. 'I canna attend two things at once.'

I wrapped my coat over my head again, and unlatched the half-door and fastened it behind me, to keep the rain from pouring in the barn.

Then I stepped across the deep puddles, keeping to the cobblestones, and avoiding the liquid manure which was spreading over the yard. I ran lightly over the wet grass and up the path to the church door, but even as I went I was suddenly filled with fear. The church door was shut and there was never a glimmer of candlelight although it was nearly dark with the pouring rain. I stopped running and walked more slowly, dragging back, yet constrained to move forward as the music came in elvish sweetness. Mrs Pluck never played like that; her music was faltering and broken, except when she thumped out a well-known hymn. This was no hymn, it wasn't sacred music at all, and for that I was glad, but it was unearthly and fairy, as if the wind had come down to earth to play a harp of willow boughs. It was unlike anything I had ever heard, and I stood in the church porch sheltering from the rain, listening, hesitating. I felt dizzy and sick and I began to tremble. I unlatched the great door and slowly pushed it open. The church was in pitchy darkness as if it were the middle of the night, and I could smell the green rushes on the floor. Then the blackness lightened and I could distinguish a figure crouched by the font, with intense white face and closed eyes. It was Arabella with a small harp in her hands. She continued to play her magical tune, and I walked over to her, as if drawn by an invisible cord. Her long white hands moved on the strings, and she seemed to sing some strange words although her lips never moved. Then she looked at me, and started as if she had only just seen me. She rose to her feet and bowed in a formal way, and smiled pleasantly, although her smile filled me with the same strange fear.

'How charming you look, Penelope!' she said. 'But you are pale, my sweet wench! Didn't my poor music please you, or don't you wish to visit this world in which we dwell? You see I know all about you, Penelope. I have some powers which my father has taught me.'

I stood motionless before her, waiting for something to happen, bound as if in a dream.

'Francis has told me about the tunnel, Penelope,' she continued in the same honeyed voice. 'I am a Babington, too, and must share the fortunes of the house. The work is going well. I have never seen it, but you have. Do you think Cousin Anthony would take me down? Or Cousin Francis? He is your friend; perhaps he would go with me if you asked him.'

There was a long silence, and I heard only the loud ticking of the clock and the rustle of mice among the rushes. The wind caught a curtain and swayed it to and fro and the door creaked on its hinges. My heart was beating rapidly, and I caught my breath to keep down my rising fear. The strangely bright eyes of the girl were fixed upon me.

Then Arabella lowered her voice and spoke in a different tone, as if reassuring me.

'Francis wants to speak with you, Penelope, privately about the queen's passage. He has something we can do to help, but we must see him secretly. He is waiting in the old ivy barn.'

'But he doesn't know I am here,' I said.

'Oh yes, he does. He knew you would come from wherever you were to give him aid, for you love the queen as he does.'

That was true, and when Arabella went towards the door I followed her. The rain had ceased, the stars shone in the clear, frosty air. We went past the brew house, where the smell of the malt was strong, and by the store barn, now emptied of its fleeces. The immense wooden bins were filled with winter corn which trickled on the floor, and hens ran there pecking in the dust. A cowhouse door was open and I saw the backs of a row of cows, small beasts, not like our Lusty and Rose. But Arabella beckoned me on, hurrying me as I loitered to peep into the familiar buildings to find somebody whom I had seen but lately.

She took me to a small stone building which I had never entered, a tumbledown place smothered in ivy. She pushed open the broken door and we stepped into a small chamber whose floor was covered with bracken and litter. The room was chill and the rough walls ran with moisture, which shone in the faint light of the doorway. I stared round at the rusty bills and broken longbows hanging on the walls, and the flail and stone-headed hammers and bits of leather and mouldy gear piled on the floor. It was evidently an old storehouse, seldom used, for cobwebs hung black from the corners, and piled rubbish lay decaying on the ground.

'It's not very pleasant, is it?' Arabella remarked cheerfully. 'It feels quite ghostly, doesn't it? A haunted barn, the servants say. That's why nobody ever comes here and Francis thought it would be a quiet place to meet.'

In the half-darkness her voice had taken on a shrill quality, and her eyes shone green like a cat's from the shadowed doorway.

'I don't think I will wait,' I said. 'I will go back to the house and see Aunt Cicely.'

But Arabella sprang to the door and put her back against it, facing me with flashing, wild eyes.

'Yes, you must wait,' she cried. 'You will have to wait a long time too. Now I have you, Mistress Penelope, and you needn't scream, for no one will hear you. Anthony's at Wingfield and your beloved Francis has gone to meet him. Mistress Babington has a megrim, and your aunt is attending her. Nobody knows you are here. Nobody at all.'

'Please let me pass, Arabella,' I said, and my voice was calm, for suddenly I felt no fear.

'Not till you tell me how you know about the future. What do you know about the Queen of Scotland? What do you know about Anthony? Is he in danger? Will he save the queen? Answer me.'

I shook my head. 'I cannot tell,' I said sadly.

'Confess, traitor! Francis and Anthony have told you secrets. They have trusted you and you are sending news to Walsingham through that spy Ballard, for I know he is a spy.'

'I've never heard of Ballard, and I know nothing of Walsingham,' I answered truthfully. 'I know less than you do.'

'You can read and write with ease which is unnatural in a wench of your position, and Mistress Babington takes your part, and would have you in her household. You are a tool of the State, and a spy against Mary Stuart, and you have wormed your way into this household only to betray them all. Is their work for nothing? Are they tunnelling this passage only for your gain?'

'I want to save the queen too,' I cried indignantly, 'but nobody can save her. She is doomed.' My voice dropped, and I swayed, sick with my knowledge.

But Arabella thrust her passionate face close to mine, and spoke in fierce rapid whispers.

'If I told the justices about you, they would burn you as a witch.'

'Even if you told them it would change nothing,' I cried defiantly.

Perhaps she meant to murder me with one of the pikes on the wall, I thought, and nobody would ever know where I was. I should be lost outside time, and never go back to those others, my dear ones, who were so very far away.

'Is all this work for nothing?' asked Arabella again.

'Why do you ask me?' I asked miserably. 'You don't believe me. I wish it wasn't true, for I can do nothing.'

'Yes you can. You can save the queen and Anthony.'

'If only I could,' I moaned. 'I want her to escape.' I put my hand to my head; I felt ill and weak.

'What will happen to Anthony?' she asked, so urgently that I wondered if she loved him, for only love could excuse the girl's wild gestures.

I shook my head. Never would I say what I knew. If I didn't speak the fateful word, perhaps life would change, and he at least be free, safe to live at Thackers in the shelter of the woods he loved.

'Tell me, tell me, witch girl!' She struck me violently across the cheek so that I reeled to the wall and blood poured down my face from a cut of the sharp stones. I could do nothing but accept her scorn, for I was filled with grief for them all.

'You've bewitched them with your cunning,' said she. 'Where is Anthony's jewel? Why does Francis ride with you? I had your wax image but it made no difference; I let it melt slowly before the fire, but you were unharmed. You were beyond my powers, but now I am going to keep you from spying any more. You will never interfere in our lives, because you will die.'

All the time she spoke her hand had been groping on the wall for a rope which hung there, attached to the floor. She pulled the rope, and the bracken at my feet parted, a hidden trapdoor swung back and the earth seemed to open. I was thrown, bumping against the rocks, deep into a hole underground. Arabella peered down at me as I struggled to my feet, dazed with pain and anger.

'Nobody will find you here, for this tunnel has been given up. So here you'll stay and here you'll die, and if ever in the future they open the trapdoor and find your skeleton they will think you were spying on their work and got imprisoned.'

She shut the trapdoor and shovelled earth over it. I could hear the clatter of a spade, and the outer door of the hut slam. Then all was silence except for the dropping of water under my feet.

I scrambled up the rough stones, clinging to the rocks, but I could not reach the door. I called and called, half-dead with fright and bruises. There was no answer. I listened and called for hours it seemed, but only a queer echo came from the darkness of the shaft. I knew only too well where

I was. This was one of the deserted tunnels, a boring which had been attempted and abandoned, and there was little chance that anyone would ever look down the shaft. I remembered how neglected was the shed, for I had never seen anyone enter, and its bad reputation kept the maids away.

I fumbled my way along the passage with my arms outstretched to feel the rocky walls, remembering the tunnel I had entered with Francis. There had been little shelters for tools and perhaps I should find something forgotten by the miners when they excavated this old cutting before they disbanded the working. Creeping slowly inch by inch, to save my scratched and bleeding skin, I moved along. Water ran under my feet, and I stooped and drank and bathed my face. At last I found what I sought, a standing-place for the miners to pass, and I searched the rocks with my fingers, tracing the cold stones. My search was rewarded, I gave a cry of joy as I touched a tinderbox and flint and candle-end. I dried my hand on my dress and struck a light. The tiny flame gave me more comfort than a basket of food would have done. I shielded it with my hands and looked about me. The tunnel ended fifty yards farther on, where solid rock blocked the way. Then back I went to the entrance and gazed up at the roof. I could never raise the door, it was too high to struggle against. I could only wait and call and wait again.

The candle flickered with the draught which came down the spring of water, and I knew I should have plenty of air. Water and air and a light now and then! The candle would last an hour if I allowed it to burn, so I blew it out and kept it for future comfort. I sat in the darkness, clasping the candle and the tinderbox, my feet tucked up out of the water, my coat wrapped round me.

I thought of Aunt Tissie and Uncle Barnabas, of Francis and Anthony, of all those I loved. I thought too of the Queen of Scots. I knew now the feelings of the queen, imprisoned like a wild bird in a cage, beating her wings till she died. It was a terrible thought which brought panic to me, so that I had to summon all my powers to keep from crying hysterically and beating my arms against the rocks. There was no sound, only the tap, tap of the falling water.

Again I lighted the little candle, and again I blew it out. I called, and then, exhausted with my cries, I sank down with my head on my coat and fell asleep through sheer weariness. When morning came I would call again, I decided, forgetting that I should not know when it was daylight. I tapped on the rocks, but nobody came, and I lay for many hours alternately sleeping and calling for help. The terror of a living grave was the worst of all, and when this swept over me I quickly lighted my candle-end and tried to sing 'Greensleeves was all my joy', and this song gave me hope although my voice was hoarse and cracked with calling.

I brought from my pocket the manikin Jude had made for me, and held it tightly in my hands, stroking it, talking to it, as if it were alive and could help me. I felt happier and warmer with my thoughts of Francis, and I blew out the candle and settled myself on some stones I had collected and fell asleep.

Each time I awoke I couldn't remember where I was. Once I thought I was in bed at Thackers, imprisoned in the bedclothes, and I said to myself: 'This is a nightmare,' but although I struggled I could not get free. I might die down there, nobody would ever find me, and the panic fear which I sometimes had that I should be left behind in that life of the past was coming true. I knew that if I didn't escape I should surely perish, and I fought vainly for freedom.

But the candle burned away at last and my strength went too. I had no desires, I sipped a little water and lay half in the stream, in a stupor, waiting, waiting, dreaming of Thackers and Dame Cicely and Francis.

I dreamed I was in the passage by the closed door, banging my fists on the wall, unable to get out. Tabitha and Margery walked in front of me, bearing hot possets, and they stopped at a door. I called but they did not heed. I ran to them and pulled their arms, but they never saw me, for I seemed to flow past them like mist. I raced in and out of rooms, my mind in a turmoil, my feet making no sound, seeking help which did not come. Nobody saw me or knew I was there.

I opened the door of Mistress Foljambe's room and Mistress Babington was there with Dame Cicely sitting by her, comforting her, holding her hands, and to me she was Dame Cicely and Aunt Tissie too.

'Dear child. Don't take on so,' she said. 'God will keep him. In life and death we are in His hands.'

'Aunt Tissie! Help! Save me!' I cried. I dropped on my knees and tried to clasp her, but my arms touched nothing. She could not feel my sorrows and I went speeding along the passage to Francis's room. He lay asleep on his narrow four-poster with the moon shining on his face. 'Francis!' I called, but my dream-voice was soundless and he tossed and turned and muttered without waking.

Down the narrow stair I pattered on my dream-feet, cold and thin as icicles, without feeling, like bones, and into the Thackers' kitchen I went. The dogs slept by the warm embers and Jude lay curled among them, his arm round the neck of Fury.

'Help! Help! Jude!' I called. 'I can't get out. I am shut in the tunnel. Help!' and he roused himself and rubbed his eyes, and the dogs growled as I called in their dreams. Then I awoke and lay weeping softly on the wet earth.

Soon afterwards there was a sound of some one entering the ivy house, and the trapdoor was raised a few inches. I struggled and tried to call but no sound came from my dry throat. I recognized Jude's snub nose and gleaming eyes, and I feebly waved, fearful lest he shouldn't see me in the darkness. He gave an excited grunt, and tugged at the door, pulling it back with the rope.

Then he slid down to me, making little inarticulate noises, rubbing my hands, and raising my head from the water.

He clambered up the rocks, and ran back to the house, banging on doors, thumping with his fists, so that Dame Cicely and Francis came out to see what was the matter. But Jude was away to the big bell in the church tower. He rang it, swinging on the rope, and all the household came tumbling out at the alarm to see what was amiss. He led them to the disused tunnel, where I lay listening and waiting with new hope. They followed the excited leaping boy over the churchyard, through the croft to the ivy-shed.

A lantern flashed into my eyes, and I heard Aunt Cicely's warm, rich voice.

'It's Penelope, down there underground, Master Francis. She's fallen in, poor mortal.' But Francis was already half down the shaft, with Anthony following. Together they lifted me from the rocks and carried me to the surface.

'She might have been killt, poor lamb,' cried Aunt Cicely. 'Art hurt badly, my chuck?' She kissed me tenderly and held me to her heart.

'No, only I thought you would never find me,' I whispered.

'My sweeting! My fondling!' murmured Dame Cicely, 'how long hast thou been down there?'

I shook my head, I had no idea. It seemed years and years of endless time.

They carried me back to the house, Jude following with leaps and bounds like a goat. Then they wrapped me in hot blankets in front of the kitchen fire which Tabitha was blowing with the great leather blow-bellows.

'Now what made Jude find her? How did he know she was down there?' they asked one another, but nobody could explain. I was too weak to tell them my dream, but I knew the dumb boy was the only one who had heard my last cry for help. He knelt on the hearth by me and touched my clenched fist, rubbing it with his cheek. Slowly I opened my frozen fingers and the little wooden manikin fell out. He pounced upon it and held it up for all to see, nodding his head to me, and then he gave it back again to my keeping. I realized that this toy of his making was the key to the mystery, that through it I had kept a contact with that strange primitive mind, which like mine could move out of time.

The maids crowded round, bringing hot possets and spiced drinks, making poultices and wrapping hot cloths round my chilled limbs. But Dame Cicely wrapped me in blankets made of sheep's wool, thick and soft, and carried me upstairs. Instead of going to her own chamber, she took me to the great best bed with the carved posts and the curtains of worked tapestry.

'Mistress Babington says you must rest here, and she'll come and doctor you. I'll sit by you, my chuck, while you go to sleep. Jude found you by a holy miracle of God, and we shall never know what led him to you.'

She gave me hot bread and milk with a dram of eau-de-vie in it, and then she drew the curtains round the vast bed.

'Was it Arabella?' she whispered, poking her head inside.

I nodded. 'Don't tell, Aunt Cicely,' I murmured.

'It will be safe with me,' she whispered back. 'Now go to sleep, little wench, and God be wi' ye as He has been ever.'

She drew the curtains close across and left me.

'I'm sleeping in the queen's bed,' I told myself. 'She will feel like I do when she gets here, all tired and cold but very happy to be in safety, escaped from prison.'

Then I sank into a deep sleep and only awoke once to ask: 'Is it a nightmare? Where am I, Aunt Tissie?'

'At Thackers, sweetheart. Safe in your very own bed. Now go to sleep and not another word.'

I felt I could sleep for ever, and when I awoke again I saw the bright fire flickering behind a screen and heard the creak of the rocking chair.

'You've been very ill, my dear child,' said Aunt Tissie, leaning over me. 'You fainted in the church porch, and you didn't come round as you ought. But I carried you up here and made a good fire and gave you brandy and sips of hot milk.'

'I remember,' I murmured. 'I got shut underground.'

'Nay my dear. That's what you said when your mind was rambling, something about underground and calling for help, and saying "Francis". But you were not shut anywhere, we found you lying in a dead faint in the church porch, all in the rain, with your head on a stone, cut where you had fallen. I would have sent for the doctor but Uncle Barnabas said no, you had been all right in the barn and no doctor ever comes here. So lie very still my dear and don't talk.'

'Please will you feel in my pocket, Aunt Tissie,' I asked. 'See if there is anything in it.'

She brought out the little broken bobbin-boy and gave him to me.

'The little bobbin-boy!' she cried, 'as I gave you once, my dear.'

'It's Jude's carved little man,' I smiled feebly, and I put it under my pillow.

'Now that's enough talking, Penelope darling. Go to sleep, and I shall be near you if you want me,' said Aunt Tissie, and she went back to the rocking chair with her knitting, murmuring: 'She's delirious, poor lamb.'

I didn't speak. I lay very still, trying to think things out. I had been over there once more and this time I nearly didn't come back. If Jude had not found me I should have died in that faint at the church door and nobody would ever have known the reason.

# 13. The Marchpane Thackers

WINTER came with snow and hurricane, the wind screaming up the valleys, the snow drifting down from the grey skies, piling in the narrow lanes and hiding the landmarks, so that I could scarcely see the two farms on the opposite hillside. Uncle Barnabas and Jess walked with heads bent like bulls tossing against the driving storms, but Aunt Tissie was blown like a ship when her wide skirts caught the winds in their folds. There was some shelter round the farmhouse, with the trees and the church walls, for the house was built on a lower slope of the hill which shielded it. When I leaned against the haystacks I could feel a real tide of warmth in them, and often I found rabbits and pheasants sheltering there and flocks of birds waiting for the food which Aunt Tissie spread on a low wall for her pensioners.

Thackers was like a hamlet in itself, with its buildings and church wrapped in the white snowdrifts. I enjoyed going round the house to look at the stores, for I assured myself by thinking we were besieged, and the enemy camped around with arrows of frost, which they shot harmlessly at the old house.

The brew house, where the Babington family brewed their ale, was a storehouse for firewood; great logs from fallen trees blown down in the gales were piled high towards the roof. There was plenty of food for the siege, salted butter in the dairy, potatoes in the pit. On the kitchen walls hung sides of bacon, frosty with glittering saltpetre, and from the hooks in the ceilings dangled enormous hams curing in the wood-smoke. So that Elizabethan household must have prepared for the winter months, I told myself.

I went to the larder to fetch and carry for Aunt Tissie, who found the stone passages trying for her rheumatism. A sack of flour stood upright on the bench, and from it I filled the baking bowl. On the shelves were rows of jams and jellies, pickles and chutneys, which we had made in the summer from the fruit of the orchard and the wild fruit of the hedgerows and fields, blackberries and crabs, sloes and bilberries. The pots stood like an army of dark men, each with its cap of white paper. On the shelf above were the Christmas puddings, for Aunt Tissie kept her plum puddings three years before they were eaten. A giant jar, which Aunt Tissie said was one of the oldest things in the house, was filled with snow-white lard, just as it had always been, I was told. Once I thought I saw the other Aunt Cicely come to the larder, and dig her knife into it and then go out, her patterns moving silently over the stones, her folded linen cap bobbing on her hair.

Next to the pantry was a narrow darkish room where the best elderberry and cowslip wine were stored, together with bottles of ginger and peppermint cordial. There was a tin of black liquorice sticks for sore throats, and pots of goose grease and bunches of tansy, feverfew, camomile, and wormwood. The air was strong with the extraordinary mixture of pungent odours, which took away my breath when I lifted the latch of the fast-shut door. This was the closet where Mistress Babington kept her dried herbs and unguents, but she called it the 'still room'.

The postman came with letters, struggling up to his knees in the drifts, and Uncle Barnabas invited him indoors to tell the news, for he was a traveller. He shook the snow from his cape and told us of fallen trees and broken telegraph wires. Then he had a cup of tea and a slice of toast and dripping and went on his way. One day a letter came from Mother, saying that she and Father were coming to spend Christmas at Thackers; Alison and Ian had persuaded them to brave the weather.

'We shall have to get ready the best bedchamber,' said Aunt Tissie, nodding her head with pleasure.

'The grand bed! Hers! Mistress Babington's!' I cried. It was indeed an honour for my parents.

'Yes. I'll light the fire at once. I will have a regular set-to and make it nice, for your father has never stayed here before,' said Aunt Tissie. 'I must ask Mrs Appleyard to scrub.'

'Let me. I'm as strong as a village woman,' I exclaimed.

'Not quite! We mustn't have you fainting again.' Aunt Tissie looked at me and laughed. 'You gave me a fright that time; I thought we had lost you! But you're different now and quite a colour in your cheeks.'

Uncle Barnabas and Jess carried five mighty feather beds downstairs and piled them in downy heaps before the parlour and kitchen fires. Three of them were from the best bedchamber, for there were only boards and straw palliasses on the four-poster bedstead. They lay roasting before the fire for nearly a week, pommelled and turned as if bread were baking.

Aunt Tissie lighted bedroom fires and Mrs Appleyard scrubbed the floors. I beeswaxed the furniture, and I opened little drawers and hunted for secret panels. Only one discovery did I make, but that gave me intense satisfaction, for it linked our life with the past. In a square oak table, with rough scrolls carved over the front and many scratches and scores upon the surface, there was an empty drawer, but between it and the tabletop was a narrow ledge where in velvety dust lay a scrap of tightly folded paper. The dust was so thick that I sprang back, thinking I had touched the furry body of a mouse. I opened it out. There was a sketch of the Babington shield with 'Foy est Tout' printed carefully upon it, and underneath, the signature, beautifully written in ink black as coal:

'Anthonie Babingtone. June 15. 1585.'

'Fancy that lying all those years and never been found! That comes of peeping and prying! I never knew such a one for hunting about as you, Penelope. Master Anthony's own writing. I'll be bound.'

'I shall keep it,' I said. 'I am proud to have it.'

'Then I will give you a box for it, one that belonged to my mother, your great-grandmother. You remind me of her. You have the same way of screwing your lips, and smiling sideways when you are pleased. I've no chick nor child of my own, so it is fitting you should have it.'

She fetched a polished mahogany box with brass corners and ivory keyhole. She turned a tiny key and showed me the treasures of her youth, which lay in the rose-quilted silk interior: a silver bracelet, a jet locket, a bead purse, and an ivory needlecase.

'There. Lay your paper inside and put your gilt locket there too. You can have them all for your own,' said she, kissing me, and looking deep into my eyes. 'This box will hold your love-letters some day I hope, Penelope.'

I shook my head. 'I shall never marry, Aunt Tissie. I shall never fall in love with anybody in the whole world.'

Aunt Tissie laughed. 'They all say that,' said she; but to myself I murmured, 'O Francis. Francis.'

A day or two later, when the snow had lessened, Uncle Barnabas suggested we should drive down to the little town by the river and do our Christmas shopping before another snowfall kept us indoors. Aunt and I were wrapped up in ancient cloaks with scarlet linings and hoods on the shoulders which we could slip over our hats if a storm came on. A bitter wind was blowing, and we drew the furred edges of our cloaks about us, so that I was sure we were not unlike the Tudor women whom I had once seen riding down the hillside to that same town. But Uncle Barnabas turned the other way when we reached the crest, and took us to Tandy Moor. He drove to a plantation of fir trees which struggled bravely against the gales.

'Choose which one you want,' said Uncle Barny to me. 'Make your choice and Jess'll come and dig it up. I've had permission.' He looked at us with a twinkle in his old blue eyes.

I looked down at the regiment of small trees, and there was one in advance of the others, perfect in shape, holding out its evergreen skirts like a ballet girl who steps from the company to dance alone.

'That is the one, Uncle Barny,' I pointed it out, and he climbed down and tied a string to the trunk. But I thought the tree nodded to me, as if it were glad to be chosen. Away across the moor rose the dark rocks half-hidden in snow, and beyond were the old mysterious woods. They all seemed to whisper together, and as we drove away I felt compelled to turn round to listen to their soughing branches, to peep once more at the little Christmas tree stepping so bravely out in the snowy waste.

Down by the river it was warmer, and we looked at the bright windows of the shops as if we had never seen such a fine display, although they were simple enough, with cotton wool dropping from strings and candles burning to dispel the moisture. I bought toys for the tree, golden balls and glass bells and birds of spun glass, and I helped Aunt Tissie to choose presents for my parents.

I had made my gifts during the long evenings of November, when I was convalescent after my faint. There was a needlecase with a cover of ancient blue taffeta, like the kirtle of Mistress Babington's gown. I had found it in Aunt Tissie's patchwork bag, where there was a storehouse of treasures, ancient silks and faded velvets, and scraps of half-made patchwork, each with its lining of stiff paper. I saw faded writing and crabbed words and odd spelling, with poems and hymns half-concealed in the squares and diamonds of the patches. Some of the paper was parchment, I was sure, but Aunt Tissie said they were only old documents she had found in an oak chest when she was a girl, and cut up for her quilt linings.

For Father I had painted a picture of Thackers, with the whitewashed porch and the great haystacks glowing in the sunlight, and the church tower in the background like a mystical guardian. It was the best watercolour I had ever done, and although I could never catch the romantic atmosphere of the place I felt proud as I called at the framers for the finished picture and carried it back to the waiting trap. Then, laden with oranges, groceries, and a bottle of port wine we drove to Thackers, happy and rich as if we were millionaires.

It was on the day my parents were to arrive that I revisited the old Thackers, and walked in the panelled rooms and spoke with those whom I had grown to love. Although I had had glimpses of moving, shadowy people, I had been unable to go to them, and I thought that my power of entering that time had gone. Then I saw them once more.

I was sitting with Aunt Tissie in the kitchen by the fire, waiting for the travellers, when I heard a noise outside, a thud of hoofs and the clang of the gate. I went to the porch and waited there, looking out across the yard, but there was nobody. When I returned to the kitchen, it was the old Thackers room, the kitchen of ancient days, with its halberds and longbows on the walls, and the skillets simmering by the fire. The oak table at which I had sat with my aunt and uncle was scrubbed and on it stood a basket brimmed with new little loaves, flat and marked with a cross. Near lay a heap of hares and rabbits and a deer cut up for distribution among the poor of the village. Earthenware bowls of dough covered with cloths were set to rise before the fire, and Jude guarded them from the dogs.

He saw me and made a sign, but no one else noticed me, and I might have been invisible as I stood there in the shadows. Aunt Cicely in a white cap and striped petticoat and stiff little lawn ruff sat warming her toes, her hands clasped in front of her apron. She had cherry-coloured ribbons in her cap, all spruced up very grand, and she nodded her head as somebody spoke to her.

'Aye,' she said. 'Aye. If 'tis to be, 'tis so. The will of God can't be altered, but we don't know what His will is. I only know what the soothsayer foretold.'

'Why does Master Anthony give all for the Papist queen?' asked Tabitha. 'He's got so much, far more than common folk – a sweet, loving wife, as he has wed only a few years, and them only eighteen at the time, and he has a mother who dotes on him, and sisters and brothers, and good health and fine looks, and a great estate that spreads across this bit of England, with manors and woods and all. Surely it is God's will that he looks after his possessions and doesn't interfere between two jealous queens?'

'Hush ye now, Tabitha. You don't know what you're saying. It's none of your business, and you mustn't call Her Grace a Papist either. She belongs to the Old Religion, and we were all of it once, but some have changed and some remained faithful. I've changed the religion of my forefathers because I can get nearer to God without a priest in the way, but I'm faithful to God and the Babington family.

'If Master Anthony can save the Scottish queen he will, and if not, then God have mercy on her, poor lady, and upon him too. I dandled him when he was a babe, and I love him as if he were my own. I fear me he is tangled in this affair more than he knows, and I don't trust that black-haired servant he brings from London. I don't trust him an ell, but he never gets a word out of me beyond good day.' Dame Cicely lifted her skirts and pushed the log with her toe.

'He'll be ruined whether he saves the queen or not, for all the money is running away like yonder brook,' said a man whom I had not seen before. He was Mistress Foljambe's lawyer, I heard afterwards. 'Mistress Babington looks like a ghost and Mistress Foljambe is troubled, for she never knows what may happen.'

'If the Scots queen came to the throne, Master Anthony would be rewarded and then he would be very rich, surely?' asked Margery.

'To the throne of England?' Dame Cicely shook her head. 'That she can never do. Even if Queen Elizabeth died, which God forbid, before her natural time, the country would not have the Scottish queen. King James of Scotland would be heir. He has no love for his mother, from what they say. It's a forlorn hope for Master Anthony, and the best he can do is to save Mary Stuart and get her across to France.'

Then Dame Cicely noticed the way Jude was staring across towards the porch, and she saw me standing there. I ran across the room and flung my arms about her. Her cheeks were firm and hard as apples, and she was real and solid as a woodnut.

'Bless me! You flit in and out and go off when you please, Penelope, but we forgives you. We're talking of this and of that before we carry in the dinner. What do you think of the decorations? Haven't Tabitha and Margery done it well? Tom Snowball usually helps, but he is hard at work digging for lead to make Master Anthony's fortune.'

The great kitchen was decked with boughs of fir and scarlet-berried holly and many a branch of bay. From a central hook in the beam hung a round bunch of holly and mistletoe intermingled with ribbons, and garlands swung in loops across the walls. 'The Kissing Bunch' Dame Cicely called the ball of berries and bade me beware of standing under it, for at Christmas everyone, young lords and all, would clip and kiss those maids they caught under its shadow. I noticed that Tabitha and Margery and Phoebe loitered much under the bunch that day.

Then Aunt Cicely pulled herself up from her chair and got to the baking, for spiced breads were wanted, and I filled the bread oven with dry wood ready for her. Mistress Babington came to the kitchen, but she was too delicate and frail to help as was the custom of the lady of the house. She nodded to me and told Dame Cicely that somebody was ill of fever in the village, and Tabitha must take calf's foot jelly and an infusion of borage which she would prepare. There were chines and strings of hogs' puddings to go to the cottages and loaves of new bread for the widows and venison haunches for the goodmen at the farms. She took some dried herbs from the bunches which hung on the walls and reached for the pestle and mortar. Then away she went to the still-room and shut the door.

'I have work for Penelope's fingers,' said Dame Cicely, and she gave me instructions. I went to the hen house to collect the eggs for the marchpane and sweetmeats. I took a basket and the keys and crossed the yard, but Francis came up, calling to me, just as if he had seen me every day, without a word of our last meeting.

'Come and see the Yule log, Penelope!' He showed me an enormous log which four men had dragged up to the barn. All the village would come to Thackers on Christmas Day, he said, to eat the roast beef and drink the mulled ale, and they would be asked to the hall to watch the Yule log burn and drink healths, the poorer sorts in barley ale, the farmers in sack and canary wine.

Then there would be gifts of food and woollen stuffs, and some of them would bring presents to Anthony. All would be on equality, with singing and music and playacting, dressed in garments from the oak chest where I had found my tunic, he added.

There would be church in the morning, and then the great feast, and I must come too, he said, no slipping away.

At their own table there would be wild boar, from the hills of the north, for boars did not live near Thackers, only deer and gentle beasts were there. Each year a wild boar was sent to Anthony Babington by the lord of Haddon, and from its flesh were made brawns and jellies, but the head and shoulders would be roasted in the kitchen and borne into the hall by the oldest man on the estate, John Darbishire, the bearded old man I had seen at the table one day. Already it hung in the killing house. It was a fine beast with long tusks and thick bristles. Would I like to see it?

Its head would be decked with a wreath of bay and rosemary. They would sing carols, and as John Darbishire carried in the boar's head he would sing in his piping ancient voice:

> *'The boar's head in hand bear I,*
> *Bedecked with bays and rosemary,*
> *And I pray you, my masters all, be merry,'*

and all would then join in with:

> 'Quid estis in convivia.'

'We are all joyful,' said Francis. 'We share our pleasures, and you will be with us, Penelope. You will hear the villagers come a-wassailing on Christmas Eve, too, and they will enter and drink our barley brew. That's why we have such a great baking and brewing before Christmastide.'

'This will be a glorious Christmas,' he added, sitting down on a stool in the barn, and drawing up another for me. He looked round, not a soul was there beside ourselves. 'The work goes on,' said he, 'and the underground passage is over a mile long.' Then he began to laugh, and he threw back his head with merriment.

'Anthony has seen the queen. It was as good as a play. He dyed his face and hands with walnut juice, and put on a pair of old torn leather breeches and a ragged jerkin. In his ears he wore brass earrings, and he darkened his eyebrows and his hair. Oh, you should have seen the sight he was, with his gold hair dipped in a bowl of walnut juice, Anthony the fastidious dandy! Nobody knew him. Mistress Babington screamed when he entered the hall! He carried a pedlar's pack heaped with ribbons and trinkets, silver beads and glass baubles, and a pomander of silver wire, some of the things so pretty Mistress Babington longed to have them. There were special things too, fit for a queen, silver toys, such as Her Grace loves, buttons of enamel and gold for her dress, seed-pearls for her broideries and bunches of silks and tinsels. Then he set off with his pack of gewgaws, and we had a to-do to get him out of the house safely, for Tabitha saw him and wanted to buy from the strange gipsy fellow, and he had to stop and speak in half-French, to bewilder her, and let her buy a ribbon before he got away. But she never suspected!

'He got to Wingfield, and then entered the little west door, where the servants go, the nearest door to Thackers, too. In he went, without any question, and soon he came to the hall, following after the servants and the crowd of rascals and fools which went in and out of the serving rooms. He got to the queen, by showing his goods and speaking of the pretty trinkets he had for the rich and mighty. Her Grace sent for him, and Sir Ralph Sadleir saw him and bought some of his things. When he was with the queen he whispered a word in her ears, and she sent her women away. Then he gave her the letters, and received others from her, and he told her of the plan of escape but not the whereabouts of the tunnel. She was full of courage, full of hope, her eye sparkled, she was ready for anything. Like a young boy, she was filled with adventure, and Anthony came back most encouraged, so much so that I feared he would do something rash.

'He walked boldly out of Wingfield, and kissed the serving wenches, who were loath to let him depart, but he came over the hills in the evening and crept into Thackers at dusk. He removed the stains as best he could, but that took him much longer than he expected and we feared he must be a gipsy all his life!'

Francis fumbled in his pocket and brought out a ribbon.

'I bought this for your dark locks, from the gipsy's pack, Lady Greensleeves,' said he. 'Put it on, and wear it for me.'

It was a crumpled green ribbon, stiff with silver thread and laced with silver love-knots, and I tied it in a fillet round my head. As I thanked him I heard Aunt Cicely call impatiently, and I sprang to my feet.

'Penelope! Where is the wench? Art' helping the hens to lay the eggses?'

I hurriedly collected all the eggs I could find, fifty or more, and ran back to the house.

'Where did you get that pretty ribbon, Penelope?' asked Tabitha. 'Ah, you needna tell me. Your blushes are enow. Master Francis gave it you, and he got it from the pedlar's pack. That was a queer gipsy as came round here, and I wish he had stopped longer. He had the loveliest things ever I saw, and he was as handsome a man as ever I saw either. Dark skin and black hair and blue eyes.'

'You liked him better than Tom Snowball, didn't you, Tabitha?' teased Margery. 'He was a pretty fellow with a fine leg, wasn't he?'

'I won't deny it,' Tabitha tossed her head and then gave a sigh. 'But that's a lovely ribbon, Penelope, and it suits you well and matches your green smock.'

Mistress Babington came out of her still room and went to the storeroom for tall waxen candles for the altar, and I polished the beautiful silver candlesticks. The bellringers rang their peal of bells, and the deep clashing sound of it went over the hills, joining with bells in far valleys. I thought of the queen sitting in her room with her ladies, listening to the bells' message of goodwill on earth, and then kneeling in her private chapel. What did she pray for? Freedom? But what else? Did she ask for vengeance for those long years of imprisonment, and did God listen to prayers for revenge?

There was to be midnight mass for Master Anthony and his wife and Mistress Foljambe who had arrived at Thackers for Christmas. Fresh straw had already been taken to the church to keep the feet of the congregation warm, and I carried my candlesticks there. When I returned to the kitchen Dame Cicely was already making the marchpane, a great bowl of almonds powdered in the mortar, pots of honey, some flour, and many eggs all mixed together to a stiff paste, ready for moulding.

'Thou shalt make it into a device out of thine own head, Penelope,' said Dame Cicely, as she worked the yellow mass together.

'A horseman came two days ago with letters from France, and Master Anthony and Father Hurd have been deciphering them,' she whispered to me. 'Now Master Anthony has gone to Wingfield to try to bribe a servant to get them through to the queen.'

'What do you think about it?' I asked, half timidly, for I was shy to interfere in such weighty matters.

'I say "God save Queen Elizabeth", but I would like the poor Scottish queen, who has seen such terrible trouble, to be safe and sound overseas,' said Aunt Cicely, and she pressed the mixture together and bound it with the eggs. 'It's a dreadful life to be imprisoned when you are young and beautiful and to be kept there for twenty years. She is a great lady, used to every luxury, with the most beautiful jewels and clothes and furniture, and there she is, living with her women, clothed in plain dresses, in a lonely country house, and no music or dancing or companionship.'

'Will they get her away?' I whispered, for my cruel knowledge was dim and lost in memory, and the present was bright and hopeful, like the wreaths of bay and holly.

'I hope so, my sweeting. We are staking all upon it. But don't worry your pretty head, Penelope. Get to your pastry shaping, for you've got clever fingers and can make roses and lilies to the life. There's jars of colouring ready for you.'

I worked hard, making leaves and flowers for the giant pasties and pies which Dame Cicely had prepared ready for cooking. Then I started on the marchpane, and I decided to make a model of Thackers and the church and tower in the sweet almond paste to surprise my aunt and Mistress Babington. First I modelled the buildings and tower, and marked the long windows and set the fifteen shields round the sides of the tower, and showed the carvings round the doorway. Then I set to work on the house, with its porch and little mullioned windows, but as I worked I found my mind wandering, so that I made Thackers as it is, not as it was at that day. The shields were broken, the house was smaller, and farm buildings stood where once were servants' rooms.

'You've done it wrong, Penelope,' said Tabitha leaning over me. 'The church and the tower are beautiful, but the shields are broken, and you've missed out the south parlour and the wing.'

Dame Cicely came to look. She bent over it a long time, while I moulded a little green rose tree with tiny red roses, and I twisted the tree up the house porch and placed the rosettes of flowers on the boughs. It was my Aunt Tissie's rose tree I had made, and Dame Cicely touched it with her blunted finger.

'There isn't enough marchpane to do all the house,' she excused my work to Tabitha. 'This little manor house is well enough. The haystacks and church are there, true as life, but I'm sorry you spoiled the shields, Penelope. The rest will amuse the mistress and delight Master Francis. You've done it beautiful, with porch and chimleys and as beauteous a rose tree as ever I seed.'

Then Jude came over to look. He clapped his hands and crowed and threw back his head. He took my hand and kissed it, as if he thanked me for letting him into a secret of the future. But I couldn't help myself. My fingers refused to work differently, I had made Thackers as I knew it.

We set the great confection on its wooden board to be dried and set in the cooled bread oven.

'It's like one of the marchpane sweetmeats they make at Hardwick Hall for the Earl and Countess Bess,' said Tabitha.

'There can't be a better one at Greenwich Palace for Queen Elizabeth herself,' said Phoebe, who had left her spinning to come and see.

'Jude has been promoted,' Dame Cicely told me, as I helped with the mince pies, and marked them with the sign of the cross. 'He's been promoted to be Master Francis's own man. The young gentleman never had a servant of his own, and Master Anthony offered him the lad after Jude saved your life. So he's all decked out in a new livery, very fine, and he seems to understand all Master Francis says, reading his lips, and even reading his thoughts we think. It's Jude's reward.'

Jude watched her speaking, and nodded his head and pointed to his silver buttons and fine new coat, much finer than that which Francis wore, I thought. Then he took my hand again and kissed it, and I laughed and stroked his head.

'Go now and see if Mistress Babington wants anything. She likes you to wait on her, Penelope. And you will see the fine decorations, which she has done herself.'

I went into the panelled hall, and curtsied to Mistress Babington, who was singing softly to herself at the virginal. The room was beautiful with leaves and berries hanging in circular wreaths and long twining garlands along the walls, symmetrical and correctly even, unlike the freedom of the boughs in the kitchen. At the far end of the room was a table laid for the Christmas Eve feast, spread with a white linen cloth and set with silver and glass and shining pewter plates, each engraved with the Babington arms. On a raised dais was a table lighted with red candles ready for the marchpane Thackers. A great fire blazed on the hearth and the flames were reflected in the thousand mirrors of holly leaves and berries, so that the air was dancing with spots of brightness.

Mistress Babington smiled and signed to me to stay still, while she went on with her singing.

> *'In that hall there stands a bed,*
> *The bells of Paradise I heard them ring.*
> *It's covered all over with scarlet so red,*
> *And I love my Lord Jesus above anything.'*

'That's a Darbyshire song I've been learning for Anthony, and I shall sing it on Christmas Day to the company which assembles here. Do you like it, Penelope?'

'Yes, oh yes,' I cried, clasping my hands. 'Is there any more, Mistress Babington?'

She turned the page, and I stood at the window by the curtain watching her serene young face as she sang to me.

> 'Under that bed there runs a flood,
> The bells of Paradise I heard them ring,
> The one half runs water, the other half blood,
> And I love my Lord Jesus above anything.
>
> 'At the bed's foot there stands a thorn,
> Which ever blossoms since He was born,
> Over that bed the moon shines bright,
> Denoting our Saviour was born this night.'

The sweet notes of the plaintive air and the tinkling of the virginal flowed through the timeless world where I stood, and I thought it was the ringing of bells of ice high in the winter sky. Then the music died away, and there was silence, and Mistress Babington bowed her head, her hands resting on the instrument, on the painted panel of our river Darrand swinging for ever through its valley of rocks. In my mind rang the carol I had heard. The bed, the flood, the thorn, and the moon shining bright, all belonged to Thackers, and in the stable like that across the yard was the holy child born. At midnight the shepherds would come from the fields to see the child lying in Thackers' manger. Even now they were on the hillside with their flock, the ancient shepherd and his companions, listening to the song of the angels.

'Penelope,' said Mistress Babington, and she rose from her seat and came to me. 'I am happy today, for I have had news from heaven itself and my prayers are answered. I am going to have a babe, to be born here at Thackers, to be brought up in this lovely country, and he will play in the garden and run round the stacks and ride over the hills just as his father and grandfather did when they were little. He will be the heir to our lands, and perhaps when he is full-grown England will be at peace, and these wounds of religious hatred will be healed.'

She put her arm round my shoulder and kissed my lips. Yet even as we two stood looking happily at one another there was a wild clatter of hooves from the road and the gate was flung open.

Anthony galloped into the yard, his horse covered with sweat and such a look on his face as filled us with terror. We both rushed to the door, and he threw himself off and staggered in with half-shut eyes, blinking in a dazed way like a bird caught in a snare. Francis followed from the stable, and Mistress Foljambe came running downstairs white as a ghost, trembling with apprehension. Mistress Babington clasped his arms as he strove to speak.

'What is it, Anthony? What has happened?' she asked.

'Listen all of you,' he panted, choking on the words. 'We are ruined. We are discovered.' He groaned and sank to a seat, shivering violently. 'The queen, Mary Stuart. We cannot save her now,' he muttered, as all waited horror-stricken.

'What is it, Anthony? Tell us, Anthony. All may not be lost,' said Mistress Babington, instantly brave to face whatever might come.

'They've discovered the secret passage at Wingfield, where it starts in the underground hall. They noticed the covering stone had been disturbed, although it was well concealed, and they found the tunnel. Then they buzzed like a hive of bees. The queen is to be moved as soon as possible, to Tutbury, to that damp and gloomy castle where she was so ill formerly. It will be her death to go. Only three months at Wingfield, and her freedom so near.'

'Do they know about your tunnel here?' asked Mistress Foljambe. 'The Wingfield tunnel was blocked, and they cannot know where it leads without many days of excavation. They will never guess it goes to Thackers.'

'That is true. It is my hope they will discover nothing, but the queen will be moved and my plan destroyed.' Anthony groaned again, but his wife took fresh life from the knowledge that the plot was not discovered.

'Only the Earl of Shrewsbury knows the connection between the two manor houses, and he showed me the shaft. His grandfather told him the story of a tunnel made through the hillside many generations earlier, and as a boy he saw the entrance. He walked along and found the way blocked, and it is this passage that has been exposed by some unlucky chance. He told nobody about the secret way, and it never seemed to have any importance until the rumour came that the queen was to live at Wingfield. Then he revealed the entrance to me, and together we explored the ground. I have told nobody where it is. The queen can face her questioners with a calm denial. I was waiting till we bored through the complete length before I unfolded my plans to others.'

'Then why should the tunnel be discovered?' asked Francis. 'They will surely see the queen couldn't escape by a blocked passage.'

'They will be rightly suspicious, for Mary Stuart has tried to escape from prison many a time. Remember Loch Leven! The least occasion sets them agog with inquiries. They may think that somebody intended to enter Wingfield that way to get in touch with Her Grace. Obviously the tunnel hasn't been used, but if we had got a little farther the queen might have been on her way to France now.'

'And Thackers would have been destroyed and all in it,' whispered Mistress Babington.

Anthony took no notice. 'They will search the farms and manors in the district for any clues,' he said, 'and as ours is the nearest house of importance, and I am already a suspect, they will come here first.'

'Then quickly fill in the shaft at Thackers and cover all traces,' cried Mistress Foljambe. 'Anthony! Pull yourself together. Call Tom

Snowball and fetch the men out of the tunnel. Even their tapping might be heard.'

'They are not in it, as it is Christmas Eve. I gave them a holiday and for two days there has been no work down there, otherwise they might have been heard at Wingfield.'

'All the better. Fill in the shaft and hide all before they come.' Mistress Babington spoke bravely, fired with new hope, for she had been wellnigh fainting as Anthony talked.

'But the queen!' cried Anthony, and he sank down again, his head in his hands. 'The queen! Why should we trouble to do anything now! We can't save her, our work was for nothing. She is going to be taken away. Do you realize? Our plan is broken and our hopes destroyed. Never was there such a great chance to save her, and it is lost! I don't care what happens now.'

'Anthony!' Mistress Babington knelt by his side, imploring him.'Anthony! Save yourself! For my sake, and for the sake of your unborn child!'

'For the sake of Thackers,' cried Mistress Foljambe, and Francis shook his arm in anger. He rose wearily and went out with Francis to call Tom Snowball and Adam. At once they carried stones and timbers to cover up the disturbed earth, but the ground was frozen and scarred, and the freshly disturbed soil betrayed them. Unlike the earlier shaft, hidden in the old barn under earth and bracken, this one was obviously a recent excavation.

I returned to the kitchen to whisper the sad news to Dame Cicely. The old woman went quietly on with her work as if she had known all the time, but it was the fatalism of her nature which made her accept so calmly the blows of destiny.

'It was not to be. Poor lady, she is doomed,' she murmured. 'But Master Anthony, we must save him,' she cried with sudden resolution. 'If they find the shaft and long tunnel they will know all, and they'll come here first as he is lord of the manor. We can keep the pretence of lead mining with the short unfinished shafts, but not with this.'

'What can we do?' I clutched her arm in my anxiety and trouble.

'We can pray to God to help us,' said Dame Cicely, and on her face came a transfigured look. Together we hurried across the little grassplat to the church. It was dark inside except for the candles burning on the altar, and we knelt down in the rustling straw and prayed for God's help, for confusion to the searchers and deliverance for Thackers. 'But if it be Thy will,' added Dame Cicely slowly, fumbling for her words, 'if it be Thy will that all be discovered, then give us courage, good Lord, to face disaster bravely and to die if needs be.' We rose from our knees confident in a Divine help for the house we both served.

The fir branches and holly wreaths which decked the rood screen shone darkly in the faint light of the candles, and a lantern flickered for a moment as Anthony and Francis went across the churchyard to the head of the shaft. We returned to the house, and went on with the cooking, for none in the village must suspect when they came for the mumming, and Sir Ralph Sadleir's men would be less suspicious if they saw the ordinary preparations of a country house in progress.

The excavations were covered with branches and earth spread over the surface. Tools were cleaned and put away, but there were many traces of broken ground and torn grassy banks, and footprints deep in frozen mud. The men could do no more and Anthony went to his room to destroy papers if the house should be searched, and to hide others in the wood stack in the orchard.

I stood in the porch and looked out, waiting for a miracle to happen, waiting for God to send fire from heaven to destroy the searchers, or a cohort of white-robed flaming angels to fly down with swords to defend our beloved Thackers. I had infinite faith in Dame Cicely's prayer.

Jude was on the hillside, on the lookout for the horsemen, ready to give warning when he sensed their approach, for although he was deaf, he knew by other means. But the old house wore its usual air of peacefulness, an ancient manor house prepared for Christmas, with horses in the stable, and cattle in the byres, and a great fire burning in the hall, and cooking and cheer in the kitchen.

Again I went to the porch and looked up in the clear sky at the glittering stars, at Orion serene over the great woods, and Sirius cold and brilliant, and the Great Bear, the homely constellation beloved by shepherds and farmers. A meteorite sped down the dark blue heavens, leaving a trail of gold, and I made my wish for Anthony. Surely God would send a host of shooting-stars to fling their arrows against the invader of this tranquillity! I thought of the sorrowing queen, and poor Anthony Babington with his hopes dashed, with cruel tragedy coming up that slope of hillside in the east, to separate him from his wife and the unborn child.

Christmas Eve! Already the shepherds were starting to Bethlehem! O God, be quick!

The stars slowly faded as I stood there, the brightness was dimmed, a cloud seemed to move over the surface of the heavens and an icy stillness made me shiver with apprehension. Then there was a sound, so faint that I felt it with my own extreme consciousness, a movement as the earth listened also. A few feathers of snow shimmered through the air, then more and more, great flakes came fluttering down, caught in their beauty by the light from an unshuttered window, heralding a snowstorm.

'If it snows the traces will be hidden, and the ground covered so that they won't find out,' I thought, my heart beating wildly. 'Will it be in time? Will it be heavy enough? Will it hide the scars before the searchers come?' I asked myself.

At the same moment I heard the dull tramp of feet. My heart leapt again to choke me. They were coming already, and the snow had not whitened the ground. I stood waiting, waiting. But merry voices came from the dark figures who turned in at the drive, and dancing gleams of light came through the bare trees. These were no horsemen seeking plotters against the throne, but villagers carrying lanterns on long poles, prancing on wooden steeds, mocking and laughing and singing snatches of song. They were the mummers, coming for the festival of Christmas Eve.

Their faces were masked, some had cow horns and the antlers of deer fastened to their heads, others wore devil's tails. Dark cloaks hung from their shoulders, concealing their multi-coloured jerkins, their painted bladders and jesters' toys and wooden swords. They came up the drive to the front of the house and the dogs rushed out barking wildly. Mistress Babington put her hand on her heart, near fainting, and Anthony caught his breath when he heard the sound, but in a minute all was laughter, as the men's voices could be heard talking in good broad Darbyshire.

'Are we ready? Are ye in good voice? Now, Dick Woodiwiss, and Will Bestwick, and Robin Clay. Get ye ready. Pipe up! Give it 'em tunefully, and don't beat so masterful on the tabor, Sam Taylor, or ye'll drown our words. Now! Men! Give it 'em.'

They all sang in harmony, with the beating tabor and a flute pipe, the wassailing song:

> '*Here we come a-wassailing*
> *Among the leaves so green.*
> *Here we come a-wandering,*
> *So fair to be seen.*
>
> '*God bless the master of this house,*
> *God bless the mistress too,*
> *And all the little childer*
> *That round the table go.*'

The powerful manly voices came ringing through the air, and the snow fell in a mad dance upon their hooded and cloaked figures, upon the flickering lanterns and the flaming torches and the wooden horse-heads which some of them rode.

'It's snowing,' I sobbed, as I rushed indoors and clasped Aunt Cicely. 'The mummers have come and it's snowing.'

'God be thanked,' cried Dame Cicely. 'He has answered our prayer. This day he has saved Thackers and all the people in it.'

She knelt down on the sanded floor and clasped her hands together, and I stood there awed by the deep content on her furrowed face. Above her hung the kissing-bunch, and the Christmas holly and bay, and the firelight played on her white coif and her dark-stained hands. Then she rose from her knees, took a lantern and flung wide the door.

'Come ye all in! Welcome! Welcome Dick Woodiwiss, and Robin Clay, and William Bestwick, and Will Archer, and all. You've come in good time and brought real Christmas weather with you. There's plenty to eat and drink, and Mistress Babington and Master Anthony will be pleased to hear thy songs and see thy playacting,' she cried.

They entered, stamping their feet and shaking their cloaks which they flung in a pile in the porch. They stood by the great fire and warmed their chapped hands, speaking of the suddenness of the snowfall which nobody, not even the oldest gaffer, had expected on such a bright and starry night.

Outside the snow fell in a thick pall, hiding the walls and buildings, covering the earth. Those at Thackers knew that no trace of the secret passage would be found as long as the snow remained, and when it melted there would be a chance of the scars being healed.

A dim shape came from the churchyard, staggering blindly in the whiteness. It was Francis with a sack wrapped round his head.

'Master Anthony is safe. Nobody can find out now,' I cried. 'The snow has come and God sent it.'

'Yes, Penelope,' sighed Francis wearily. 'It's snowing hard. A blizzard sprang up like a flash. It's a miracle. We are safe, thank God.' Then he saw the cloaks and staves and lanterns in the porch.

'What's this? Are they here already? Have they come on foot? Why didn't Jude warn us?'

'It's only the mummers, Francis, come a-wassailing,' I whispered, touching his arm, and reassuring him.

'Ah! Thank God!' He sank back exhausted. From the kitchen came the laughter and talk of the mummers and the clink of tankards.

'Francis,' I said, kneeling by his side. 'They'll ride from Wingfield and search the house, but they will find only Christmas festivities, and the table laid, and my marchpane Thackers there, and the wassail cup moving from one to another, and the mummers drinking, and perhaps Mistress Babington singing her sweet carol. They will never suspect, will they, Francis?'

He laughed softly, and put his arms around me. 'I think you are right, Penelope. We are safe this time. We have another chance. Thackers is delivered too. Penelope! Penelope!'

He stooped over me and kissed me, and for a moment I lay in his arms. 'Don't leave me, Penelope,' he whispered.

But I sprang to my feet. 'It's still snowing,' I cried, pointing to the sky, and when I turned to him again, he was gone.

## 14. The Snow Falls

'IT'S STILL snowing, and they will ride over from Wingfield but they will find nothing,' I said aloud, and I held up my hands to catch the dancing flakes. 'Nothing! Nothing!' came a ghostly echo, and the songs of the mummers and the laughter of the serving maids died away. But the warm touch of Francis's arm, and the look he had bent on me remained, and I waited there, longing and despairing. 'Nothing!' whispered the falling snow petals, and my heart took up that cry: 'Nothing.'

I leaned against the porch, fumbling with trembling fingers for the stones, sinking half-dead upon the snow-covered seat. For a moment I heard the harsh clatter of swords and the neighing of horses and shouts of men, and then all was silent. A shadow moved over the yard, and a lighted lamp sent its beams on the snow from the kitchen window. Aunt Tissie sang in her cracked old voice as she walked about the room, and the words came to me as I bowed myself in sorrow by the door. 'Abide with me, fast falls the eventide,' and I too whispered, 'Abide with me, Francis. Abide with me.'

Then the sound of a horse's hooves trotting down the road came beating rhythmically out of the night, and Jess hurried from the stable, buttoning his coat.

'They're here,' he called, and he ran down and opened the big gate. The horse came clicking up the drive to the house. The light from the trap lamps moved in long jagged beams on the walls. I saw Mother and Father, with Alison squeezed against Uncle Barnabas's bulky form and Ian shutting the gate after them.

'Welcome to Thackers,' cried Aunt Tissie, running to the porch with the warming pan in one hand and a lighted candle in the other. 'I was just going to run this over their bed, Penelope,' said she as she saw me, 'and here they come before their time.'

There was such a confusion of people talking and dogs barking that I felt this was the unreal life and the tragedy going on at the same time in the unseen part of the house was the reality. For once I did not want to come back, not even to see my own mother and father, who spoke a different language with their high polite voices, instead of the sweet low burr of the country folk, of Aunt Tissie and Uncle Barny, of Tabitha and Dame Cicely and even of Francis and Anthony Babington.

'Aren't you pleased to see us, darling Penelope?' asked Mother wistfully, as I stood staring blankly at them with never a word or smile, not even returning their embraces.

'Yes, only I didn't expect you,' I faltered.

'Why, my dear, I wrote to say we were coming, and Uncle Barnabas came to meet us! Are you asleep Penelope? Aren't you well? What is the matter?' Mother's voice was sharply anxious as she drew me to the light and looked keenly at me.

'Yes – No – It's the snow, Mother,' I stammered, shivering. 'I've been watching it, and I feel dazed with its dancing,' I excused myself.

'She's been sitting in the porch,' explained my aunt, and she brushed the snow from my hair. 'I thought she was looking out for you, she sat so still. But come along, dear Carlin and Charles. I'm very glad to see ye both and I hope ye are quite well.'

Aunt Tissie enveloped them all in her arms, and led them to the fire in the parlour. I followed with slow reluctant steps, half-glancing back into the kitchen, peering for the mummers, listening for other voices beside those of my parents. But I was quickly called to attention, to carry the cloaks and hats to dry in the brew house, to fetch cans of hot water for the bedrooms, and to refill the kettle for cups of tea.

'How beautiful it is,' sighed my mother, as she held her hands to the fire. 'You don't know how I have been looking forward to bringing Charles to see you, dear Aunt Tissie.' And my father wandered about the room, uneasy and curious in the old country house.

'Take them upstairs, Penelope,' said Aunt Tissie. 'Get the candles and take them to their rooms.'

'All the bedroom fires are lighted, my dear Carlin,' she turned to my mother, 'and you need have no fear of damp beds, for we have been airing them for a week. I have put you and Charles in the best bedchamber, and there is a monstrous fire burning, and I beg you to take care and not set the house afire by putting more logs on!'

'I'll take care, Aunt Tissie,' laughed Mother. 'We won't set darling Thackers ablaze.' I went to the candle cupboard and got out the pewter candlesticks which were polished and fitted ready for the guests, and I lighted them, stooping over the fire, lingering as long as I dare.

So I led the way, but as I went up the crooked stair, carrying my candle aloft, I felt I was taking strangers to Anthony's house, and they had no right to be there.

I flung open the door of the best bedchamber, where the fire burned brightly, and shadows swept up and down, mopping and mowing like dark travellers themselves, seeking in walls and cupboards evidence of guilt. I could have sworn that some of them had plumed hats and swords in their hands, as they dived away before my upheld candle.

The beautiful bed was ready, its four carved posts polished and reflecting the firelight, the little angels, or cherubs, whichever they were, and the babe seated on a tun, 'poor Babington', all with shining faces after my morning's work with the beeswax. The bed curtains had been freshly washed and they moved gently in the draught from the window, swaying outwards as if somebody were already in the bed, listening to our voices. The best patchwork quilt with its satin and silk hexagons looked dark in the shadow, but Mother ran with uplifted candle, raised the curtain and looked at it with admiration.

'Look, Charles, darling, look.' She pointed with her forefinger to one of the 'patches' of claret-coloured embossed velvet.

'Look! That was a bit of my own mother's wedding-dress. Mother showed me the dress once. Aunt Tissie's sister, you know.'

Father bent his head, and touched it gently, smiling at her excitement.

'What a conglomeration of scraps!' said he. Then, 'Here's a lovely bit of ancient stuff.'

He picked out a piece of embroidery, a scrap of tapestry work, inserted oddly in the border, for it didn't fit in with the patterns of silks and velvets.

'Do you know what that is? By Jove, it's very old. I wonder what it is. I can't make it out, but it is antique, I swear.'

Mother didn't know, but I recognized it with a queer excitement that set me trembling, so that I backed away lest they should notice my shaking hand. I couldn't tell them that it was a sheaf of corn, with the sun behind it, one of Joseph's brethren, cut from the embroidered strip which Mistress Anthony Babington's long white fingers had worked over three hundred years ago. Why it had been cut and where the rest of it was I never discovered, for Aunt Tissie could only say it was very old, and it had lain in her grandmother's oak workbox for many years till she had begged it for the quilt.

Ian was already in his room, unpacking his suitcase. 'Uncle Barny, will there be any pheasant shooting?' I heard him call as he galloped noisily downstairs. 'Can I be a beater? Will the Squire let me go with the beaters?'

Alison was eager and excited to be back again. She leapt upon the feather bed and thumped it joyfully, and then ran round the room, looking at the old things, pulling out tiny drawers in the looking glass, peering at herself in the dim speckled mirror, and I leaned over her shoulder.

I saw my own pale face as I had seen it when first I came to Thackers, but older, more mature. I saw Penelope Taberner in the glass, and I felt very near those who loved her, so that I longed to slip through the hidden door to that unseen world where hearts were aching for a captive queen and a broken cause. But there was my sister Alison, laughing and talking of London, teasing as she turned over the contents of my mahogany workbox and saw the jewel and the precious signature, then opening her suitcase and displaying her clothes.

She showed me the morocco bag she had bought for Aunt Tissie and the briar pipe for Uncle Barnabas.

'Uncle Barny doesn't smoke,' I objected. '" 'Ware candle and pipe in barn and in house" he once told me.'

'Oh dear, I'd quite forgotten,' cried Alison.

'He will treasure it all the same,' I told her; 'and Aunt Tissie will say the bag is too grand for the likes of her, but she will wrap it in a linen handkerchief and love it.'

'You've grown very wise, young woman,' mocked Alison.

'Yes. You can't live in the depths of the country without acquiring some wisdom,' said I quietly. 'Besides, I am an experienced traveller.'

'Traveller! You! You've been nowhere, have you?' she asked, surprised.

'A traveller in time,' I replied, and Alison gave me a quick glance and shook her finger at me.

'Oh, Penelope! You're incorrigible! But you'll grow out of it,' she assured me.

Her words made me very unhappy, for I didn't want to lose this possession of mine, which gave me the power of passing into other layers of time, to share the lives and love of those who dwelt there. I went out of the room with aching heart and stood on the landing. From my mother's room ran spreading fans of firelight and low voices talking, and from our own room came Alison's voice humming a song.

As I stood there the firelight faded, and I was in the darkness with the latch of another, older door within my reach. I lifted it and stepped silently down the little flight of stairs to the corridor below. I walked along, past Mistress Foljambe's room, where another fire burned and the strange birds and beasts of the woodland seemed to come to life and move among the painted trees on the wall. The round gold watch ticked noisily, the fire spattered as the snow fell down the chimney on to its blazing logs. Mistress Foljambe sat there, with the Book of Hours in her hands, and she turned the pages slowly, not reading. I passed on to Master Anthony's room and walked inside, waiting for him to speak.

He saw me at once, and put his finger to his lips for silence, so that I knew the priest was in the secret chamber.

'Are you safe, Master Anthony?' I asked. 'Did the snow hide everything?'

'Yes, Penelope,' he whispered, in a voice soft as a breath. 'They came galloping over the hills but there was nothing. We were sitting at the feast, listening to the mummers. They were in their masks with their bladders and hobby-horses, acting a play, and we were laughing uproariously when Sir Ralph rode up, for Jude had warned us they were near. No, we knew nothing of doings at Wingfield. We were too much occupied with our festivities. So we gave them cups of sack and invited them to join us. They admired your marchpane Thackers immensely, and tasted the red roses, and took away the sweetmeat tower. They had no desire to go farther in the blinding snowstorm. They rode back without paying any more visits, for the night was cruel wild, and they wanted to get back.'

'And the queen? Mary Stuart?'

'Alas, she is to be moved to Tutbury in January, in a few days time. Even the villagers are sorry, for they were profiting by the trade with Wingfield, and some thought they were going to make their fortunes.'

'And you, Master Anthony?' I asked gently.

'I have my strength and youth, and I shall devote my life to her service. I shall rescue her, never fear. Even now I am arranging to go to Paris to make fresh plans. My work has only just begun.'

'Master Anthony, don't go. You can't save her, and you may ruin her,' I pleaded with him.

'One has only to die once, and I'll outwit them. They shan't get Thackers. They shan't get all my estates. I'll will them to Francis and George. I'll make my will now and give my lands away before I go to France, and so defraud the cunning crown. The lawyer is in the house, and he shall help me and Father Hurd shall be witness.'

He seized his quill and ink-horn and dragged a piece of parchment from his desk.

'Father Hurd,' he called, and the priest moved in the hidden chamber, but I prepared to fly from the room.

'Goodbye, Master Anthony,' I said sadly. 'Goodbye and God be with you.' I knew that the end had come, that I should not speak to him again.

He looked up but did not see me, he had already forgotten me, and I went softly to the door.

'Farther Hurd. Come quickly. I'm going to make my will and outwit these foxes. Ah! They shan't have Thackers and its chapel and homestead. They can have this body to break, but not the home of my childhood, and not my faith. *Foy est tout,* Father Hurd. Come write. "Thackers and my meadows, Westwood, Squirrels, Meadow Doles, Hedgegrove, I bequeath them and my horses, Stella, Silver –"'

I shut the door and ran weeping along the passage to the head of the stairs, but no farther could I go.

Down below in the hall I saw Mistress Babington playing chess with Francis, moving the ivory figures with slow hesitations, listening, her face uplifted, as if she awaited Anthony. Dame Cicely entered with a covered silver cup.

'Drink this broth, dear mistress,' said she tenderly. 'It will put colour in your cheeks. Remember you have another life to think of now.'

Mistress Babington sipped and smiled at the round homely face bent over her.

Then she saw me, leaning on the rail, gazing down at the room from which I was separated by a veil I could not penetrate.

'Look! Look! On the stairs! Penelope is there!' she cried, and Francis sprang to his feet and ran across the room. 'Penelope! Stay! Never leave us!' he implored, but even as he called the scene faded, the air lost its luminosity, and Francis was but a shadow moving on the wall. I went along the passage, moving fleetfoot, unreal. The steps were there, one, two, three, under my feet, and I unlatched the waiting door and it closed behind me.

From the bedroom across the way came my mother's voice warning my father against spilling the candle wax, and laughing when he asked where the bathroom was. Alison was singing as she brushed her hair, and I caught my breath as I heard her song.

> 'Greensleeves was all my joy.
> Greensleeves was my delight.
> Greensleeves was my heart of gold,
> And who but Lady Greensleeves.'

'Stop! Stop!' I cried running into the room. 'You mustn't sing that.'

'Penelope! What's the matter? I thought you were going downstairs? What's the matter?' she asked, in surprise.

'Why do you sing that song?' I demanded.

'Greensleeves? We danced to it at the folk-dance class. Don't you like it, Penelope?'

'Yes,' I said slowly. 'Yes. But I don't want it tonight, please'; and even then I thought I heard a faint whisper, a breath vibrating the ether. 'Penelope! Stay!' it said, but I shook myself free and went downstairs.

That Christmas Eve, as we ate our mince pies and drank the hot spiced ale and the posset which Aunt Tissie warmed by the fire, the dogs began to bark, and on a sudden there was a burst of music outside. The village choir had come to sing their Christmas carols. They stood in the garden path with their lanterns shining across the snow, some with pieces of music in their hands, others with trumpets and flutes, and I thought they were like those other singers I had heard so recently in the very same place. We opened the door and invited them into the kitchen, and they stamped their boots and left their coats and sticks in the porch. They stood round the fire, and the older men sat down on the settle, and we all laughed and joined in the merriment as they ate their mince pies and sipped the mulled ale Aunt had prepared for them.

'We can't stay long, Miss Taberner,' said the leader. 'We've got to go up to Bramble Hall, and o'er the hill. Goodnight to all on you. Goodnight all. Thank you kindly. The compliments of the season. Don't forget to ring the midnight bell, Master Taberner.'

Uncle Barny replied that he had never forgotten bar once, when the spiced ale was too potent. There was renewed laughter, and away they went.

I said goodnight, for my head ached, and I wanted to be alone. I went upstairs to my bedroom where the fire was burning brightly. I leaned out of the window, and far away up the fields I could see the lanterns bobbing in the snow as the waits trudged to other farms. The singing was lost in the soughing of the trees, and the murmur of the brook as it fought its battle against the ice which strove to bind it.

As I waited there, listening to the crackling sounds of winter, with the frosty sky above and the stars blinking fiercely among the dark trees, I heard a voice down on the lawn where the cedar tree had once stood, and as I stared into the blue-shadowed distance the old tree's flat, powdered branches swam into my vision, and below I saw a cloaked figure with a pheasant's feather in his hat. I heard the mocking voice of Francis Babington, half plaintive, half defiant, singing to the open spaces around him.

> 'Greensleeves now farewell, adieu!
> God I pray to prosper thee;
> For I am still thy lover true,
> Come once again and love me.
> Greensleeves was all my joy,
> Greensleeves was my delight.
> Greensleeves was my heart of gold,
> And who but Lady Greensleeves.'

There was a clatter of hooves from the courtyard and Master Anthony rode out with two horses. Francis sprang to his mare's back and away they went, down the drive and along the winding valley. I waited there, shivering with cold, but the hoofbeats were only the clamour of the brook's waters, and nobody returned.

The peacefulness of Thackers which had held the seasons for five hundred years flowed through me, giving me strength and courage as it had done to those others, uniting me to them. I knew I had seen them for the last time on this earth, but some day I shall return to be with that brave company of shadows.

ALISON UTTLEY

A Traveller in Time

| | |
|---|---|
| 1884 | Born Alice Jane Taylor on 17 December in Cromford, Derbyshire |
| 1892 | Goes to Lea School in Holloway, two miles' walk from Cromford |
| 1897 | Wins a scholarship to the Lady Manners School in Bakewell, where her favourite subject is science |
| 1903 | Attends the University of Manchester and becomes only the second woman to graduate with honours in physics |
| 1908 | Having trained as a teacher at Cambridge, takes up the position of physics teacher at Fulham Secondary School for Girls in London |
| 1911 | Marries James Uttley |
| 1924 | They move to Bowdon in Cheshire and live there until 1938 |
| 1929 | Her first children's book, The Squirrel, the Hare and the Little Grey Rabbit, is published |

**1930** *Her husband, James, tragically dies. Alison (her pen-name) turns to writing full-time to support herself and her teenage son*

**1931** A Country Child, *a memoir of her childhood experiences at her family-farm home in Derbyshire, is published*

**1934** How Little Grey Rabbit Got Back Her Tail *is published and over the next twenty years she writes many more stories about Little Grey Rabbit*

**1938** *Settles in Beaconsfield, Buckinghamshire, in a house that she names Thackers after the manor house in* A Traveller in Time

**1939** A Traveller in Time, *the first of several novels for older children, is published*

**1940** *First publication of the series of stories featuring mischievous Sam Pig, which were to strengthen her reputation as a children's author. Other characters follow, including Tim Rabbit, Brock the Badger, Little Red Fox and Little Brown Mouse*

**1966** *Publishes a cookbook for adults called* Recipes from an Old Farmhouse

**1970** *She is awarded an Honorary Doctor of Letters degree by Manchester University in recognition of her literary achievements*

**1976** *Dies 7 May in Buckinghamshire, aged ninety-one*

**1978** A Traveller in Time *is serialized for BBC TV*

# WHERE DID THE
# STORY COME FROM?

*Alison Uttley grew up on a farm in Derbyshire, only a
few miles from the old manor farmhouse at Dethick,
which was once the home of the Babington Family. This
was the inspiration for Thackers, the setting for
A Traveller in Time. Alison's love of the countryside and
her attention to detail helped her to bring the story to life.
She was also interested in the study of dreams and fantasy,
and she combined them with historical
fact to create a vivid timeslip novel.*

# GUESS
# WHO?

**A** *I found myself pressing close to him, for he had a smell of something delicious . . .*

**B** *On her thick hair was a fold of linen, like a cap, snowy and fresh, and her apron was gathered and pleated in many folds round her large waist.*

**C** *'Why do you say such things? Are you a soothsayer? Can you foretell the future?'*

**D** *I espied another face, a boy older than I, with fair hair and keen, blue eyes.*

**E** *'Didn't my poor music please you, or don't you wish to visit this world in which we dwell? You see I know all about you, Penelope. I have some powers which my father has taught me.'*

**ANSWERS: A)** Uncle Barnabus **B)** Aunt Cicely **C)** Penelope **D)** Francis Babington **E)** Arabella Babington

# WORDS GLORIOUS WORDS!

*Lots of words* have several different meanings – here are a few you'll find in this Puffin book. Use a **dictionary** or look them up online to find other definitions.

**boggart**  *a naughty spirit*

**dumbledores**  *a colloquial word for bumblebees*

**besom**  *a historical word for a broom*

**garb**  *clothing of a distinctive or special kind*

**madrigal**  *a song for two or three unaccompanied voices*

**mullioned**  *referring to windows divided by vertical bars of stone*

**verdigris**  *a greenish-blue deposit that forms on copper or bronze surfaces*

*Here are some old words from the story – some are still used today.*

**doublet**   *a man's tight-fitting buttoned jacket that is worn over a shirt*

**farthingale**   *a hooped structure worn under a skirt to support the shape*

**kirtle**   *an item of ladies' clothing that has a close-fitting body and a full-length pleated skirt*

**marchpane**   *a sweet paste, similar to marzipan*

**pennon**   *a type of flag*

**posset**   *a spiced drink made with cream, eggs, and wine or ale, and served hot*

**syllabub**   *rather like a posset; made from cream and wine, and served cold*

**virginal**   *a keyboard instrument of the harpsichord family*

# QUIZ

*Thinking caps on –* let's see how much you can remember! Answers are at the bottom of the opposite page. (No peeking!)

**1** To what year does Penelope go back in time?

a) *1582*

b) *1640*

c) *1492*

d) *1750*

**2** What does Penelope see when she first goes back in time?

a) *A small spaniel dog*

b) *Some children playing*

c) *Four ladies sitting round a table, playing a game*

d) *A maidservant wearing a white cap*

**3** What is the new song that Francis Babington sings?

a) 'The Holly and the Ivy'

b) 'Greensleeves'

c) 'Three Blind Mice'

d) 'The Children of the Wood'

**4** Where does Anthony Babington plan to hide Mary Queen of Scots?

a) At Thackers

b) At Wingfield Manor

c) In an underground tunnel

d) In the hayloft

**5** Why is Penelope disappointed when she goes on a family outing to visit Wingfield Manor?

a) Because she wanted to go there by herself

b) Because it is nothing but a ruin

c) Because it was boring

d) Because she expected to see Mary Queen of Scots

ANSWERS: 1) a 2) c 3) b 4) a 5) b

# IN THIS YEAR

## 1939
### Fact Pack

*What else was happening in the world when this Puffin book was published?*

ALISON UTTLEY

A Traveller in Time

The **Second World War** breaks out when *Britain and France declare war on Nazi Germany.*

*The very first film version of* **The Wizard of Oz**, *starring Judy Garland, is shown in Hollywood.*

*The* **prime minister** *of Britain is* **Neville Chamberlain.**

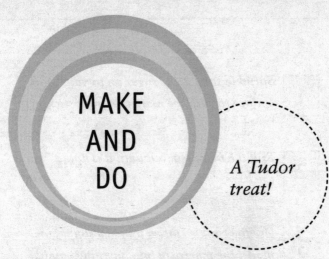

# MAKE
# AND
# DO

*A Tudor treat!*

*Marzipan, which is similar to the marchpane that Aunt Cicely made to decorate her pies in Tudor times, is great for modelling sweet treats and decorations. It's so easy – why not have a go!*

## YOU WILL NEED:

* 1 box of icing sugar
* 1 packet of ready-made marzipan
* Cookie cutters
* Dried fruit or nuts
* Paint brush
* Food colouring

1   *Sprinkle some icing sugar on to your work surface to stop the marzipan from sticking.*

2   *Roll the marzipan out until it is about 7cm thick.*

3   *Use the cookie cutters to make shapes, or model the marzipan into anything you like, such as a rose.*

4   *Decorate your shapes with dried fruit or nuts, or paint them using food colouring.*

5   *Leave to firm up, and then enjoy!*

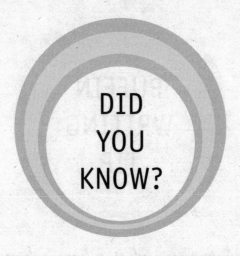

# DID YOU KNOW?

*There really was a person called Anthony Babington who plotted to rescue the imprisoned Mary Queen of Scots. However, his plot was discovered by Queen Elizabeth's secretary, Sir Francis Walsingham, and as a result Babington was executed in 1586.*

*Alison Uttley wrote over one hundred books, mostly for young children, including over thirty in the Little Grey Rabbit series.*

*There is a commemorative blue plaque on the outside of Castle Top Farm, near Matlock in Derbyshire, where Alison was born.*

*While she was an undergraduate, Alison lived in Ashburne House, which later became Ashburne Hall, and was the University of Manchester's first hall of residence for women.*

# PUFFIN
# WRITING
# TIP

Ask: *who, what, where, when, why and how?* It'll help you to dig deeper and find out more about your characters.

If you enjoyed reading *A Traveller in Time* you may enjoy travelling even further back in time with *The Sword and the Circle*.

# 1. The Coming of Arthur

IN THE dark years after Rome was gone from Britain, Vortigern of the narrow eyes and the thin red beard came down from the mountains of Wales, and by treachery slew Constantine of the old royal house and seized the High Kingship of Britain in his place.

But his blood-smirched kingship was little joy to him, for his realm was beset by the wild hordes of Picts and Scots pouring down from the north, and the Saxons, the Sea Wolves, harrying the eastern and southern shores. And he was not a strong man, as Constantine had been, to hold them back.

At last, not knowing what else to do, he sent for two Saxon warchiefs, Hengest and Horsa, and gave them land and gold to bring over their fighting men and drive back the Picts and the Scots and their own sea-raiding brothers. And that was the worst of all things in the world that he could have done. For Hengest and Horsa saw that the land was rich; and at home in Denmark and Germany there were many younger sons, and not enough land nor rich enough harvests to feed them all; and after that Britain was never free of the Saxon-kind again.

They pushed further and further in from the coasts, sacking the towns and laying waste the country through which they passed, harrying the people as wolves harry the sheep in a famine winter; and many a farmer died on his own threshold and many a priest before his altar, and ever the wind carried the smell of burning where the Saxons went by.

Then, seeing what he had done, Vortigern drew back into the dark fastnesses of Wales and summoned his wise men, his seers and wonder-workers and begged them tell him what he should do.

'Build yourself a mighty tower and lie close in it. There is nothing else left to you,' said the foremost of the seers.

So Vortigern sent out men skilled in such matters to find the best place for building such a stronghold, and when he had listened to their reports, his choice fell upon Eriri, the Place of the Eagles, high in the mountains of Gwynedd. And there he gathered together workmen from the north and the south and the east and the west, and bade them build him a tower stronger than any tower that ever had stood in Britain before then. The men set to work, cutting great blocks of stone from quarries in the hillsides; and the straining teams of men and horses dragged them up to the chosen place. And there, on the cloudy crest of Eriri, they began to set the mighty foundations that should carry such a stronghold as had never been seen in Britain until that time.

But then came a strange thing. Every morning when they went to start work, they found the stones that they had raised and set in place the day before cast down and scattered all abroad. And day by day it was the same, so that the stronghold on the Place of the Eagles never grew beyond its first day's building.

Then Vortigern sent again for his seers and magicians and demanded to know the cause of the thing, and what they should do about it.

And the seers and magicians looked into the stars by night and the Seeing-Bowl of black oak-water by day, and said, 'Lord King, there is need of a sacrifice.'

'Then bring a black goat,' said Vortigern.

'A black goat will not serve.'

'A white stallion, then.'

'Nor a white stallion.'

'A man?'

'Not even a man who is as other men.'

'What, then, in the Devil's name?' shouted the High King, and flung down the wine cup that was in his hand, so that the wine spattered like blood into the moorland heather.

And the chief of the wise men looked at the stain of it, and smiled. 'Let you seek out a youth who never had a mortal father, and cause him to be slain in the old way, the sacred way, and his blood sprinkled upon the stones, and so you shall have a sure foundation for your stronghold.'

So Vortigern sent out his messengers to seek for such a youth. And after long searching they came to the city of Caermerddyn; and in that city they found a youth whose mother was a princess of Demetia, but whose father no man knew. The princess had long since entered a nunnery, but before that, when she was young, she had been visited, as though in a dream, by one of those who the Christian folk call fallen angels, fair and fiery, and lost between Heaven and Earth. And of his coming to her, she had borne a son and called him Merlin.

All this she told freely to the High King's messengers when they asked her, thinking no harm. But when they had heard all that she told, they seized the boy Merlin and brought him to Vortigern in the fine timber hall that he had caused to be set up in the safety of the mountains hard by Eriri. And Vortigern sat in his great seat spread with finely dressed wolfskins and cloth of crimson and purple, and pulled at his meagre beard and looked at the boy through the smoke tendrils of the hearth fire. And the boy stood before him, lean and whippy as a hazel wand, with dark hair like the ruffled feathers of a hawk, and stared back at him out of eyes that were yellow as a hawk, also, and demanded, as a man demanding of an equal, to know why he had been brought there.

The High King was not used to being spoken to in that tone, and in his surprise he told Merlin what he asked, instead of merely ordering him to be killed at once.

And the boy listened; and when it was told, he said, 'And so my blood is to be shed that your tower may stand. It is a fine story that your magicians have told you, my Lord King, but there is no truth in it.'

'As to that,' said Vortigern, 'the matter is easily put to the proof.'

'By scattering my blood upon the stones of your stronghold? Nay now, do you send for your magicians, and bid them stand before me, and easily enough I will prove them liars.'

Vortigern tugged at his beard and his narrow eyes grew narrower yet. But in the end he sent for his wise men, and they came and stood before the boy Merlin.

And Merlin looked them over from one to another, and said, 'The Sight and the Power have grown weak in you and your like in the long years since the passing of the true Druid kind. Therefore, because you are darkened to the truth, you have told the King that my blood shed upon these stones shall make his tower stand. But I tell you that it is not the need for my blood that causes his stones to fall, but some strange happening beneath the ground which every night engulfs the work of the day. Let you tell me then in your wisdom, what thing that is!'

The magicians were silent, for their powers had indeed grown dim.

Then Merlin turned from them to Vortigern. 'My Lord the High King, let your men dig beneath the foundations until they come to the deep pool that they will find there.'

So the King gave his orders and the men set to work, and in a while they broke in through the roof of a vast cave; and all the floor of the cave was one deep, dark pool, from the depth of which slow bubbles rose to the surface as though some great creature lay asleep and breathing deeply far below.

Then Merlin turned to Vortigern who had come from his hall to look on, and to his magicians behind him, and said, 'Tell me, oh workers of wonders and walkers in secret ways, what lies at the bottom of this pool?'

*The Sword and the Circle* is
available in A Puffin Book

A PUFFIN BOOK

# stories that last a lifetime

Ever wanted a friend who could take you to magical realms,
talk to animals or help you survive a shipwreck? Well, you'll find
them all in the **A PUFFIN BOOK** collection.

**A PUFFIN BOOK** will stay with you **forever**.
Maybe you'll read it again and again, or perhaps years from now
you'll suddenly **remember** the moment it made you **laugh** or
**cry** or simply see things **differently**. Adventurers **big** and **small**,
rebels out to **change** their world, even a mouse with a **dream**
and a spider who can spell – these are the characters who
make **stories** that last a **lifetime**.

Whether you love animal tales, war stories or want to
know what it was like growing up in a different time and place,
the **A PUFFIN BOOK** collection has a story for you
– you just need to decide where you want to go next . . .